LOST AND FOUND

Lost and Found

Danelle Helget

NORTH STAR PRESS OF ST. CLOUD, INC.

Saint Cloud, Minnesota

Special thanks to:

Jared

My amazing husband. Thank you for entertaining the kids while I wrote. And for believing in me.

Kristin

My BFF. Thanks for the countless hours of listening to me babble about this journey. Also thanks for your semi-pro editing skills and strong opinions.

Molly

My Writer's Group friend. Thanks for your editing skills and support. I enjoy sharing stories and coffee with you.

Jeremy

My policeman friend. Thanks for your help and expertise in the details of the story.

Sara Kuck

My photographer. You do amazing work. Thanks for sharing your gift with me for this book.

Seal and fellow staff

My publishers. Thanks for believing in me, and for all your professional help that made this dream into a beautifully finished product.

Copyright © 2011 Danelle Helget

ISBN: 0-87839-430-3

ISBN-13: 978-0-87839-430-2

Printed in the United States of America

Published by

North Star Press of St. Cloud, Inc.

P.O. Box 451

St. Cloud, Minnesota 56302

www.northstarpress.com

For Jared, Brooke, and Taylor,
with love.

1

W E'D BEEN DRIVING FOR WHAT FELT LIKE DAYS, and I thought we would've been there by now. "Jake, I think we should stop and check the directions," I said. "Jake? Jake!"

"What?"

"I said I think we should stop and check the directions." I looked at him, and he seemed a million miles away. We'd been married for four years, and lately I'd felt like I didn't know who he was or where he was for that matter. He was so distracted.

"No, it should be right up here," he said, and he was right back to staring at the road.

I put my arm up and lightly scratched the back of his head with my nails. Jake was six feet and 190 pounds, most of which was lean muscle, like other Martin men. He had soft, tan skin and a head full of thick dark-brown hair. "What's wrong?" I asked him, "You seem so lost lately. Is everything okay?"

"Yeah. I'm sorry, Sara. I'm fine. I was just thinking about work."

Jake worked hard but what could possibly bother him so much? He was a construction worker. Pouring foundations for buildings shouldn't be so stressful that you had to bring it home with you. I, on the other hand, had deadlines and court dates to be ready for and tons of paperwork I should have brought with me but didn't because this week was suppose to be for relaxation and rekindling. I worked the family law department of a large firm. Mostly I did wills, trusts, and health directives, but once in a while I took on bigger cases. This past week was really busy for me. I had a lot to finish up before I left.

We hadn't vacationed in a long time. One week, in a rented cabin in the woods, with our closest friends, Lily and Mark, should do the trick. Hiking trails, the lake, use of the boat and fire pit, and best of all, miles from everyone and everything. I couldn't wait. And the weather forecast was perfect for the week, high seventies and sunny, lows in the mid-fifties.

I'd found the cabin listed in our local paper, fully furnished, on a lake and not too far from home. The price was great, and when I called the number and spoke with the property manager, Harold, I was instantly sold. Harold described the property. He said an older couple owned it but lived in town, in a house closer to their jobs. They hired a property manager to take care of the upkeep and reservations and rented it out for extra income.

I heard my phone ringing. My cell was getting a signal out here? That surprised me. It was Lily. After convincing her that we were headed in the right direction, I passed the phone to Jake so he, too could tell her to relax. They were following close behind us in Lily's car.

Jake rolled his big, brown eyes and took the phone. "No, I promise I know where we are. Don't worry, I'll get us there. Just think about which bottle of wine you want to open first, okay? Five minutes, I promise." He disconnected and passed me back the phone. "She's so worried all the time. Doesn't Mark have any pull with her? He's the one who downloaded the directions," he added.

I shrugged and shook my head. Smiling, thinking about how Lily would never survive on her own. She couldn't even make it through a haunted house with her eyes open. I probably couldn't either though. I was afraid of the dark, always had been. I could admit it though. *I, Sara Martin, am afraid of the dark. There, it's out! I'm okay with it. Really.*

The roads seemed never ending. We took Highway 10 north out of the Cities and stayed on it for what felt like hours, then took 371 into Brainerd. I was officially bored. We'd gone through Brainerd, a larger city with lots of stuff to look at, but that felt like years ago already. Since then it had been long, boring roads with a farm maybe here and there. There were a lot of cornfields out there, too. It was almost spooky, yet peaceful at the same time. This city girl would get lost in a second out here. I wasn't feeling any better as tar turned to dirt. Just the lack of street signs made me nervous. I really needed to get one of those GPS things. Our final destination was Nisswa, a quiet smaller town. The cabin was on a lake named Hawsawneekee, far from the big cities, but technically not too far from civilization.

Finally, the never-ending dirt road brought us up a driveway to a sweet little log cabin. It was absolutely adorable. It looked pretty new. Both the cabin and the grounds were very well kept. The yard around the cabin was good sized, freshly mowed, and had lush, green grass. The lake in the background looked really blue, not what I was used to seeing in Minnesota. The lake was completely surrounded by large trees that came all the way to the banks. On the left, behind the cabin, the elevation was much higher. The property around the cabin was covered with huge oak and maple trees, thick with leaves. The very tops were starting to change color already. The trees in the yard were nothing compared to the thick woods behind the cabin. The woods seemed to go on forever. At the very edge I could see a little, well-manicured trail leading into the woods. The pontoon at the dock was new and looked big. A nice fire pit area off to one side of the yard was surrounded by chairs, tiki torches and a large pile of split wood. It was beautiful, breathtaking. Perfect. I rolled down my window and took a deep breath. Ah, fresh, clean air.

"Are you seeing this?" I asked Jake, to make sure he was still with me. He put the Jeep in park and sat back in his seat, looking around the grounds.

"Yeah, wow, I feel better already." He turned the key back and we both jumped out. Mark and Lily were already at their trunk digging in the cooler. A moment later we were all standing in awe, drinking cold beer, leaning back on their car.

"This is going to be a great week," Mark said, tipping up his beer.

Mark Berens was in real estate, so I was sure he was never impressed with properties—he saw them all day long. He loved his job, and he was good at it, too. Mark, a hard worker and a handsome man, with light, blond hair, cut short and always was clean shaven, was about six-foot-two and the perfect weight, not too thick, not too thin, and he worked out some so he was well toned. Over the last few years he had bought and sold a few fixer-uppers. He knew a lot of contractors and could see the potential in places most people would walk right past. If I remembered correctly, he currently had two rental properties. But that changed often. Usually Mark rented out single-family homes and as soon as people got settled in, he'd feel them out. If it sounded like they liked the place and planned to stay in the area, he'd throw a great price on the property and offer them first dibs. They almost always took it, and then he'd be on to the next property a few months later. It helped that Lily was a mortgage broker and could get him locked in at great rates with low closing costs and easy terms.

Lily Kowalski, my BFF, had been dating Mark "officially" for four and a half years. They'd been living together for three of that. The four of us had been really close since the eighth grade. They had a really nice apartment about ten minutes from us, in Bloomington, so we saw each other often. Lily went to business school for a year, dropped out and then worked at a bank for a while. While she was there, she got a great job offer from a client that she immediately accepted. Although she had currently been at her job for about five years, she never loved it, but it was easy work, a comfortable environment with good pay, plus she got nice bonuses and amazing benefits. So she didn't love it, but felt sort of stuck with it since she had no desire to go back to school. Lily always told me she was going to marry money, so she wouldn't have to work. Mark was good at his job but far from rich; she might have to settle.

"To great friends, great places, and new memories to be made." Lily held up her beer in salute. We all clinked bottles and said cheers.

"Sara, did you bring the pool floats?" Lily asked.

"Yes, and I remembered the foot pump!" I smiled at her, remembering our last trip to the beach.

"Great," she yelled, "let's go!"

Lily took off running, stripping off her shirt to reveal a teeny bikini top. She was tossing flip flops and hopping on one foot trying to get her jean shorts off on the run. She was in incredible shape. She worked out a few times a week with Mark, and it showed. She was making her way to the beach slowly, stripping on the run, all the while trying not to spill her beer. We all just stood there and laughed. She was the wild one of the group, always ready to go.

Mark slammed the last of his beer and slapped Jake on the back. "Well, Martin, let's unload and find the grill. I've got steaks thawed out, and I'm starving." With that Mark and Jake turned toward the trunk and started grabbing stuff.

"That sounds perfect. You two cook supper and I'll catch up with Lily and keep her afloat," I said with a smile. I walked down to the beach and found her waist deep in the water twisting back and forth, taking sips of her beer with her face to the sun. It was a beautiful picture, so peaceful.

"Hey, you gonna help or not?" I yelled. "Start pumping these up, and I'll go get the cooler." I tossed the two floats and the pump on the sand and ran back to the car.

At the car I met up with Mark. "So you ready for a little R&R and a lot of beer?" he asked, with a wink.

He smiled as he folded his arms and sat his butt back against the car. I couldn't help but notice that he may have put on a few pounds, which was working in his favor. "How are things with you?" I asked.

"Good, I guess. Business is good and we're here. Hopefully this will be just what Lily and I need to reconnect. We've been struggling lately," he said, his voice dropping. "She seems so out of reach. She's crabby and distant and says she's just been tired lately, but I don't know what to think. She just acts different and seems annoyed by my presence," Mark said sadly.

"Really? I'm sorry," I said and reached out to rub his arm. "Jake's been the same way, work stress I guess, but maybe this week will help everyone. We have seven days to forget about the world and just think about each other." I punched his arm and nodded as to not give him a chance to argue that point.

"Yeah, you're right and that's exactly what I had in mind." Mark pushed off the car, reached in the trunk, grabbed the last cooler out and slammed the trunk shut. "Well, give us about an hour to get things settled and the steaks grilled, then we'll eat," he said.

I grabbed the beer cooler from our Jeep and headed back to the beach. As I came around the side of the house, I saw that one float was inflated and Lily and Jake were standing near it laughing and smiling. "Hey, guys!" I yelled, "Can someone help me with this cooler?" They both looked a little startled. Jake jogged over and took it from me. He set it over by the beach chairs and returned to the house to help Mark.

"So," Lily said, "What's the plan for today?" A little urgency in her voice made me think for a second that I may have interrupted something. She grabbed the other float and started stepping on the foot pump quickly.

"Well, I guess we get to drink cold beer and lay in the hot sun while the boys cook and unpack. It doesn't get much better than that."

"That works for me," she responded.

We clinked our bottles together and grabbed the floats. I stripped to my black, one-piece suit and followed her into the lake. The water was warm. The lake was a smaller one, and in Minnesota small lakes warmed faster, but our summers were short so you had to enjoy every second of it. Once we were settled on the floats, we tied ourselves together and then tied one end to the dock.

"Nice boat," I said. "I can't wait to spend a day out on the water."

"No kidding, this place is amazing. It's absolutely perfect. If I lived here I'd never want to leave. I feel so good just lying here, warm, buzzed and happy knowing that for the next week I have nothing to do but have fun," Lily added. She was very easy to please.

I figured as long as she had a beer in her hand, it wouldn't matter where we were. We floated silently for a while. I could feel the air cooling down, it was about 6:00 P.M. and the sun's heat was weakening.

"So how have you been lately, Lily? How's work going?" I asked.

She opened her eyes and looked at me. "Okay, I guess," she took a long pull on her beer. "I've been kind of short with Mark lately. I think he's starting to notice it. I don't know, sometimes I look at him and I think, you're not the man for me. I feel like we've been drifting apart. He's great, ya know. He helps around the apartment, cooks, cleans, does laundry and is attentive to me, but I just don't have the vibe for him like I used to."

"Wow, really?" I was shocked by this, they had always been such a great couple. "I'm sorry. If you ever need to talk, just let me know. Have you thought about talking to him about your feelings or trying a counselor?"

"No, I guess I've been just living like it's not bothering me. But lately I feel like I'm too old to be playing games. I'm not getting any younger, and the clock is ticking. I want a wedding and kids soon. I know he does too, but I just don't know if I want it with him," she said bluntly.

"Wow, that's a lot to deal with. I think you should talk to him. Maybe just opening up to each other will help, or maybe he feels the same."

Lily and I had been friends since the eighth grade, and I had never seen her with a boy for longer than a month. When she and Mark started dating, I really liked him. He was new in town and really nice. I was glad after the first month was over and he was still around. "Maybe you two are just in a rut. It happens. Relationships have lots of ups and downs. Maybe this is just a down part. I bet after some quality time together this week you'll feel differently."

Lily nodded but didn't look convinced.

"Are you cold? Should we go get changed for dinner?" I asked.

"Yeah, let's go in. I'm starving. We'd better stop by the kitchen and make sure the guys have it under control in there," Lily said with a grin.

We gathered up the floats, brought them up to the cabin and tied them to a chair so they didn't blow away during the night. We carried the cooler through the back door of the cabin and set it down. The most amazing smell was coming from the kitchen. I walked up behind Jake at the stove and slid my arms around his waist. He jumped and stiffened up a little.

"Oh, sorry, didn't mean to scare you. It smells so good in here. What are you making?" I tried to peek over his shoulder but he was much taller than I, so instead I kissed his shoulder and came around his side. He was sautéing green peppers, mushrooms, garlic, and onions in a pan with oil. "Mmm. Looks great, even better with you cooking it!" I said, with a wink. "Lily and I are going to go clean up and change." I glanced over at Mark and Lily, and they were both looking at me. They hadn't said two words to each other yet.

"Come on, Lily!" I said, to ease the awkward quiet between them. She followed me to the back of the cabin.

The cabin was on the smaller side, one level, but perfect for us. The kitchen was a nice size. It had all the usual stuff and an island counter with four bar stools. A glass, sliding door with a paved patio just off the kitchen, opened to the lake. The appliances were all new, stainless steel, and the counter tops were a light, beige granite. Across from the kitchen wall was a family room with a fireplace, two small but comfy-looking couches, and two recliners. A coffee table separated the couches that faced each other in the middle of the room, perfect for playing board games. The two recliners had an end table between them and were placed in front of the large, bay window that looked out to the driveway. Just down a short hall was a small bathroom with all the essentials and a huge soaking tub with lots of candles around it. You could fit two in there easily. The walk-in shower could also fit two. There were two bedrooms straight across from each other at the end of the hall. Both had a king bed with a night stand and a dresser, and a full-size closet.

I walked into my room, and Lily went into hers. I set down the bag I'd grabbed from the living room and went to the window. It was such a beautiful property, nothing like in the city, when you look out and all you see are the neighboring apartments and their lovely, trash-ridden, parking lots. This was so serene. I could literally feel my blood pressure drop.

I opened the window to let in the now cooler air. I inhaled and filled my lungs. My view was of the driveway and back yard which was nice and backed up to the large, thick woods. That was the side of the yard where the elevation was higher. If there were neighbors nearby, you wouldn't be able to see them or hear them through that. I saw our cars in the driveway and noticed that the window was still down on my Jeep. I better remember to shut that later. I didn't think it was suppose to rain but better safe than sorry.

I pulled on some jeans and a red tank and stopped by the bathroom quick to throw my hair in a ponytail and swipe on a quick fresh coat of mascara. I was one of the blessed who had nice skin tone and medium beige color so I didn't wear a lot of makeup, but I always put on mascara and eyeliner. It helped to make my brown eyes a little bigger. My thick, long, wavy hair, however, took some work, and I didn't want to deal with it right then, so I said a quick, mental thank-you to the inventor of the pony tail and sauntered to the kitchen.

Lily was made up nice, sporting a cute, yellow, ruffly, sleeveless shirt and white capris. Mark and Jake were just putting a few things out on the island counter top. They looked like they were preparing a buffet-style line. I added some napkins to the beginning of the line, and Lily grabbed four cold ones from the fridge.

"Go ahead and start," Jake said. "I think it'd be nice to sit out on the patio. What do you guys think?" We all agreed and start dishing up all the great-smelling food.

There was a nice, four-person, glass-top table and chairs set on the patio. It had an umbrella in the middle that I noticed a cord coming from, so I turned the handle and the umbrella opened. This exposed a switch for a light, I spun it, and lo and behold, we had light! Perfect. It had started to get pretty dim as the sun had already set. We all gathered around and started in.

"Boys, the food is amazing. Thank-you for cooking," Lily said, with a smile.

"Yes," I added, "thanks. It was so nice to relax while you made it. We owe you one. Tomorrow we'll make brunch for you guys. I know Jake said on the way up that he wanted to get the boat out before dawn. So when you get back, we'll have it ready."

Mark smiled and nodded in agreement. When he finished chewing, he asked Jake what he put in the potatoes. Jake told him it was his grandmother's recipe.

"It's just peppers, onions, garlic, and mushrooms, sauteed in chicken stock. Then you add a little fresh thyme, mix it into the already smashed spuds, sprinkle it with shredded cheddar cheese and you've got the best potatoes in Mille Lacs County," Jake said proudly. Jake's grandma had lived in Milaca a small town of about three thousand. She'd been well known there for her cheesy potatoes. She died about two years ago and left Jake the recipe.

We all finished and eased back in our chairs. It was pretty dark, and the bugs were getting bad, so we decided to move to the fire pit and start a fire. I ran inside to grab the stuff for s'mores. Mark followed me in to get more beer. I was rummaging though the cupboards, trying to find the marshmallows when Mark backed up against the counter next to me, arms folded across his chest.

"Did Lily mentioned anything about the distance between us?"

"Yeah," I said slowly, not wanting to get caught in the middle. "She just said pretty much the same thing you said, that she just felt that you two are kind of drifting apart." I saw the hurt in his eyes and added, "Maybe this weekend will help. I think we all need to reconnect, ya know. We have all been busy with our jobs, and life just gets in the way. Jake and I have our ups and downs too. Everyone does."

"I hope you're right, I don't want to lose her. She's my world. I've loved her since the first moment I saw her, and I can't even bear thinking about a life without her." He turned and looked through the cupboard near him and handed me the marshmallows. We headed back outside to see Jake and Lily talking and laughing, and they'd just clinked bottles as we came out the door.

"What are we toasting to?" I asked.

Jake raised his beer and said, "To great friends and peace and quiet." We all lifted our beers and took drinks. While tipping mine up, I looked around and again got the feeling that I'd walked in on something. I looked at Jake, who was looking at Lily, and they were smiling. Then I looked to Mark who was looking at me as if to say, "Yeah, I noticed it too."

"Well, who wants a s'more?" I asked, reaching for the marshmallows. We all enjoyed the warm fire, gooey s'mores, and a couple more beers. "I'm beat," I announced. Not really but I was tired of the uncomfortable thoughts I was having and thought maybe a change of scene would do me good. "I think I'm going to call it a night. Jake, are you coming in with me?" I asked.

He looked over at me and smiled. "Yeah, I'll be right behind you."

I grabbed my empties and the s'more stuff and went in. After I put everything away. I remembered my Jeep window was open, so I went out the front door with my keys in hand. I was a little hesitant because the porch light wasn't very bright. I walked slowly, fear in my gut, thinking the whole way how childish I was. You'd think that by the time I was an adult I would've outgrown being afraid of the dark. I got to the Jeep and opened the door. I stuck the key in and quickly raised the window. Then shut and locked the door. As I was walking back to the cabin, I noticed something to my left move. I froze in place and slowly turned my head. It was so dark, I couldn't really make out what I was seeing. It looked like a young girl in a white dress standing in the woods. She was waving. Then she turned and walked farther into the woods, all the while waving like—follow me, this way. I stood there not knowing what I was seeing. I was scared, and there was no way I was going to follow her into the dark woods. I closed my eyes. When I opened them again a moment later, she was gone. What the heck? Did that just happen? Was it just a weird shadow? Wait, shadows don't wave. I ran as fast as I could back to the cabin and shut and locked the door behind me.

I stood there for a minute, my back to the door, wondering if I should tell the others what I'd seen. But I wasn't even sure what I had seen, and they'd probably think I was crazy. So I decided that a shower and sleep would be my best plan of action. If that girl did exist and needed help, she knew where to find me. I jumped in the shower and washed up quick. After I dried, I pulled on a t-shirt and sleep shorts and combed through my wet hair, which fell to the middle of my back and was getting pretty heavy when it was wet. I might need a trim soon. I'd dyed it dark-brown about six months ago and had kept that look. It was nice and easy to throw up for court dates. The firm where I worked wanted the lawyers to look professional. Making women lawyers put their hair up, in this day in age, was a little old fashion, but whatever. If they kept paying me what they did, I'd shave my head for them, if they asked. I chuckled at the thought. I brushed my teeth and headed to the bedroom. Jake wasn't there yet, so I flopped down in the middle of the bed, and I was out instantly.

2

I WOKE TO JAKE SNORING, LOUDLY. It was light out, and he was in bed still, which meant he'd overslept on his plans to get the boat out before dawn. I looked at the alarm clock. Eight-fifteen. The alarm was set. I pushed the button and sure enough, it was set for evening. "Jake? Jaaake," I gently rubbed his belly. "It's eight-fifteen, you set the alarm wrong. Do you want to get up?"

"Unn ahhh," was all I heard as he flipped over. He buried his head in his pillow and made a few more noises.

"Hey," I said quietly, "what time did you come to bed?"

"Huh? I don't know. One maybe," he mumbled. He stayed under his pillow and didn't move.

One, huh? I thought that he was right behind me, and I'd taken a shower first. Guess there must have been good conversation going on, too good to join me.

"Good morning," Jake said, about five minutes later as he rolled over to hold me. He grabbed me and pulled me in close, and I could feel that he was in a good mood.

He kissed the back of my neck and asked if I was in a hurry. I turned to meet his lips.

"Nope," I said. "I have all day!" He moved in closer, if that was possible and a half hour went by.

We were laying there quietly, when we heard Lily and Mark come out of their room. "I bet they're still in bed." Then BAM BAM BAM on the door. "Hey, you horny fools, get up! Where's my breakfast, Sara, huh?" Mark yelled.

"It's coming right up!" I yelled back. That got everyone laughing.

"Yeah, I bet it is." Mark replied. "Hey, Jake, that alarm in your room working?"

"Ah, yeah, it will be in about twelve hours. Sorry, buddy."

"No worries. I was tired too," he said.

We rolled out of bed, threw on some lounge wear, and I padded into the kitchen. Mark and Lily were already digging in the fridge. They threw together a quick and easy breakfast while Jake was in the shower. We finished our eggs and toast and discussed our plans for the day. We all agreed that we should pack a light lunch and head out on the boat for the day. The guys could fish and Lily and I could read, swim and fix our pedicures. Sounded perfect to me.

After the dishes were done, the guys went to the vehicles to get their tackle and poles. Lily and I stayed in the kitchen to make sandwiches and snacks for the boat. Then we went to our rooms to grab everything we needed for a day in the sun and met the guys on the dock.

"Geez, girls, it's a twelve-person pontoon and half a day," Mark said.

I guess it might have looked like we overpacked, but the "never know what you might need" was a good rule to live by.

"Did you grab a cooler and beer?" Jake asked. I looked around at all the stuff we'd just sat down on the pontoon and then looked at Lily.

"Shoot, Lily," I said in a bad, southern accent, "we done gone and forgot the beer!"

"Are y'all sure there's room on this here boat for all that?" Lily asked, in her own southern accent. "Gee, Sara, we best be gettin' back to the cabin to round up what we can. Whada ya say?"

"Sure thing, little lady. I'm right behind ya," I said, with a giggle.

The boys laughed and rolled their eyes. Mark added, "Don't forget toilet paper." Toilet paper? Cool, the boat has a toilet. That's awesome.

A half hour later, the boys had decided on the perfect spot and finally dropped anchor. Lily turned on the radio and actually got a station to come in. It was a variety station, so we were all happy except Jake, who was convinced that we were scaring away all the fish. Oh, well, guess only the deaf fish would be biting then. Lily and I started moving stuff around and settled down in to our seats with sunglasses, cold beers, and magazines. The guys were readying their poles and talking fish talk that I didn't pretend to know anything about. It was so relaxing. I looked around the lake. It was a nice, smaller-sized lake, and was very undeveloped. We only saw a few houses around the shore, and all three were right next to each other. Rumor had it that one family owned most of the land and just refused to sell it. Must be nice to pretty much own your own lake and only have a few neighbors, too. What a dream. It would be an awesome place for a moderately sized house, nothing too big. I didn't enjoy cleaning, so just what I needed and nothing more. Throw in a couple of great kids and a dog and a handsome, loving husband and you've sold me!

I looked over at Lily, and she was comfortably stretched out on the back of the boat, drinking her beer. I turned my head to see Jake just letting go of his line over the side of the boat, reeling up and getting ready to cast.

"Five bucks on the first catch, Mark?" Jake asked, confidently.

"Oh, yeah, but I should warn ya, this here's a new reel and she's special, Jake. This is a one of a kind, and it'll bring in the big boys," Mark sassed back.

"Really?" Jake asked, turning around to check it out. "Where did ya get that?"

"Ebay," Mark said and did a so-what head shake I hadn't seen since kindergarten. I was half expecting a tongue to stick out, too. We all chuckled. It was so nice to be out on the water. I didn't really feel like drinking much. My stomach was a little uneasy. I mentally blamed it on the boat and put my head back in my magazine.

It was quiet on the lake. The boys were casting and retrieving. Lily was reading, the radio was softly playing. There was a slight breeze. I looked up from my *Glamour* slightly to see Lily looking to my right. I turned just my eyes, which were hiding behind my sunglasses, just in time to catch Jake winking at her. She bit her bottom lip and looked back at her magazine. Jake cast again and didn't miss a beat. I turned my eyes to Mark, who was happily fishing and hadn't noticed anything.

What the hell was that? Now my stomach was really turning. Was that totally innocent? Was I overreacting? We'd been friends for so long, I was sure it was nothing. Or, we had been friends for so long, maybe it was something. No way! Lily would never hurt me like that. And Jake too, he would never cheat on me. *Oh, my gosh, they're having an affair!* No, no ... I was so quick jumping to conclusions. I overreact a lot. I would not this time. It was just a friendly gesture, I was sure. But now I was thinking about last night and Jake seeming so distant lately. And Mark, he said that Lily had been working hard lately. Does that mean, working late? I sat there looking at her from behind my sunglasses. She had an amazing body and knew it. Her bikini was as small as could be and she filled it just right. I was sure I wasn't the only one in the boat who noticed this. I took a sip of my beer and stood up. I needed to stretch and shake the thoughts from my mind. I decided to let it go, so instead I took my sunglasses and cover up off and walked to the front of the boat and looked over the edge.

"You gonna brave the water?" Mark asked.

"Yea, I think I'll take a dip, cool off a little." *More than you know.* I responded with a smile. I dove in, came up and said what else? "The water's great. Come on in!"

"I think I will," Mark said, and sploosh, a cannon ball splash not two seconds later.

"Hey, how am I gonna catch fish with you two making all that ruckus?" Jake yelled.

"Don't bet on it. I'll catch the first fish. You know I will," Mark yelled back and threw some water up at Jake.

"Come on, Lil!" Mark hollered.

"Not yet. I'll come in later. I want to be good and hot first," she yelled back.

"Are you gonna join us, Jake? Come on, the water's great and the fish already left the area," I said.

Jake looked at me smiled and said, "Okay, but if we're swimming, then we're all swimming." Then he set his pole down, turned around and scooped Lily up and jumped in with her in his arms.

Lily was holding on for dear life and screaming, "Noooooo!" *Splosh!* They came up laughing, and she was playfully hitting his arm, saying, "You jerk," while holding onto his neck. I couldn't see where Jake's hands were but it didn't look good to me. Now I was beyond annoyed. I paddled over to the boat and climbed up. After I grabbed my towel and wrapped it around me, I slammed the rest of my beer.

"Hey, are you done already, Sara? We all just got in. Come on, you're right, the water's great. Get back in here," Lily said.

I bit my tongue at what I wanted to say and instead used the beer and bathroom as my excuse. If they were having an affair, I wanted to be sure before

I said something that might hurt people's feelings or make them uncomfortable. I noticed Mark's face as I walked to the bathroom and it was about as gray as mine. I bet he was thinking the same thing.

3

I T WAS ABOUT FOUR BY THE TIME we got back and unloaded the boat. "Let's not forget that we made dinner last night, so I think it's the girls' turn tonight. Don't you think, Jake?" Mark asked.

I jumped in, "Ya know what, Jake, I think that you and I should make dinner tonight since Lily and Mark made breakfast this morning. We could make spaghetti and meatballs with salad and garlic toast. And spaghetti is your specialty."

"Sure, sounds great," Jake responded, but didn't seem excited.

"If you two want to enjoy some time together while we cook, we can plan on dinner at eight," I added.

Everyone agreed and we all headed in. That gave us some time together as couples, which I thought we would all benefit from. I needed to use this time to feel closer to Jake so that I could shake the feeling I was having.

I showered quickly and threw on a t-shirt and my best-fitting jeans. Then did a quick, five-minute make-up job and squeezed some mousse in my hair. I hit it quick with the blow dryer and voila! Good enough. I headed to the bedroom, but Jake wasn't there, so I walked down the hall to the kitchen. He had his head in the fridge and was talking to Mark, sitting at the island counter finishing a beer and granola bar. "Hey, shower's open." I announced.

Jake looked at Mark and said, "You go ahead, then you and Lily can go on that walk in the woods while we cook dinner."

"Okay, thanks, guys. Have fun," Mark said as he threw his bottle and wrapper in the garbage and headed down the hall.

I heard Lily say, "No way, me first," and then a slap and Mark mumble something. They both disappeared into the bathroom. Next, I heard a giggle and the lock click into place. Guess we're preserving water.

I grabbed the meat and salad from the fridge. Jake was already started on the sauce. In his family, nothing came from a jar, which I thought was great except when you're in a hurry. Jake was an excellent cook, and he enjoyed cooking too, which was a benefit to me.

"So, how are you?" I asked, as I started working on the salad.

Jake looked at me, tipped his head kinda sideways and asked, "What?"

"Nothing. I just think we need to talk, and so I thought I'd start there," I replied, while looking at the vegetables I was working on.

"Oh, what now? Did I do something wrong? What are you mad about?" He asked, annoyed.

"I don't know. There just seems to be a lot going on with you lately, and I feel like you're a million miles away sometimes. I see you smile a lot, but it's not usually in my direction. It seems like you have lots to talk about when I'm not around but as soon as I walk up you get quiet. So I'm just trying to figure out where you're at." I wanted to be gentle in case I was way off in left field. I waited, what seemed like forever, before I continued. "I have fears, Jake, like a lot of married people. I'm afraid we're drifting apart, and it scares me."

Jake seemed irritated and was shaking his head as he continued chopping the tomatoes. He looked very lost in thought and really upset. It wasn't that he was mad, but really more like, I don't know, upset. He wasn't responding to me or looking at me. I really wished he would've just looked at me with loving eyes and told me he was sorry, that it was just stress, that I was being silly. Anything. But he didn't. It was like he'd left the building. Just kept chopping tomatoes, face down, deep in thought.

"Jake, will you please say something?" I demanded.

"What? What do you want me to say?" he practically yelled at me. "I told you on the way up here that it's been really busy at work and I'm just stressed."

Wow, he had never used that tone with me before. He didn't even look me in the eyes either. Now I was mad, too. He was guilty of something. Why else would he have snapped like that? Whenever he talked to me it was always in a loving fashion. He couldn't even look at me. God, I hoped and prayed that I was wrong, but my heart was telling me I wasn't. Crap, I was going to throw up. Shit, Lily and Mark were still in the shower, giggling. Sick. She was playing both of them! I grabbed a cup and drank some water. I needed to hold it together. If I threw up in front of Jake, he would know that I was really upset. I made the decision to act normal until I had solid proof.

"Okay, well we're on vacation so try to forget about it for now. There's nothing you can do about work while you're out here in the middle of nowhere," I said. I put on my best fake smile and walked over to him. I slipped my arms around his waist and hugged him from behind. I nuzzled my face in the back of his shirt and inhaled. He smelled so good. I prayed I was wrong. Was I? Man, I hated the fight in my head. *I'm right… I'm wrong.* Ugh, I needed a beer. I went to the fridge and grabbed two. I set one by Jake. He said thanks.

We continued cooking without much conversation. About twenty minutes later, Lily and Mark passed through the kitchen and went out the door for their hike. "Bye. Have fun and don't get lost," I said to them, gritting my teeth.

"We won't," Lily said, "Dinner at eight, right?"

"Right, and if you're late, there might not be any left," Jake said back, with a wink.

They put on their shoes and light jackets and left. The kitchen smelled awesome, the sauce was simmering, and the salad was prepped and back in the fridge. Jake worked on browning the meatballs, while I set the table. The sauce had to simmer for a while, and the rest of the stuff was done. So, after the meatballs were brown and in the oven on warm, we both sat down at the table.

"I really wish you would take this time to enjoy us and our time together and try to keep work at work. It's going to be a long week if you're like this towards me the whole time," I said, not realizing I was talking until a sentence into it.

Jake finished his beer and grabbed another one. Then he looked at me from the fridge and wiggled a beer at me in an effort to ask if I was ready for another one. I shook my head. He opened one, slammed it, walked around to where the trash was and tossed it in. Then he sauntered over to where I was and put his hand out, palm up. I put my hand in his not knowing what he was doing. As soon as my hand touched his, I felt my heart skip a beat and my whole body relaxed. He pulled me up to my feet and pressed his body into mine and hugged me, so tight. I loved full, body-length hugs. I felt a rush of heat move through me. I loved him so much. Right then I thought, *what a paranoid wife. Geez. We're fine.* Mark and Lily were fine too. We had just seen that.

Jake moved his face from my shoulder up to my lips and kissed me softly. I inhaled deeply and melted into his lips. He was so soft and warm, and I was starving. The kitchen smelled like spaghetti sauce and Jake, two of my favorite things. Bad feeling gone. We continued kissing, and he slid his hands down to my hips and picked me up and set me on the island counter top in front of him. Lips still touching, he didn't miss a beat. Jake was kissing my neck when I felt him fumbling with my zipper. I opened my eyes and looked into his. Our eyes locked for a long moment, and I felt better. *See, he loves me. I am crazy,* I thought, as I lifted off his shirt.

Twenty minutes later, I was wiping up the sauce-splattered stove while Jake took a shower. I threw the rest of the meal together and put it on the table. Jake came out clean and dressed, just as Lily and Mark walked in. We all enjoyed our dinner together and retired to the living room for a movie. It had started to rain outside, so we'd decided to forego the campfire. Each couple snuggled up on one of the overstuffed couches. The TV was little and old but there was a DVD player, and it worked. The guys put in an action movie, and we all grabbed adult beverages and I added a large bowl of popcorn in the middle of the coffee table. We watched the first half hour of the movie, and I decided I didn't really like it. The cool air and dark sky outside made us all snuggle up nice and close, so I felt a nice romantic comedy would have been better.

I heard my cell phone ring tone coming from the other room. Yay, I still got service. I quickly jogged to the bedroom, but I missed the call. I checked my voicemail. My mother. She just wanted to talk, but I didn't need to call her back. My heart ached for her. Her mother had passed away a year and a half ago. They had been close, and my mom was an only child. My grandfather passed away four years before, and we knew Grandma would soon follow. My grandparents were very old fashioned; they kept everything in life simple. They were very rich but most people didn't know that. Ken and Pauleen Taybro kept their finance details to themselves. When they were first married, they lived in Alaska for two years, in a tiny apartment, in the basement of a house that belonged to a member of their church.

They bought a hundred acres of land super cheap with the plan to build a home and maybe farm there in the near future. Shortly after, Grandpa got a great job offer as an assistant director of sales, for the Ford Motor company. That moved them around a lot, but he made good money, so he stayed with them. Grandma worked her whole life even though she never had to. She loved feeling needed and important. They lived simply and well below their means. "It's not about the money," she'd tell me. "You have to do something you love and makes you feel important in the world, or you'll lose yourself in it." Good advice. Pauleen was a patient assistant to birthing mothers in the hospital for most of her life. She loved it and it showed.

I couldn't even imagine what it must have been like for them when they found out that the land they bought was the central location for the biggest oil find in the U.S.A. ever! Stubborn as they were, they didn't sell. They rented the land to the oil company, so each month they received a huge check in the mail. Not only that, they made a percentage on each barrel of oil that the company extracted as well. There were a lot of barrels extracted every day, year in and year out. I can just picture Grandpa at the table with the big oil executives pounding his fist and making demands. It made me smile, little people beating big people in the corporate world. The other nice part was that my mom was an only child and so was I.

When Grandpa passed, Grans sold the property to the oil company for a lot of money. She never told anyone how much she got for it, just said that she got what she wanted, and her family would be taken care of for generations to come. Her passing had been tough on my mom, but at the same time a blessing. My mom was a hard worker all her life but unfortunately did not love what she did. Now she was able to quit and still live very comfortably the rest of her life. My mother and father, Jan and Will Lewis, were still happily married and had lots of plans to travel in the near future. My father quit his job the day the lawyers told them the details of the estate. My dad had been a mechanic his whole life, and he'd worked only for the paycheck.

Grans had set up a trust for me as well. She wrote me a letter, that I was to read after she passed. In it, she stated that it was her wish that I continue to work, at least part time, doing something I loved and to make sure I didn't lose myself in this world. The trust, from what I understood, would give me a one-time gift of three million dollars on my thirtieth birthday and ten thousand dollars a month for the rest of my life. My thirtieth birthday was last month, but the estate was going through probate. My mom had set another meeting with Grans's attorney for the next week. Probate could take up to a year, some of that had passed already but in the meantime, I had set up appointments for later in the month with three different financial advisers. I hoped, out of those three, I'd find one I was comfortable with so I could start planning investment strategies. Ten-thousand dollars a month was way more then I needed, and I didn't want to blow it. I thought I was responsible and had made good choices in life thus far. Life could only get easier from here, right? Right.

I had only told Jake about the estate and asked him to keep it on the downlow. I didn't want people or friends to change their feelings towards me. The money was in my name only and was legally set up as my inheritance so that it would always be mine and could not be considered as part of any divorce issues. Grans insisted on the pre-nup, too. She wouldn't tell me why but insisted firmly. I figured I'd get an inheritance, but I had no idea when or how much. I told Jake that if he ever divorced me, I'd be rich and he'd be lonely. He just laughed and told me he'd surely love me forever.

I asked my mom why Grans never asked me to be her lawyer, and she said Grans wanted to enjoy her time with me when she saw me and not let money or business get in the way of our time together. She was such a smart woman. I hoped I'd become half the woman she was. I was excited and nervous. It really changed how I looked at the world. I thought a lot about what I could have now, what I could do, where I could go. It was as if a million doors had just opened and I could pick which one or ones I wanted to walk through. It was very calming. Grans would tell me stories when I was a kid about people with lots of money, how they got big heads, got stupid and then lost it all. They usually ended up sad and alone and broke.

I had planned to keep working, but to drop back to part time or maybe just do pro-bono work. It was really nice never to have to worry about money again. Life was full of problems but at least, no matter what else happened, I knew I would be able to pay my bills and put food on the table.

I texted my mom back and told her all was good, the place was in the middle of nowhere, it was really beautiful and that we'd be back next Sunday afternoon. I said I'd call then, if not before. When I got back to the living room, both the boys were sleeping and Lily was rolling her eyes. "So much for couple's cuddle time," I said.

"No kidding. It's not like they worked real hard today. Remember the old days when they stayed awake for our dates."

"Yeah, I think so. That was the first two dates, right?" I smirked back. "The good news is now we can watch a different movie. What did you bring?" I asked Lily.

She went over to the TV and read through titles. "*Mama Mia, Sweet Home Alabama, Fried Green Tomatoes,* and *Dirty Dancing.*"

"*Dirty Dancing* for sure!" I said. "I haven't seen that in forever! I was so sad when Patrick Swayze passed away. He was such a heart throb in that movie. Yay, date night just turned into girls' night! You get it started, I'll go get two margaritas." I told her. I went to the kitchen and returned five minutes later with drinks in hand. I passed one to Lily and sat on the floor in front of the couch.

When the movie was over we left the guys on the couches to suffer and went to bed.

I woke up at about six and couldn't fall back to sleep. It was still raining. The weatherman said it should clear up soon. Good, I thought, because he promised nice weather the whole week. When I padded out to the kitchen and started the coffee, I noticed Mark was still asleep on the couch. Jake had climbed into our bed late, mumbling something about his back hurting and asking why I hadn't awakened him. I rolled over and asked why he didn't stay awake. He sighed, and that was the end of that conversation. I rummaged through the fridge and found the flavored creamer. Then I dropped a Pop Tart into the toaster. I was still in my lounge pants and long-sleeved tee that I'd slept in. My hair was up in a messy bun. I was a little concerned for Mark. If he woke up and saw me sans makeup, he might get a little freaked out.

I'd settled at the island counter on a stool with my version of breakfast and a magazine. I'd brought about ten with me since I wasn't much of a book person. I flipped through it very quickly, then shut it. Okay, I was officially bored. This was bad because everyone was asleep, and it was wet out. No cable TV, only a radio, which was playing old-time country. I wasn't a fan of whiny country, especially in the morning, so I decided to take a shower. I dressed for warm weather, praying the news anchor on the radio was right. I squeezed some mousse into my wet curls and let them air dry. I added a couple swipes of mascara, Chapstick, and slipped a ponytail holder onto my wrist for later. If it rained early and then was suppose to get hot, that added up to frizz in my book. A girl scout is always prepared.

I sauntered back to the bedroom, and Jake was gone. I could smell his cologne, so I figured he must be up and dressed. While walking into the kitchen, which was getting brighter, I noticed he and Lily were on the patio, both dressed and sipping coffee.

"Good morning." I said. They both looked over, smiled and said hello. "So do we have a plan for today yet?" I asked them.

"Lily was just saying that it'd be fun to drive north. Her co-worker, Scott mentioned there was a great, little town called Nisswa about twenty minutes north of here, off County Road 18. It has a cute little main street with a bistro, bar, restaurant, and ice cream shop, and a bunch of little souvenir shops. We were thinking that would be a good plan for the morning since it's still pretty wet out." Jake said.

"Yeah, he said it's kinda fun. It'll give us something to do for a bit while the weather clears. I already mentioned it to Mark, and he's in, so what do you think?" Lily asked me.

"Sounds great to me. I'll just go throw some things together," I said and I grabbed a cup of coffee and headed to my room. I tossed a sweatshirt, iPod, hairspray, sunblock and a wallet in my shoulder bag, and I was set. I headed back to the patio with the pot of coffee, topped off Jake's and Lily's cups. "I just heard Mark shut the shower off, so he should be out soon." I told them.

Jake went in to grab his things. Lily and I picked up the breakfast mess, then she headed to her room for her purse just as Jake and Mark announced they were ready.

4

WE DECIDED TO TAKE OUR JEEP, just in case there were good mud puddles on the back roads along the way. Of course there were, so Jake gave us a wild ride through the back country and didn't miss a one. We arrived in Nisswa about ten-thirty. It was a cute town. Like something out of an old-time movie. The main street was about two blocks long, and all the stores were connected. The fronts were all painted different colors but were built like a strip mall. The heights of the roofs, the colors, and shapes of the stores were different but complemented each other. They had a long boardwalk out front, and it was the same on the other side of the street. There were tables and chairs out on the boardwalk by the ice cream shoppe, and large flower pots outside the saloon. A cute bar and restaurant had wood picnic tables covered in vinyl, red-and-white-checkered tablecloths. And the best part, there was a speaker system. We could hear old-time, country music all the way down the street. The place was alive with people. Jake found a parking spot right in the middle of the block, and we all got out.

"This is super cute!" I said, as I stepped out of the Jeep. "Wow, Jake, nice job on the Jeep." It was pure mud on the bottom half and the rest was splattered here and there.

"I didn't want to stand out like a sore thumb when we parked in this redneck village, and now we don't. And we won't have to worry about anyone stealing our ride, lil' lady." Jake said, as he slung an arm around my shoulder.

"Well, you ladies are the pros. Where do we start?" Mark wanted to know. He reached out for Lily's hand, and she took it.

"We'll start over here," she said and pulled him toward the boardwalk. Jake and I followed, and we slowly checked out a couple stores. About thirty minutes later, we were at the saloon, and the boys were begging to go in and stay. They said they'd wait for us while we hit the rest of the shops, maybe three or four more. We agreed they could have a beer and wait there for us. But no more than one before we got back, and no eating because we wanted to go to the cute place across the street with the picnic tables for lunch.

Lily and I kinda split once we were in the next store. It was the biggest one so far called "Lost and Found." All the little rooms were themed—home décor ranging from antiques to modern stuff. There were candles, purses, clothing, everything. I found my way over to the jewelry, and I was looking at some really cute, handmade earrings when I heard a voice.

"Pretty lady, you must be lost, because around here we don't grow such beauties."

Awww, who was this sweet old man? I turned around to see a short, old man, about seventy-five years old, maybe older. He wore a nice button-down shirt, black slacks, and leaned on a cane. He was looking up at me smiling.

"Oh, thank you. You're sweet," I replied, feeling my cheeks get hot. "You're right. I'm not from around here."

"I hope you're not on your honeymoon, because if this is where your husband takes you on your first trip it's not too promising a future. You might just divorce him now and run away with me. I'll take you somewhere really nice, with some of those tall trees with the coconuts and sandy beaches," he said, in a raspy voice that was just too cute for words.

"That's a great offer. I'll have to keep you in mind, should I ever get divorced." I told him, smiling ear to ear.

"Reggie, you leave her alone."

I looked over to see an older woman about the same age dressed almost the same. This must be his wife, I thought. I quickly checked for rings, and there they were. She was adorable too. Lots of make-up on, hair aqua-netted into a round shape that suited her well. "Don't mind Reggie. He's always making the ladies blush. He's harmless. Well, unless you're me. I fell into his trap of compliments fifty-one years ago and look where it got me," she said, winking at him. She walked on, carrying a small box of items. He smiled at her as she passed and at the last minute he poked her in the butt with his cane. She jumped a little, shook her head and continued walking to the shelf in the back. Cute.

"So do you like the earrings?" Reggie asked me.

"I do," I said, "I'll take them."

"Okay, love. Bring them up here to the counter," he said. I followed him to the front of the store. "These are handmade by my granddaughter. She makes all the jewelry you see in here. She's about your age, lives closer to the cities. Stays at home with her daughter and makes jewelry in her spare time. She ships us new stuff every month."

"Really? That's great! She does amazing work, please tell her that for me," I said.

He nodded, "Where are you coming from today?" he asked. "I mean, you said you weren't from around here. Are you on a vacation or just out for a drive?"

"We're staying in a cabin about twenty minutes south of here. Rented it with another couple for the weekend. We're staying for the week. It's on a lake named Hawsawneekee. Very pretty property, tons of trees, nice cabin and a great price."

"Really, Lake Hawsawneekee. I know where your talking about," he said. He looked at my hand and reached for my credit card, but instead he placed both hands over mine. He leaned forward on the counter, toward me, like he had a secret. His eyes looked very concerned. I instinctively leaned forward and looked him in the eye. But then I suddenly felt a little uncomfortable. He lowered his voice and said. "Strange things happen on that lake. People in town say they see things around there . . . like ghosts. It changes people. I'm not into all that weird stuff, but I'm telling you what I know. Just be careful," he told me.

"Okay," I said, "I'll be careful, I promise." I freed my hands and placed the card on the counter. He took it and rang up my earrings. He handed me the card back and handed me a cute little paper bag with the "Lost and Found" logo on it.

"Sorry if I scared you. I don't mean to. Just that I like you. You seem like good people, and I'd hate to hear that anything bad happened," he said apologetically. He seemed really sincere.

"Oh, it's okay. You didn't scare me." Lie. "I appreciate the advice," I said, as I gathered my bag and purse. "And I will be careful. Thank you."

I looked over to see Lily walking towards me. "All done?" she asked.

"Yup, a new pair of earrings," I said, lifting my little bag. I decided to keep the crazy conversation to myself.

We quickly passed through the remaining shoppes and headed over to the saloon to collect the boys. I entered first through the authentic, swinging, wood doors. "Yo, Martin, Berens, y'all ready to take us lil' ladies to lunch?" I asked, in a southern accent. I wasn't sure why I thought I needed to use a southern accent. We were in Minnesota for heaven sake, pretty far north too. Maybe it was the redneck feel of being in the country. I didn't really know. I added a wink for effect.

Jake smiled and said, "Sure, pretty ladies. Let's go across the street to the fancy restaurant." He stood between me and Lily and put his elbows out to his sides and said, "Shall we? Mark, get the tab, will ya buddy? I got my arms full." With that, Lily and I took an arm and let Jake lead us to the door. Jake could be so cute sometimes. It helped a little that he hadn't shaved this morning, so his dark facial hair was looking mighty fine in this setting. He had that naturally dark skin from his Italian and French connections. And thick, dark hair all over. He was naturally handsome, and I felt lucky to be holding his arm. A rush of heat moved through me, taking my mind back to the island counter in the kitchen.

We enjoyed a country style Bar-B-Que lunch and decided that we'd had enough of this town for a day. We swung through the gas station on the edge of town that we'd noticed on the way in. Jake topped off the gas tank and took a spin through the car wash. Oddly, on the way back, the puddles were not as much fun. The weather had cleared up, and it was getting hot. I instinctively pulled my hair back into a pony. Frizz was on the way. I gazed out my window and noticed three deer munching on corn in the field. Neat.

5

W HEN WE GOT BACK, we decided to hang at the cabin. Lily and I changed into our swim suits, Jake and Mark into their swim shorts and tanks. The boys set up the bean bags and golf game, while I untied the floaties and grabbed extra rope to tie them to the dock. Lily carried the beer, and we headed out to the water. It was perfect, warm water, warm air, cold beer. No noise at all, which I thought to myself was really odd. No boats, no kids, no cars. It was total silence, I wasn't sure how I felt about that. It was nice but almost uncomfortable. I'm sure I could get use to it though.

A few moments later, Lily and I were floating, tied to the dock and each other so we wouldn't float away. I laid my head back and closed my eyes. Lots of thoughts raced through my mind, but I quickly pushed them out. I was going to remain positive. I found myself thinking about the old man. He was so sweet and kind and so concerned. Honestly, he had me a little worried, not really sure what I was worried about but it was a strange conversation. I took a long pull on my beer, then tipped my head back and closed my eyes again. Complete relaxation. Moments later, I heard water splashing so I slowly opened my eyes. I saw a boat off in the distance. It was about a hundred yards from me. Was that what I heard splashing? It couldn't be. Must have been a fish jumping. Lily looked like she was asleep and I could see Mark and Jake up by the far side of the cabin tossing bean bags. I looked back to the boat. It looked small, like an old fishing boat. It was made of wood and the white paint was peeling off it. I could see someone in it. I put my hand up to shield the sun from my eyes. It was so bright and the sun was reflecting off the water, so I couldn't see well at all. It looked like a girl or a young woman in the boat. She appeared to be looking at me. I kept looking, blinking my eyes to try to see better. She was standing up in the little old boat. She was going to fall! What was she doing? I sat up a little, still shielding my eyes. Was she waving at me? It looked like she was waving, a big "come over here" wave. I looked at Lily. Still sleeping. Should I wake her? What if this girl needed help? "Lily," I said, "look. Do you see that boat over there?" I pointed.

She sat up and asked, "Where?" shielding her eyes with her hand. I looked over and pointed further, but when I looked again the boat wasn't there.

"What the heck? I just saw a boat out there. Now it's gone." I told her. I kept looking all over the lake, but I couldn't see it anywhere.

"Oh, was it big or what? What did you want me to see?" she asked me.

"Umm, no. It was nothing…never mind. Sorry, I thought I saw a girl in a boat waving like she needed help. It must have just been a weird reflection. It's probably the beer mixed with the heat." I added, hoping I wasn't losing my mind. "Do you want a margarita?"

"Sure," Lily said.

"Okay, I'll be right back. Save my spot." I told her. I hopped in the water and waded to shore. When I got to the cabin, I turned around and looked one more time for the boat, but it wasn't there. Weird. I said, "Hey," to the boys, who looked like they'd just finished the game.

"Margs anyone?" I yelled to them. They both said yes.

I came out of the cabin door carrying four strawberry margaritas and a pitcher full for the next round. I looked out to the lake and Lily was still on her float. Mark was hanging on to the side, and Jake had taken over mine. I passed out drinks and Jake sat up. After I set the pitcher on the dock, I jumped on the float with him. It sank a little but it was holding. I looked out at the lake as Lily filled them in on my "vision." I defended myself by smiling, slamming my drink and reaching for a refill.

"It's really good tequila!" I informed them, to lighten the moment. Noting to myself—never slam a margarita. Major brain freeze. Ooooow!

We spent another hour on the water and were all feeling the burn, and our skin was wrinkly from being wet, so we decided to take a break. Jake and Lily carried the patio table over to the shade of a big tree, and Mark and I grabbed chairs. We all sat down and wasted another hour chatting. Mark was pretty quiet. Lily was trying to include him in the conversation but he wasn't biting.

When I got up to grab more drinks, I asked Lily if she wanted to help me. She said sure and joined me in the kitchen. She was busy slicing a lime while I collected four Coronas and popped them open. After we poked the limes in, Lily grabbed two and so did I. I followed her out the patio door. She walked over to Jake and handed him one, so I gave my extra to Mark. They both thanked us and again, I felt suspicion. I took a long drink of my beer and mentally noted that I needed to stop after that one or have a lot more to make it through the night.

We decided on frozen pizza for supper, with chips and salsa. No one wanted to volunteer to cook I guess. I think we are all feeling the effects of laziness, alcohol, and sun. I had an extra piece of pizza to help soak up the alcohol, and then decided to have at it with another shot of the tequila. I was getting pretty drunk.

"Wow, the room is starting to spin," I stuttered.

Lily chimed in, "It's spinning for me too, and it's a good thing we don't have to drive anywhere." The last time the four of us got drunk, we forgot to designate a driver and ended up paying for a very expensive cab. Lily did another shot.

I looked around the table. I thought they all looked as drunk as I was. Jake stood up and suggested we start a fire. We all slowly sauntered outside, Mark brought out the portable stereo and put on some music. Lily was instantly dancing. I was watching Jake stumble around the fire pit trying to get a fire going, giggling softly. He wasn't having much luck because it was pretty windy and his balance wasn't good.

Lily walked up and put her arm around him and slurred, "It's okay, Jake. I still love you." He smiled and they both start laughing.

Then he put his arm around her and said, "Let's go in the house and get out of the wind. Mark, put the tunes on in there," Jake stammered.

We all moved in, and Mark shot me a look. I half smiled back and finished another beer.

We moved into the living room, and everyone was kinda dancing in their own way. Mark went to the kitchen and filled up four shot glasses with tequila. We followed him and took another shot together. Pretty soon the room was spinning faster, and Lily had now fallen over twice, both times I had picked her up.

"I think you've had enough Lily," Mark scolded.

"Mark, you're such a jerk. Just let me have fun," she stammered at him. "I wish you'd lighten up and be more like Jake here." Lily returned her eyes to Jake and changed her voice. "Jake is tons of fun. Aren't you, baby?" she said, as she slung her arm around his neck, her face inches from his.

Mark stepped in and grabbed her other arm, "It's time for bed, honey. Tell your friends goodnight," he told her, while trying to pull her toward him. But she ripped her arm free and put that arm around Jake, too. Now she was seriously pissing me off! Jake was reaching behind his neck and trying to unhook her hands.

"Jake, you're so much fun. We have fun, don't we?" she asked.

"Yes, we do," I answered loudly. "Tons of fun, but I think Mark is right. We've all had enough. I think we should call it a night." Jake was staring really hard into her eyes and looked mad.

Mark reached for Lily's hand again, and she pulled back. She shot me an "I hate you" look and marched off to her room. Mark apologized to us and followed her.

"Well, that was entertaining," Jake said and finished his beer. He went to the radio and turned it off. Then started picking up the kitchen. I was fuming. That was all a little too much for me, plus I was drunk, so that made it worse.

"I think Lily's been a little too friendly lately. She seems to think she needs to make extra efforts towards you." I said, quite frankly and leaned back against the counter and folded my arms across my chest.

"Oh, geez. Let's not make a big deal out of this, Sara. She was drunk and just having fun. She's our friend," he replied, looking at me like I'd just done something wrong.

"Yes, I'm aware she's our friend, Jake, but she's crossing lines lately, and actually I think you are too. Is there something going on I should know about?" I asked, trying my hardest not to slur my words.

"What?" Jake said, as he snapped his head toward me. "Are you actually implying I may be having an affair with your best friend? What the hell, Sara? Now I think you've had enough too. I'm going to forget you said anything. We're going to go to bed and forget this night ever happened." And with that, he walked to the bedroom.

Shit, now I was concerned he was right. I may have just said something really hurtful. I basically just told him I had no confidence in him or our relationship and that I didn't trust him. If I was wrong, I'd forever regret that.

I turned all the lights off except the one above the stove and shuffled to the bedroom. Jake was in bed and the room was dark. I climbed in and stayed on my side of the bed. I noticed the clock, about eleven-thirty. Jake didn't move. I closed my eyes, and the room started spinning. Man, I hated that! Why did the room have to spin? Slowly, I started to relax and eventually fell asleep.

6

I WOKE UP WITH A START. My tequila wanted out! Shoot, I really hated throwing up. I lay there with my eyes open in the dark and tried to ignore my stomach and swelling tongue. It wasn't working. I rolled over and sat up. It was one, and oddly Jake was not in bed. Maybe he was sick too. Then I heard something . . . voices, quietly whispering. I tippy toed across the room and put my ear to the door to hear better. It was Lily and Jake, but I couldn't make out what they were saying. Shit, I needed to throw up very soon, but I really wanted to stay here and spy on them. I stepped back from the door and the floor creaked. Oops! I jumped back into bed and covered up. Moments later, Jake opened the door quietly and peeked in. Then he closed it and walked back down the hall. I jumped back up and ran back to the door, and I heard the deck door slide open and shut and then I heard nothing. I slowly opened the door and peeked out. They were not in my sight, so I jumped across the hall into the bathroom. Moments later, I was feeling better stomach wise but now what should I do, go back to sleep or spy? Geez, seriously I never thought that I'd have to ponder that in my life. Fact of the matter was, it really bothered me, and I needed to know if I was being cheated on by my husband and best friend.

I quietly slipped out the front door of the cabin, and crept carefully along the side to the back. I got to the patio corner, stopped and backed up against the logs. I could hear them now, so I stayed out of sight and listened hard.

"I said sorry. I don't know what else to say, Jake. This is really hard for me. I have to watch you with her the whole week and pretend it doesn't bother me. Then I have to sit around and be her friend. You know it's not easy even to look at her. I love you and want to be with you, but I don't like sneaking around. I can't stand this. Plus it's been four days, Jake. I miss you and I need you," Lily said.

And there it was! The truth. My suspicions were confirmed. I couldn't believe it. I tried to control my breathing and put my hand over my mouth to help. I felt tightening in my chest, and my knees suddenly couldn't support my weight. I couldn't breathe, and I really wanted to scream and cry, but I couldn't. I thought I was going to hyperventilate. My blood was pounding so hard through my veins that my heart was literally knocking on my ribs. This wasn't happening! I loved Jake so much, and he loved me. No, no, no! My mind was racing as fast as my heart. I shook my head and tried to control my heart rate. I was shaking from head to toe. It was like nothing I'd felt before.

"Lily, we have to be careful," Jake said. "Just get through the rest of this week, and then it'll be easier. We'll figure out what to do when we get back. For now, you need to behave and stay calm. And lay off the alcohol a bit. We don't need anymore outbursts. We need to get back in there."

"Okay," Lily said, "but I don't like it. It seems like you're still in love with her. Are you? Do you want to end this?"

"It's hard for me too, Lil, and I'm not in love with her anymore. I haven't been for a while, but I do still care about her. I don't want her to get hurt, but I know she will, and it's all my fault. I feel awful. But, Lil, I'm in love with you. We'll make it through this." Jake said, in his soft, affectionate voice.

Then it was quiet. I couldn't hear anything. I peeked slowly around the corner and saw them kissing. Fuck! I can't believe this! I turned and ran, quietly, to the front door. I needed to beat them in or they would know that I knew. I got inside. From the front door I could see through part of the patio door, and they were still kissing, hands moving everywhere. I didn't know if I should confront them or not. I didn't know what my next move should be. I stopped by the bathroom and threw up again, not from tequila this time. Then quickly jumped back into bed. About twenty minutes later, Jake finally came back to bed. I laid very still, pretending to be asleep, tear after tear falling down my cheeks.

I tossed and turned all night. When I finally got up, it was seven-thirty. I padded into the kitchen and started some much-needed coffee, then grabbed some clothes from my room and went to shower. I dressed, and threw on some make-up, taking note to use the waterproof mascara. I spent a little extra time on my hair, not really sure why. It wasn't like Jake was going to notice me anyway. I looked at myself in the mirror and told myself I was an adult and I'd handle this with dignity and grace. I would be fine. I smiled at myself and noticed how sad I looked even with a smile. I hurt ... so bad ... my body felt like it had had the flu for a week. I hurt ... physically ... everywhere. I was not at all hungry, but I took a deep breath and headed to the kitchen to start with coffee. I felt so weak and achy, I hoped the coffee would help some.

I took my cup out to the patio and sat down in the rising sun. I pulled up another chair to prop my legs up. One sip and a deep breath and there I was, in full-on tears. I was unsure what I should do. Should I grab the keys to the Jeep and leave? I didn't know my way back at all. Should I stay? Should I wake up Mark? Should I tell Jake and Lily that I knew? Should I act like nothing happened? I felt completely out of control. I closed my eyes and prayed hard for strength and guidance. I heard the deck door slide open and looked over to see Mark, still in his lounge wear, coming out with a coffee cup. He pulled up a chair.

"Good morning," he said, "You're already showered and dressed? What time did you wake up?" he asked.

"I couldn't sleep last night. It was a long night, to say the least," I responded without looking at him.

"Sorry about last night. Lily had too much to much to drink, I hope she didn't make you or Jake too uncomfortable. She hasn't been herself lately. I think she's under stress at work." Mark said apologetically, with a half smile.

"Mark, do you think Lily would ever cheat on you?" I asked, sternly without returning the smile.

"What? No, Sara, I don't. I think she was drunk and made herself look stupid last night. But I don't think she's cheating on me," he said.

I could tell I'd hit a nerve. I just looked back out to the lake.

I was so angry. I just wanted everyone to know so that I could move on with my life. I didn't want to spend one more second married to Jake. I just wanted to pack my things and leave.

"Sara?" Mark asked, "Where did you go there? Do you think Lily's cheating on me? Is she, Sara? Did she tell you that?" his voice was getting louder.

"She didn't tell me," I said, plainly.

"What do you know Sara? Tell me. My god, if you know something tell me, now!" he yelled, leaning at me in his chair.

"Ya know what, Mark, if you want to know something, go to your girl-friend and ask her. Maybe she'll tell you what you deserve to know," I told him. We sat there in silence for a while. Both of us staring out to the lake. About ten minutes later, Lily came out dressed in jean shorts and a fitted t-shirt. She was showered with coffee in hand.

"Good morning," she said, with a smile to which neither of us responded. "Look, you guys, I'm sorry for last night. I had way too much to drink, and I was behaving like an idiot. I'm so sorry," she said in a disgusting voice that made me ill. I got up and walked inside to the coffee pot and refilled. I was standing there facing it, wondering what to do. It felt like my world was moving in slow motion.

I turned around and saw the two through the glass door talking. Mark looked mad, and I secretly wished I would have left the door open so I could eavesdrop. I had a horrible headache, so I went to my room and got some Tylenol. When I return to the kitchen, they were coming through the door. Mark marched past me to the bedroom. Lily headed to the entry and started lacing up her shoes. When Mark came back to the kitchen and grabbed a water bottle from the fridge, he was dressed in jeans, a polo, and tennis shoes.

"We're going on a walk in the woods to talk for a bit," Mark told me. I nodded. "Sorry about my attitude this morning," he added and gave me a quick kiss on the cheek.

Lily looked at me sadly and said, "Sorry again for last night . . . I'll talk to you when we get back." I didn't nod to her. I just looked straight into her eyes. She locked eyes with me and looked really scared. I wondered if I looked as scary as I felt. I bet she wondered if I knew.

They shut the door behind themselves, and I went back out to the patio with my coffee. It didn't seem to be helping, but considering my last twelve hours I didn't think they made coffee strong enough. I was staring out to the lake when I heard the door slide open and out walked Jake dressed and showered.

"Good morning," he said, and kissed my cheek as if it were any other morning. He pulled up a chair next to me and sat back. "Are you hungover at all?" he asked.

"No, I'm not." Gosh, just the sight of him made me so angry. It was hard to believe that just hours ago, I was madly in love with him. Right now I was feeling rage like never before. My heart was thumping again, and I just wanted to get away from him.

"I'm not too bad either considering how much we drank. I'm surprised you didn't have to throw up last night. Usually when you get that hammered you're up puking a couple hours later," he said with a smile, like he was funny.

"Actually, I did throw up last night. Twice," I said. And I let that hang there for a minute. I looked over to him and got eye contact. Then I added, "You must not of heard me get up. It was about three." I turned my eyes back to the lake and took a sip.

"Yeah, I guess I didn't," he said, and I could tell that his mind was racing. He looked like a deer in the head lights.

"Where are Mark and Lily?" he asked.

"They went on a walk in the woods. I think they had a lot to talk about. Mark was pretty upset with Lily this morning," I said, while staring at the lake. "That was quite the fiasco last night."

Jake and I sat there in uncomfortable silence for about thirty minutes. My mind was racing. I was so tired and my headache was still pounding. I didn't really know where to start, so I said nothing. I told him I was going to lay down. Maybe I'd be able to sleep if he's wasn't laying next to me. I lay down and closed my tear-filled eyes and I was out.

Three hours later, I woke up. I couldn't believe I slept that long. I was still behind a few hours but wanted to get up. I made my way to the fridge for a bottled water and noticed the house was very quiet. I stepped outside and looked around to see where everyone was at. I spotted Mark and Jake in the back yard near our Jeep, talking. They looked like they were having a very intense conversation. Both men were sweating through their shirts, and Mark was pacing. Jake was using a lot of hand gestures and looked like his blood pressure was through the roof. I guess Mark must have found out.

I walked out the front door, Mark noticed me and said something to Jake, and they had a quick discussion I know they didn't want me to hear. Jake nodded and turned around and looked at me. He looked like he'd been out for a run. I guess getting busted having an affair with your best friend's girl turns the body's internal temperature up. He was literally sweating it. Good, I was so angry, and full of piss and vinegar I wanted him to suffer the hurt like I did. On the other hand I felt sorry for him. He looked really lost and worried. I kind of wanted to hold him. But I hated him so bad, I wouldn't.

"What's going on?" I calmly asked, "Where's Lily?" Jake looked at Mark, who looked awful, like he'd just been hit by a truck. Mark's eyes looked like they had a lot to say but he stayed quiet. It almost looked like he was pleading with Jake. Jake faced me straight on and stumbled over his words.

"Look, Sara, there's something we need to tell you," Jake said. He reached for my shoulder, and I stepped back. *Do not touch me.* He looked surprised by my reaction. "Can we go sit down on the patio?" he asked. We all walked to the patio. Jake looked at Mark who was sitting down next to me and wasn't saying a word. He was bent forward with his face in his hands. I put my hand on Mark's back and rubbed gently. I felt bad for him. He loved Lily so much, and she totally betrayed him. She betrayed me too, but Mark loved her on a much deeper level. What a mess.

"Okay, Jake, what is it?" I said, showing no emotion. I crossed my arms over my chest and stared at him. He looked really uncomfortable, like he was struggling to find the right words. Finally, after a few breaths and glances at my face, which was stone cold, he spat out his confession.

7

ARA... I'M SO SORRY TO TELL YOU THIS ... I never meant for anyone to get hurt. I don't know what I was thinking . . . or what I was doing. I made a horrible mistake. I need you to know that none of this was intended to hurt you."

He struggled with each sentence, and I let him. Then he started crying and taking deep breaths and naturally, I cried with him. No one cries alone in my presence. As much as I hated him, I didn't like to see him cry. I had this urge to reach out and touch him and tell him it would be okay but I fought it hard. I loved him and hated him all at the same time. I didn't ever want to see him again, but I really needed my Jake right now. This person sitting in front of me was a stranger, and I missed my Jake. This was going to be the worst day of my life, and normally I would run to Jake for support, but I couldn't in this situation because he was the cause, the monster that handed me all this pain, stole my life, my husband, and my best friend from me. I couldn't believe the person I loved more than anyone else in the whole world would do this to me. Why? What had I done to deserve this? How long had our relationship been a lie?

Finally he blurted out, "Lily and I are having an affair." He looked at me, and he was crying pretty hard. I kept calm and nodded, tears rolling down my cheeks, but I would not give him the satisfaction of seeing me break down. *Stay strong, Sara,* I repeated to myself over and over.

"Okay then," I responded. I took a few deep breaths and looked over to Mark. I rubbed his back again and told him that I was sorry for his hurt. Then I stood up from the table. "Where's Lily?" I asked, "Does she know that we know?"

"Yes," Mark answered, "she told me on our walk a little bit ago. Then she got back and took the car and left. She said she never wanted to talk to me again," he added in between sobs.

"Mark, I'm so sorry." Jake said, shaking his head. "I don't know what to do to fix this."

"You can't, Jake, you stupid son of a bitch! You can never fix this!" he yelled. "You're no longer my friend. I fucking hate you, you lying, cheating bastard!" Then, Mark stood up and looked like he was going to attack Jake, so I placed myself between them. I thought Mark had every right to punch Jake in the face, but I didn't want to see it.

"Well, I'd like to leave, too. So if you two want to get your things together, we can drive back. Let's get everything packed and leave right now, and Jake, when we get home, you'll get your things from the apartment and leave, forever. We're done." I said, very calmly. I surprised myself at how well I was handling it. He nodded and put his head down.

Less than an hour later, we were packed into the Jeep with had the cargo of four people. Lily had taken nothing with her when she left. She just grabbed the keys and took off. We locked the cabin when we left, and I called Harold, the manager, to let him know that we departed early because of a family emergency. I drove, mostly because I needed something to do besides think about everything. Jake sat in the back and Mark in the front. No one spoke the whole way except when I suggested that Jake call his girlfriend and let her know that he had her stuff and the cabin was locked. He dialed and said that he left a voice mail because she didn't answer. It took over two hours to get back, and by the time we got home my eyes, head, and stomach had had enough for the day, and it was only four.

I dropped Mark and all his cargo at his apartment and asked him if he wanted Lily's stuff. He said no. Jake and I both helped him carry his stuff in.

Jake set the last of the load down in the entry, "Mark . . . I'm so sorry . . . I'll call later," Jake said.

"Don't bother," Mark told him as he walked out the door.

I gave Mark a big, long, tight, hug. "I'm sorry," I said to him. He nodded. "Call me tomorrow if you want to talk," I added.

"I will," he said and kissed my cheek. I walked out, tears flowing again. Back in the parking lot, I hauled myself into the Jeep. Jake was sitting shot gun, but I didn't acknowledge him, I just drove silently to our apartment. I parked by our other vehicle, a newer Grand Prix. I told him I'd be taking the Jeep, and he could have the Grand Prix, so he could load his stuff in there. He didn't argue, and we walked up to the apartment. He walked into our bedroom and sat down on the side of the bed and started crying hard. I went into the bathroom and had a talk with myself in the mirror. When I was pulled together enough, I came out and told him to get going.

"Jake," I said in a firm and steady voice, "I really don't want to drag this out into a night of drama. Please just get what you need and go. You can come back later for the rest of your stuff, when I'm not here. You can take anything that was solely yours and make a list of anything that was ours that you're interested in and send me a copy, I'll look it over and give it to my lawyer. And, Jake, get a lawyer right away, I plan to push this through quickly."

"Sara, please, can we talk?" he begged.

"No, Jake, there's nothing to say. It's over. You and Lily can have the life you always dreamed of now. I hope she makes you happy, Jake, I really do." I said, without any tears. I hoped he'd leave soon because I didn't know how much longer I could keep this up.

"Okay, I'll go. Not because I want to, but because you want me to," he said.

Seriously? "Aw, thanks, Jake, for thinking of me and my feelings. You're great. Such a sweet husband," I replied with as much sarcasm as I could fit in. "Just get what you need and get out."

He got up from the bed and grabbed a duffel bag from the closet. In the kitchen I gathered a bottled water and couple Tylenol. I debated calling my mom. If I did, she'd probably rush right over, and I didn't really know if I wanted company right then. Normally I would call Lily, but I wouldn't be doing that either. I felt really alone. It seriously felt like someone had ripped out my insides. It felt different just to breathe. I sat down at the kitchen table and started thinking about how long a divorce took and all the repercussions that went with it. I was not looking forward to the next few months. I hoped Jake wouldn't fight me on anything or drag it out. If he didn't fight it, I had friends at the office that would put a rush on it for me. I couldn't believe this was happening to me. I fought back more tears.

Thank God for Grans's inheritance. At least I didn't have to worry about paying the bills. I didn't know how people made it work financially after a divorce. The cost of the divorce alone could cripple a person but how did anyone afford their own place, car and all their other expenses in this day in age? Thank goodness we didn't have children. We didn't have children now…and we never would. A couple more tears escaped. Jake and I had been together for so long, we had grown into adults together, and we always planned to raise a family. I had mentally pictured him so many times holding our babies, now there would never be any little Martin babies. That thought made a bunch more tears come.

We had talked just recently about starting a family in the near future, but we wanted to see where the inheritance would take us first. We didn't know for sure if we would move or stay, work or not, or maybe travel the world. Everything was so up in the air, we decided to wait until we were more sure of our long-term plans. Or maybe Jake was too busy planning his future with Lily. That thought took my breath away. I wondered if they talked about children. I remembered her saying recently that she wanted to get married and have kids soon, she just didn't know if Mark was the guy she wanted to do that with. Sick, I sat there and listened to her gripe, when all the while she was moving in on my life.

Now everything was changed. I felt really ripped off. My life had been stopped and destroyed without my permission. I had dreams, plans, goals, and a husband who I'd made these with and now, nothing. It was all gone. I was so angry. I needed to scream and cry, but I didn't want to do it in front of him. I wasn't going to give him the satisfaction.

Jake slowly came into the kitchen and dropped his duffel bag by the door. He slithered over and knelt down by my feet. He reached for my hands and looked into my eyes.

"I'm so sorry, Sara. I never meant to hurt you," he said from his knees. "I don't know what came over me. This has been the worst thing I've ever done. I've hurt so many people and I've become someone I despise. I can't even stand to look in the mirror at myself. I don't expect you to forgive me. I just want you to know that it was a huge mistake, and I'm so sorry that you were hurt in all this," he cried. "I never meant to hurt you, Sara. I know what I've done. I've lost a wife who was loving and faithful, kind, compassionate, successful and so beautiful, inside and out. Sara, I love you so much. I don't want to lose you. Please don't file. I'll do whatever it takes to fix this. Please just give it some thought and time," he whined some more.

I was tearing up but telling myself not to break down. I felt bad for him. I didn't want him to hurt. I hated seeing him like this. I wished a hug would fix everything. Then suddenly, I got an image of them last night on the patio table, and then an image of us on the island counter in the kitchen. Wow, he had quite the weekend, Lily, too. Ugh!

"Jake," I said steadily, "There's nothing you can say that'll ever take back all the lying, hurt, and deceit. There's no future for us. I'll never be able to forgive you ... or trust you ... or be your friend again. You have completely destroyed my life. I gave you all my love, and you threw it away. Never again, Jake, never. When you figure out where you're staying, text a message. I'll text you back about when you can get your things."

"Sara, please."

"No, Jake. Get out," I interrupted. Then I pulled my hands away and walked down the hall toward the bedroom. A moment later, I heard the door open and close. He was gone. Right on cue, I completely lost it.

I spent the next five hours or so, sobbing and feeling sorry for myself. I didn't call anyone because I just needed to be alone and have a good cry. I was really glad I didn't have to work until Monday, that gave me four more days, and my Monday schedule only had two things on it, so that would only be half a day. I looked at the clock. Almost midnight. After a long, hot, teary shower, I dressed in jammy pants and an over-sized t-shirt. I grabbed a wine glass opened the fridge. I only had one bottle of red, which would work just fine as a therapist and sleep aid.

8

THE NEXT MORNING, I woke up on the couch, and the TV was still on from last night. I got all cleaned up, then dressed in jeans and a tank. I knew I needed to call my mom and my friend Kat. Kat and I had been friends for the last eight years or so. We'd met at a work conference, and she later transferred to my building. She was in the divorce and family court department. I didn't see her much day to day, but we got together every Thursday night for ladies night at O'Bryan's with a couple other girls from the office. Lily always met up with us too. We'd done many shopping outings together and whatever else we could squeeze into our schedules. She was single so that made it a little easier.

I wondered about Mark and how he was doing. Maybe I should call him. I knew what it was like to need alone time, but at the same time I wanted to be there for him if he needed me. Hopefully he'd stay strong through all this. He was a great guy, and Lily didn't deserve him. I texted him and told him I was stopping by at ten with coffee and bagels. He replied, "Okay." Then I called my mom and filled her in. She bawled on the phone, and I agreed to meet her for lunch at one, at a mom 'n' pop restaurant near her home, which was about a ten-minute drive from my apartment. I put off calling Kat. One thing at a time.

I walked to the parking lot. On the way out I made a mental note to move as soon as possible. I didn't want to be in the apartment Jake and I had shared. I needed a new bed too. I didn't want to be around anything I'd shared with Jake. I started thinking about all the stuff we had and how intertwined our lives were. I made another mental note to get a new cell phone number and plan, too. I didn't want to be on the same plan he'd called her on, and I didn't ever want to talk to Lily or see her again. I was actually kind of surprised she hadn't called me, though. Or was I? Really, what was she going to say to me? "Oops, I'm sorry I ruined your life. Can we still be friends?" I guess I didn't expect her to call, it was just strange not having my husband or best friend to turn to when I needed them most.

Nonetheless, I had to take it day by day and make sure I moved forward. I knew I'd done nothing to deserve this. I would be fine. I just needed to keep reminding myself of that. Lily and Jake were both very selfish people, and I didn't need them in my life. I wasn't going to let them steal one more day from me. Oddly though, I missed them both. I hated them and loved them and missed them, all at the same time. Ugh, I was such a basket case.

In the grocery store I picked up an assortment of bagels and donuts. Then, I took a turn to produce and grabbed a container of fresh strawberries. Back in the car, my phone beeped. It was a text from Jake.

"So sorry, Sara, I miss you. Couldn't sleep last night knowing the pain you're in cuz of me."

Mentally, I told him to go to hell and threw my phone back in my purse. I drove to Star Bucks and got two foo foo coffees and headed to Mark's. I half expected Lily to be there crying, but she wasn't. He was up and dressed but looked like hell. We sat at the table and ate a few bites of strawberries and dough-nuts, but neither of us had an appetite. Then we moved to the living room and sat on either end of the couch facing each other, both of us sipping coffee. "How was your night?" I asked. "Did you sleep?"

"Yeah, after I drank a ton, I slept pretty good," he replied. He looked like he hadn't slept in a week. "Did you have any idea, Sara?"

"No, at least not until this weekend. There were definitely some signs this weekend, but other than that I had no idea. When did you find out? How did she tell you?" I asked.

"When we went for a walk in the woods," he said slowly, staring at his foot that was folded up on the couch in front of him. "She just blurted it out. Then said she was done with me and walked back, got the keys and left."

"Did she say how long it'd been going on?" I asked, not sure I wanted to know the answer.

"No, she didn't say much at all. When she told me, Sara, it was like I was talking to a different person. I looked at her eyes, and it's like it wasn't Lily. She was so cold and uncaring, she didn't even say she was sorry. It hurts so much. It just hurts so bad," he continued sobbing through his words, "I just can't believe she's gone."

"Has she tried to contact you at all? Has she sent messages or called? Have you tried to call or text her?" I asked.

"No, I don't think she will either. She's not in love with me, and I don't think she has been for a while. Looking back, I wonder how long they were doing this. They'd both been odd for a while. I don't think I'll hear from her again. I don't want to either. I have nothing to say to her," he said.

"Where do you think she went?" I asked, "Her mom and dad are here and her job is here."

I think she'll move to New York and start a new life there. That's what she always talked about, from the day we met she's always dreamed of New York," he said, still staring down.

"Do you think she and Jake will stay together?" I asked, again not really wanting to know the answer.

"No," he answered. "I don't think so. I guess I don't know for sure." He looked up at me, and I just shook my head in disgust. I took a deep breath and we both sat there for a while in silence.

Then out of nowhere, Mark started sobbing again. "We talked last week about marriage and kids, and she seemed like she was planning a future with me. She'd been distant, but I thought it was just work stress. Now all I can do is think about when they were together. When did he fit into her schedule, or was Jake the reason she's been so busy at work lately? I can't get it out of my head. How many times were we together after they were? It makes me sick, and my best friend, too! Why couldn't it have been a stranger or someone I didn't know. Now I don't even have a best friend to lean on right now. This is killing me."

"I know, Mark," I said, and I put my hand on this calf. "I'll be here for you, if you'll be here for me," I said through tears. "We need to remember that we are good people, and that this was not our fault. We need to stay strong and help each other get through this. We'll be okay," I said, unsure.

We sat there talking for another hour and when I stood to leave, I told Mark to call me anytime night or day. I gave him a big hug and walked out the door.

I had about an hour and a half before lunch with my mom, so I touched up my makeup in the car mirror and pulled into the Hom Furniture store parking lot. I shopped quickly for a new bedroom set and found one that was the exact opposite of what we'd had. I told the lady I'd take it. I put it on my credit card and prayed that my inheritance came before that bill did. It had to be ordered, and it could take five to ten days to get in. They would call when it got there to set up a delivery time.

I jumped back into my Jeep, and drove over to the gas station and picked up a couple magazines on apartments and got a paper, too. No time like the present to get a new place and start a new life. I didn't want to spend one more second in that place I used to call home. Everything in it reminded me of Jake.

In the parking lot of the restaurant, I checked the time. I was fifteen minutes early but I could see my mom in the window, waiting for me. I walked to the booth where she was seated and she got up and gave me a big hug.

"I'm so sorry," she said through tears.

We sat down as the waitress brought over waters. Mom ordered a coffee, and I ordered a diet soda. We talked for a while, and I filled her in on the details, not that I had a lot, but I told her what I knew. She just shook her head in disgust. We ordered but when my food came, I couldn't really stomach it, Mom couldn't either, so we ended up putting it into to-go boxes.

"It's very important to eat and take good care of yourself," Mom said, "and try to remember never to try to blame yourself or think that you caused this in anyway."

I nodded, "I'll be fine." I considered myself a strong, independent woman, and I hoped I'd be fine. But right now I felt like I needed another few hours of crying. I heard my phone beep and it was a text from Jake.

"U OK? Can we talk? I need you. I miss my Sara. SO SORRY. PLZ reply."

Not going to happen. Gosh wasn't it just two nights ago he was doing Lily with me in the other room. I showed it to my mom. Why didn't he text Lily instead?

"Get a new number," Mom said sternly.

"I plan to do that on the way home," I assured her with a half smile.

My mom was a very smart woman. She'd chosen a wonderful man to marry, and he was so good to her. Still after all these years, they're so happy. That's what I wanted. Mom told me she told Dad and that he really wanted to come to lunch today but decided that maybe it should be just the ladies for now. I loved my dad. We were close, but I bet he thought it would be really hard to listen to me and Mom cry and fight the urge to kill Jake. I didn't have children, but I could see how hard this was on them, as parents, too.

We sat there for an additional hour. Mom offered me my old room, at home, if I needed it. I declined but thanked her.

"I had a meeting with the estate planner about the probate situation, and it is awaiting final approval from the judge. It's expected to be closed out in a month, two tops. The lawyer told me that it was very well put together and an easy push because there was only me and you involved," she said with a smile.

Then, being the mom she was, she asked, "Did you find a financial planner yet?"

I told her about the appointments I'd set up and that I'd keep her updated. She said she'd called the lawyer earlier today, after she had talked to me and asked if this separation would have any effect on the trust or the one-time gift. She assured my mom that my grandmother was very careful about how she set it up, and we would not have to worry about Jake getting any of it. It brought me back to the conversation we'd had not so long ago about if Jake and I didn't make it, how I'd be rich and he'd be lonely, so sad. Again, I found myself feeling bad for him. What the heck? I realized there were stages of grief, but I hoped the hate and missing and feeling-bad-for-him emotional bull shit passed soon.

I thanked Mom for lunch and promised I'd come over for dinner tomorrow and eat whatever she made. I told her to give Dad a hug for me, and then I gave her one.

At the gas station, I filled up and then drove to the mall to check out cell phones and plans. I was kind of excited to get a new iPhone. When I got to the mall, I went to the kiosk and talked to the sales person there and asked about how to get out of a joint contract. She helped me with all the paperwork and set up my new phone with a new phone number. I immediately activated it and turned the other one in for recycling. There, no more texts from Jake, and I didn't have to worry about Lily calling either.

I headed to the food court and grabbed a quiet bench near the back wall. I called my office and let them know I had a new phone number, and instructed them to pass the new number on to the important people but not Jake. Then I called my mom and gave her my new number. I tried Mark at home, but he didn't answer, and his cell was off. I started toward my car but then turned a one-eighty and headed back to the food court. I asked a guy at the Subway register if he knew where I could get moving boxes.

9

"DUDE, YOU'RE IN LUCK!" HE SAID. "I have a gazillion boxes you can have for free. They're even collapsed. I just moved into a new apartment not five blocks from here, and I need to get rid of them. My girlfriend will kill me if I don't get them out of there. I paid for them from U-Haul. They're in great condition, and I don't need any money for them. I just don't want to toss them in the trash," he added.

He was maybe twenty-one, twenty-two, clean cut, if you could get past the pierced eye brow. He had great teeth, clear skin, a thin build and stood about six feet. And, hey, he was at work in the middle of a weekday, so he could be trusted, right? I could tell he knew what I was thinking.

"Oh, I understand if you're hesitant. I wouldn't go to some strange guy's apartment with him alone either. So I tell you what, my girlfriend is at the apartment right now. I can call her, and you can meet her there, if that's okay with you. She's way smaller than you. If she tries anything funny, you could totally take her," he added with a smile.

I laughed. Wow, that was the first time I'd smiled or laughed in two days. It kind of took me by surprise. "Okay, I'll take them," I said. I thanked him and exchange numbers, and then he called her to okay it. He gave me the directions and thanked me for helping him out with removing them.

I drove the five blocks over to the West View apartment building. Thankfully their apartment was on the bottom floor. I pressed number nine, and a woman's voice yelled to come on in. I walked down a short hall, turned a left, and nine was right there on the corner. Good because I was not feeling physically strong right now and would rather not have to climb stairs or walk long halls. I knocked on the door, and a beautiful, young, twenty-something woman answered.

"Hey, girl, you must be Sara," she said, sounding winded. Then I noticed she was very pregnant. "I'm so glad to see you! I've been on him every day about getting rid of these. We just moved in ten days ago, and I took the week off to unpack and get set up before this baby comes. I'm Kristin. Come on in," she said stepping back and opening the door further.

"Oh, congrats. When are you due?" I asked.

"Two weeks, but my doctor said I could go anytime. It didn't plan out well at all. Our lease at our old place was up, and we had been on a waiting list for this place. It all fell together at the wrong time. But, what do ya do? I spend the days unpacking, and Joey's been working part time at Subway to help with extra money for my maternity leave," she added. "He's so excited to be a daddy. I, on the other hand, could use another month." She giggled and waved me into the apartment. "The boxes are all flattened so it shouldn't be too much work. There's about sixty of them," she added, hands on her back, leaning back in a stretch.

"Well, thank you so much! They look really nice. Are you sure you don't want any money for them?" I asked.

"No, really, we're just glad we found someone who needed them. I'd hate to throw them out, but we really don't have storage room," she said, sounding winded again.

"Okay, well thanks. I have my Jeep backed up to the the door, so I'll make a few trips in and out. Do you have something I can prop open the door with, so I don't have to keep buzzing you?" I asked her.

"Oh, yeah, and here I'll help you," she said, as she bent down to pick some up.

"Oh, no. Really I can do it. I don't want you to work so hard. Seriously, I'll just make a bunch of trips," I told her.

"It's okay really. I'm fine, and I've been unpacking all week. Empty boxes are nothing," she laughed. I chuckled too and grabbed an armful and followed her out the door. She propped the door open with the garbage can that stood nearby as I unlocked the Jeep. I folded the back seats down so I had plenty of room for all sixty boxes. It was probably a few too many, but I'd take them anyway.

We were on load three and almost done when she said, "Oh, shit!" I turned around and saw her light gray, sweat pants gradually getting wet in the crotch.

"Holy crap!" I yelped, covering my mouth. "Did your water just break?"

"Uh, I think so. This is my first baby, but I'm pretty sure." I ran over to her and grabbed the boxes she was still holding. I tossed them down and told her to come back to the apartment. I yanked my phone out and called Joey. He sounded really excited and said to keep her there. He'd be there in five minutes.

I walked her into the living room and put a blanket down on the couch and then another and one more for good measure. That seemed to be all the blankets in the room. Then I told her to lie down and not push. She laughed and said okay. After I told her that Joey was on his way, I quickly took the last two loads of boxes to my Jeep, then went back to wait with her. I asked her if they knew if it was a girl or boy, and they didn't. My cell phone rang. Cool, first incoming call! It was Joey.

"Hello?" I answered, thinking I'd change the ring tone as soon as I had a chance.

"Hey, it's Joey," he said out of breath, "I went to my car and the dang tire is flat again, so I'm running there as fast as I can. I'm two blocks away. Is she okay?"

"Oh, no! Yeah she's fine. She doesn't seem to be having contractions, her water was just . . . spilling out." I said, looking over at her, smiling. She was just lying there smiling back. I looked around the room and saw a lot of boxes left to unpack. I felt kinda bad for her.

"Tell her I'm coming," he said, out of breath and hung up.

"Okay. That was Joey. He's on foot and running here right now. I guess the tire on your car was flat again."

"I told him last week it has a slow leak. It's low every time I go to use it. I had to put air in it four times last weekend. He promised he'd take care of it," she said, rolling her eyes.

"Are you guys going to need a ride to the hospital?" I asked.

"Um, yeah, I guess we could use one, if that's okay. Are you in a hurry?"

"No, I can take you. It's no problem. We'll throw Joey in on top of the boxes and you can ride shotgun. Do you have a bag packed?" I said, thinking about her water leaking all over my Jeep.

"Yes it's in the bedroooooooom! OOOOOOHHH!" she yelled and sat up higher on the couch, pulling her belly in with her hands.

"Oh, shit! Is that a contraction?" I yelled back.

"OOOOOOH! Yup, I think so," she took a deep breath and did some quick exhales.

I ran to the back bedroom and got the bag she had packed and set it by the door. Just as I turned around, a hard-breathing, bent over, too-winded-to-talk Joey came flying through it.

"Kristin! It's okay! I'm here, honey!" he yelled, between gulps of air. "Are you okay? Is the baby coming? Don't push. It's okay. We're going to be all right!" he continued, trying to breathe and talk and it wasn't working well. He walked over to the couch and put his hand on her stomach and kissed her forehead. He was still trying to catch his breath. I updated him on the plans for me to drive them to the hospital in my Jeep, her riding shot gun and he on the boxes. He thanked me and then ran to the back room to change quick and get his things. He was still very out of breath. When he got out of ear shot I asked her if he worked out much, and she laughed hard which caused another contraction. I apologized.

Joey heard her moaning and came running out, still winded, he took one look at her breathing through it and started to hyperventilate. He was wide eyed and wheezing a hundred miles an hour.

"Oh, shit, seriously? Kristin, do you have any paper bags?" I asked, starting to panic a little myself.

"Yes, in the closet next to the entryway. Grab him a paper one and me a big plastic one."

I ran over, opened the door, located the two bags and ran back to the living room. I threw the plastic one to Kristin and set Joey up with the paper one. He was breathing into it, making it go in and out.

Two minutes later, Joey was calming down a little, and we were walking slowly to the Jeep. I was glad I'd backed up to the door. We got to the passenger side, and Kristin ripped the bag open and spread it out on the seat. Genius. I had no idea what she was going to do with it, but I wasn't about to question a pregnant woman in labor. Joey climbed in the back the best he could, and we took off. We were only about six miles from the hospital. Kristin had a another contraction on the way. I asked Joey if we should call the hospital and tell them we're coming. He nodded and dug his phone out to call.

When we arrived, I parked in the ER drop off zone, and helped them out. Joey was still a little winded but trying his best to keep up. When the doors opened, a nurse with a wheelchair called Kristin by name, so I assumed she was in good hands. Kristin sat in the chair and the nurse took one look at Joey and grabbed his wrist to take his pulse.

"Grab the other wheelchair behind you, by the door," she said to me. "You," she said pointing at Joey, "sit, breathe and don't cause any problems." Joey gladly sat.

Kristin started another contraction.

"How far apart are they?" the nurse asked me.

"Um, about six minutes maybe. I didn't even think about timing them," I admitted. "Her water broke about a half hour ago," I said.

So I pushed Joey, who was still puffing into his bag, and she pushed Kristin. Off we went to the maternity ward. This was all happening so fast, I noticed I was shaking. The nurse entered a room and helped Kristin stand, then handed me a folded gown and booties.

"Here ya go, you can help her get into these," she said then turned to the computer. Joey was still in his wheelchair with his bag in his hand. We were all smiling at each other uncomfortably.

"Oh, oh," I said in a singing voice, "I think we forgot your bag in the car and I parked in the ER drop off zone, I better go move it. Here, Joey, help your girlfriend get dressed in these, and I'll bring your bag up" Joey agreed and seemed okay to stand, so I left the room and told them I'd be back in a few minutes.

On the way to the lot, I stopped by the cafeteria and grabbed a banana and coffee. I was really starting to feel the physical affects of my crazy life. I sat for a moment and consumed them. Then I went back out to my Jeep, moved it to visitor parking and grabbed Kristin's bag. I stopped by the gift shoppe on the way and got some flowers.

Settled in the room, Krisitin had been wired and was leaning back in her bed holding her belly and breathing hard. Joey was sitting calmly beside her breathing normally and holding her hand. So precious! It momentarily reminded me of Jake and me. I set the flowers down and put the bag in the far corner.

"Thank you for everything you've done for us," Joey said.

"It's no problem!" I told them. I liked them, they seemed really nice.

"Do you want me to call anyone for you?" I asked.

"No, I'll make calls in a few minutes. Both our parents live in Colorado. That's where we grew up. We moved here three years ago after I graduated college. They're not planning a trip up for about three weeks," Joey told me.

"Our parents are going to fly together and then share the car and hotel expenses because our apartment can't fit everyone comfortably, but I'm not suppose to be due for two weeks. So this, again, is not happening on a well-planned schedule. I hope I find time to finish unpacking," Kristin said looking at Joey.

"Oh, wow. Well, that'll be nice. Are they staying long?" I asked.

"Only Thursday through Sunday night. All four are in full-time jobs still, so it makes it hard," Joey answered.

"If you don't mind my asking, how old are you guys?" I threw it out there.

Kristin laughed and said, "I'm twenty-five. Joey's twenty-six. "

"Oh, sorry. You just both look really young, and then you mentioned graduating college, and I was confused. I hope I didn't offend you."

"No, not at all. We both get that a lot," Joey said with a smile.

"Well, is there anything else you need?" I asked.

"No, thank you so much. I don't know what we would have done without you," Kristin said. "Really, you're so nice, and we don't have much for friends up here. You're such a blessing. Thank you."

"Oh, you're welcome. Well, I'll leave and let you guys get to business. Good luck and thanks for the boxes," I said with a wink and let myself out. I was feeling weak, and happy and incredibly sad, all at the same time.

10

I GOT ON THE HIGHWAY AND CALLED Mark's two numbers again and got voice mail on both. I left a message on his cell, telling him I was just checking in, that I'd check back later, and I left my new number, with strict instructions not to give it to Jake.

When I got home, I grabbed a bottled water and went to my room. I was so tired, I just wanted to sleep. I looked at the clock. Only six but it felt like midnight. I hit the pillow and thought I'd be out right away, but found it hard to sleep with all the tears.

It all felt like a bad dream. I wished the pain would go away. I talked to God for a bit and asked Him for healing and guidance. I hadn't been to church in a couple months, so I wondered if He heard me. Jake and I belonged to the church where we were married, but we were kind of hit and miss on attendance. I better start going on a regular basis, I thought as I drifted off.

I heard someone yelling my name. It was muffled and sounded far away. I didn't recognize the voice, but I could tell it was a woman's. I got up and walked towards it. I stood at the edge of the woods, near the cabin area from the trip. I was at the start of a path. It was cold and damp and morning or dusk. I wasn't sure, but it was dim and foggy and the air was heavy.

I stepped on to the dirt path and headed into the woods. I could hear her yelling my name over and over, "Saaaaarrrrra!" It was far away. I wasn't sure I could get there. Who was it? It was dark, I didn't want to go. I was afraid of the dark. I wished I had someone with me. I needed a friend. I was scared, not sure if the sun was coming up or setting. I was hesitant to continue. I walked slowly and then stopped. "What?" I yelled back, "Where are you? What do you want?" I came to a steep hill. I climbed, still on a path but it was steep. I couldn't see well. On the pontoon looking around the lake, I remembered seeing a big rocky cliff, like a small mountain, off to one side. This must be it. I climbed and climbed, until my legs and chest hurt. I couldn't breath in the thick, heavy air. The higher I got the worse the fog got, too. I saw something at the top of the hill. A person, I blinked and stared harder. It was a girl, young. She was still yelling my name.

I answered, "What?" I was out of breath. "Who are you. What do you want?"

She was waving a big "come here" wave. It was the same girl from the wood boat and the edge of the woods when I was locking my car! What was she doing here? I stood up and started walking towards her. She moved away. I was losing her. "Wait!" I moved faster and got to the top of the mini-mountain and looked around. I couldn't see her anywhere. The area was very rocky. I noticed a small opening in the rocks in the distance. I wondered if I could fit in it. I started to walk towards it.

"Help her! Help us!" she pleaded, her voice far away and distant. I looked around again and still couldn't see her anywhere, I heard her though. "Please help us."

"Where are you? I can't see you. What do you want me to help you with?" I yelled.

I heard something ringing. It, too, was far away. I didn't know what it was, but it was getting closer, louder. My breathing was getting faster. I looked around. I couldn't find her. What was ringing? It was loud! I opened my eyes.

I woke up in my bedroom, in my apartment, out of breath, and sweaty. *What's ringing?* I suddenly remembered I had a new cell phone. I got up and ran to my purse. My mom, just checking in. I told her I was fine and just had a bad dream, that I'd call her in the morning.

A glance at the phone showed ten-thirty. Great. Wide awake. It was going to be a long night. After making a PB and J sandwich and pouring a glass of milk, I tried to eat, but I wasn't hungry at all. I took two bites and drank the milk. Then I grabbed the mailbox key and walked down to the lobby to get my mail. No one was in the hallway, thank goodness, because I looked a fright. I paged through the stack of mail, on the way back to the apartment. Nothing interesting. I grabbed the paper, and the apartment-guide magazine and circled a few options. I decided I could be picky, since I'd have a really nice budget to work with. I'd probably build a home soon, but I wasn't sure when or where that would be. In the meantime, I wanted to be comfortable and happy.

I set that aside for the time being. I needed a drink or two. On the drive to the liquor store, for more wine, I remembered the time. They were closed. Duh! The grocery store wasn't, so I got chocolate, a Bacardi mixer, and some ice cream. Soul food, right? On the way home, I tried Mark again. Still no answer. I texted him that I was worried and he needed to reply or I was sending cops over to do a welfare check on him. He replied right away that he had gotten my messages, new number, and threats. He said he was fine, just wanted time alone and he'd call me tomorrow. I replied with a smiley face.

While I cried through bites of chocolate, sips of a strawberry daiquiri, and the movie *Titanic*, I realized that the chocolate-daiquiri-love story therapy wasn't working and went to bed again. I hoped I didn't have any more weird dreams. It had been very scary and seemed too real. I wondered if I was losing it. The first two times I saw that girl-ghost was when I was mostly sober and awake, and last time it was in a dream. I had no idea what it meant. I tried to forget about it and put on my jammies and crawled into bed. I lay there awake and alone. The bed seemed so big. I missed Jake so much, but I hated him so much more.

The next morning, I carried in the boxes and packed up all of Jake's things. I emailed him that his things were packed by the door, ready for him to pick up, and asked if there was anything else in particular he wanted. He replied back that he was on his way right now. I replied back that I didn't want to be here, and to give me an hour and then I'd leave for an hour. I hit send and jumped in the shower. I dressed in jeans and a nice white blouse, silver jewelry, and tan high-heel sandals. Fashion always cheered me up. I did my hair and make-up quickly, and I was surprised that it turned out good. I came around the corner, and there was Jake sitting on the couch. He looked like hell. I was so glad I'd jumped in the shower and was having a good hair day. He looked awful, and I looked good. Perfect.

"What are you doing here? Didn't you get my message to give me an hour?" I asked, irritated.

"No, I'm sorry. I left as soon as I replied to the first one," he said. "I'm sorry. I'm glad I got to see you though . . . you look great," he said with an exhale. "I miss you so much, Sara. Please, can we talk?" he begged. "I tried your cell but I couldn't get through."

"Ah, no, Jake, there's nothing to say. I'm filing first thing Monday morning, and I already have a good start on moving on," I said firmly. "I changed my phone number and service contract. They'll be mailing you the info. Why don't you call Lily if you want to talk to someone?" I said in a snotty voice. "Those boxes are yours," I added, pointing at the pile of ten by the door. "If you want anything else you should get it out today. You can have the bedroom furniture and anything else you want. If you leave it here, I'll donate it or give it away. I don't want the memories. So take it if you want it. There's a pen and paper on the table. Leave me your info of where you're staying, and I'll forward your mail. I'm looking for a new place. Do you and Lily want this one or should I cancel the lease?" I asked.

"No, Sara, I don't want to live here with Lily. I haven't spoken with her since we all split. It was a terrible mistake. I want you," he said, through tears.

This had me laughing out loud. Once I recovered, I lowered my voice, looked him straight in the eye and said, "Never going to happen. Do you want the apartment or not?"

"No," he said softly. "I could never afford it on my own."

I told him he had until the the end of the day to get his stuff all out. I tossed my purse over my shoulder and marched out the door. I promised myself that I wouldn't cry. I hauled myself into the Jeep and pulled out of the lot.

I didn't want to see him, but part of me was glad that I had. I didn't know why really. I didn't know how to be without him. He had been by my side every day since the eighth grade. We'd been together longer than we'd been apart. This was going to be a whole new world now. Jake was my first and only boyfriend, I couldn't even imagine dating again.

At the local Perkins, I ordered a muffin and juice. While I was waiting, I grabbed my phone and the apartment guide out of my shoulder bag and set up four apartment showings all an hour apart. A couple were on the other side of town but not too far. I wanted to stay close to work, for a while at least.

I called Mom. I told her about the box/baby story, and she laughed and said she was thankful she'd raised such and strong, sweet girl. I told her I loved her and disconnected. When I checked out at the counter, I got two more mammoth muffins to go.

Parking at the hospital was not fun, but eventually I was on my way to the maternity ward. I had been thinking about Joey and Kristin all morning and thought I'd drop by. It'd be hard to have a baby and have no one come to see you. I got to the room, and the door was wide open. Both Joey and Kristin were there. Kristin was on the bed and Joey on the pull-out couch. There was a baby wrapped in pink, in what looked like a clear, plastic box on wheels. I tapped lightly on the door and they both looked over.

"Hey, guys," I said gleaming, "Can I come in and meet your new arrival?"

"Oh, hey, Sara," Joey said. "Yes, please, come on in. Dude, it's a girl!" he added and was absolutely glowing. He got up and picked her up out of the box and walked over to me.

"I get to hold her? Oh, my gosh, she's so pretty. Congrats!" I said, while I set down my purse.

"Wait!" Kristin said, "Tell me what's in the bag and then you can hold my baby."

"Oh, just a couple mammoth muffins from Perkins," I responded nonchalantly. "I heard the hospital food was really good so you probably don't want them," I said, waving the bag.

"God bless you, Sara," Joey said and grabbed them from me. "Here you go. You take the baby while we eat."

She was beautiful, lots of blond hair, just like her mom and dad. They were both really nice looking blondes, thin, great teeth and skin, and they made beautiful babies together.

"What's her name?" I asked.

"Marissa Lynn Spencer," Kristin proudly announced.

"Well, hello, Marissa. I'm Sara Martin," I said, "That's funny how I didn't even know your guys' last name. I feel like we know each other so well."

We all laughed, and Kristin said hers was Smith.

Then Joey interrupted and said, "Not for long though," he pointed to her finger, and there was a ring on it, "I asked her to marry me last night."

Kristin laughed and said, "Yeah, while the baby was ready to come out and I'm pushing my hardest, this guy asks me to marry him. He even had a ring

Lost and Found

pulled out. What was I going to say?" They both laughed, and he kissed her cheek.

"Well, congratulations again! Wow, what a night to remember," I said, smiling. It felt good to be around these two, well three now. They made me forget my problems and made life seem so great. "So, how long do you have to stay?"

"We can leave tomorrow if they both stay healthy, eat their food, and void properly," Joey said with a crooked smile. I laughed and told the baby to be a good girl so she could go home soon.

After another half hour, I had learned more about the three of them and then excused myself to go apartment hunting. I wished them luck and told them if they ever needed anything or a babysitter, they had my number.

It was a short drive to my first apartment appointment. I took a look at the first room and the grounds. It was okay but not really for me. The second one was awful. It looked clean, but the smell said otherwise. I asked if they would repaint and replace the carpet, and they said no, so I said no, too. The third apartment was the closest to my work, and it had everything and more to offer. The pool and hot tub area outside were absolutely grand. There was a nice park two blocks away, all the conveniences I needed close by. The apartment had a washer and dryer in the unit, the floor plan was very open, and it was huge! There was a fireplace in the living room and in the bedroom, and a nice patio that over looked a prairie field in the back. The appliances were all one year old and the building was only five years old. It had a heated, tuck-under garage with reserved spots, and security twenty-four-seven. The place was well maintained and had working elevators. Easy moving, easy in and out to the main road. I loved it! It was the most expensive of the three, but I could afford it. I filled out the application and took the manager, Jamie's, number. She seemed really nice, maybe a couple years older than I was. She said she'd lived there since the day they opened and had no complaints.

I got in my Jeep and motored to the last appointment. I was thinking it was probably a waste of time and it was. I thanked the lady and left shortly after arriving. I called Jamie and told her I loved it and asked when it was available. She said they just need to do the cleaning and shampoo the carpets, so a couple days if the ap-

62

plication was approved. She told me they needed a deposit and first month's rent to sign the papers. I asked her to rush it if she could and call me as soon as she knew anything. She didn't think the application would be a problem, and I could be in as early as Monday if everything went well and the carpet dried. Great! I thanked her and had a big smile on my face when I disconnected.

I called Mom and Dad and made sure we were still on for a get together. I hadn't seen Dad yet since all this happened, and I needed one of his great Dad hugs. I traveled over there and spent an hour talking with them over coffee and cookies. Dad was really angry and told me he was proud of how I was handling it. I thanked him. I still looked for their approval, even at my age. After I hugged them goodbye, I promised to touch base with them everyday.

I tried Mark's phones and again got his voice mails. I didn't bother leaving a message. I picked up a pizza and two liters of pop from the grocery store and went over. When I got there, I knocked. Nothing. I knocked louder, and told him to let me in. He finally opened the door. What a site! He looked like hell, smelled like he hadn't showered in two days and his face was in need of a razor. I pushed past him and told him to turn the oven on.

"I'm not in the mood for company," he slurred.

Drunk. I set everything down and walked over to him and gave him a huge hug.

"Look, I know how you feel. You're hurting. You're in pain. You hate everyone and the world. You feel like someone stole your life and you have no control over it. I get it. I know this is hard, Mark. It's not easy for me either but you have to keep going. Your life will get better. Every day you'll have a little less pain than the day before, and one day you'll be you again. But, Mark, really, getting drunk to mask the pain is not going to help. You need to understand that you didn't cause this. You are a nice, handsome, successful man, and there are tons of women out there who would love to be with you, and they won't cheat on you either! Mark, you can't let Lily and Jake steal even one more day from you," I said. Then I grabbed his arm and started leading him toward the bathroom. "Now, you're going to get in the shower, and wash up . . . twice, and I'm going to get a pizza ready and we're going to get this place cleaned up," I demanded. I shoved him into the bathroom and shut the door.

I went back into the kitchen and grabbed a garbage bag and picked up all the trash and empties in the living room. It appeared as if he'd been living on beer, whiskey, and chips. The couch was rumpled and looked like he hadn't gotten off of it in two days. I heard the shower turn on. Thank goodness! I got all the trash in the bag and then dug the vacuum out of the closet and gave it a quick spin across the floors and the couch. I ran some hot, soapy water in the kitchen sink and washed off the coffee table, kitchen table, and the counters. The oven beeped so I threw the pizza in and brewed a pot of coffee. I heard the bathroom door open and then another door close. He was clean and getting dressed. It was a start. I went to the deck door and slid it open. Fresh air was nice, and the weather had been slowly cooling into fall mode. I was sweeping the kitchen when Mark came into the room. He came up behind me and put his arms around my waist and gave me a big hug.

"Thank you. The place looks nice."

After I poured him a cup of coffee, we sat at the table and chatted about what he'd been feeling and what he thought he'd do now.

"Have you heard from Lily?" I asked.

"No, and I haven't bothered to call her either. Jake's called me and left voice mails, but I didn't want to talk to him, and I don't think of him as a friend anymore," Mark said.

I nodded. I didn't see anyone sweeping this under the rug.

The pizza was done, but again I couldn't really eat. Mark ate three pieces. I stayed for another hour, and then told him I'd be back to check on him and that I expected him to be healing and not just drinking.

When I got home, I was feeling better, until I walked into my apartment, and Jake was still there with a few buddies. They were hauling out the bedroom furniture.

"Hey," he said. "Sorry, it took me a while to get the guys together and line up some trucks. We'll be out in a few minutes."

"That's fine," I said. "Take everything you want. I don't want to keep any of it. Do you want the wedding pictures?" I asked.

"What?" he said, shaking his head. "Yes, I want some. Don't you want to keep some?" he asked, and I could tell it hurt him.

I just walked to the closet and got the box of pictures out and sat it on the table. "Take what you want and take the table, too," I said. I couldn't help it, the anger I felt every time I saw him was overwhelming. Rage filled me when I looked at him. I had never wanted to hit someone so badly in all my life. At the same time though, I looked at him, and it felt like he'd been gone on a long trip. I just ached to hug him, to feel his arms around me. I just wanted him to hold me. I wanted to put my head on his chest and hear his heart beat while I told him about the bad week I'd had. And have him kiss me and make it all better. But then I remembered that he caused this, that he was the enemy, and I was back to anger again. It was exhausting. I was so tired, so sad, and so consumed with every single emotion that one could possibly feel that every bone in my body hurt. I seriously ached through to my bones.

Jake's friends said they were sorry and gave me the sad eyes. I thanked them and kept moving boxes to the door. About two hours later, the boys said goodbye and walked out.

Jake sadly stepped to the door. "Call me anytime … I'm staying with Scott, the address and number's on the pad in the kitchen. I'm so sorry, Sara," he said and slowly closed the door.

I locked the door behind him and looked around the now nearly, empty room. No couch, no coffee table, no overstuffed chair, no kitchen table, no bedroom furniture. The apartment was pretty much gutted. I knew I had the money to get new stuff, but it made me cry to see what was once our home, now just a sad, empty apartment.

I sat in the middle of the living room and had another good cry. Then I got up, grabbed a glass of wine and padded into the bathroom for a bubble bath and did a bunch more crying in there. After I'd put my jammies on, I called my mom and then my friend Kat. Kat, short for Katherine, was already half way to my house when I hung up with her.

11

I RAN A VACUUM THROUGH QUICKLY, then blew up the air mattress and put it in the middle of the living room. It was the only thing I had left to sit on. Kat arrived at about ten, with a bag of assorted chocolates, two bottles of wine, and the movie *Sweet Home Alabama*. We sat and talked for hours. We cried and laughed, and she vowed to never talk to Lily again, which made me feel mean and victorious at the same time. Kat told me she was mad I'd waited so long to call her, but I explained that I needed time and had actually been really busy that last few days. Then I gave her the whole update.

"Saturday night I'm taking you out for dinner, my treat," Kat said. "And after dinner we're going to do something fun, so plan on the whole night."

I agreed, but I made her promise no night clubs. I wasn't ready for that scene yet. Kat was single, and I never had been, so we'd be like oil and water at a night club. She rolled her eyes. I asked her if she could stay, and she said that she'd packed her bag just in case it was a long night. We drank both bottles of wine and ate most of the chocolate. After watching the movie together, we both fell asleep on the air mattress.

At five I woke with a stiff neck and headache. I sauntered to the bathroom and downed a bunch of water with a couple Tylenol then lay back down. I woke up again at nine-thirty to my phone ringing.

"Hello," I answered. "Oh, great. Thank-you so much! Monday at three is perfect. See you then."

"Who was that?" asked Kat, through a yawn.

"That was Jamie, the landlord of the apartment I toured yesterday. She said that the application was approved and cleaning was scheduled, so I can move in at three on Monday," I said very excitedly. Then it hit me ... this would be my last weekend in my old home.

It must have been written all over my face because Kat got up and gave me a hug and said, "Look at it like a new beginning, not an end. None of the past was your fault. You can't change it now, so be in charge of the new you, the new life, and the fresh start. Focus on that and let Lily and Jake do the suffering. It'll be exciting! Come on, let's get breakfast, and then we'll come back here and start packing."

We went to breakfast in separate cars because Kat's dad said that I could borrow his enclosed trailer, so she would go over and pick it up after breakfast. I'd go get more packing tape.

We were just finishing up breakfast when my phone rang. I seriously need to change that ring tone. It was Joey. Turned out they could leave the hospital that day, but his car was still flat in the mall lot. He was wondering if I could give them a ride. I told him I'd be there in an hour.

Kat and I checked out. She drove to her dad's. I headed to Target to get box tape, toilet paper, and more Tylenol. I gave Kat an extra key in case she beat me back.

On the way to the Target, I called a friend, Tim, at the repair shop where I always brought my Jeep. I asked him for a favor. I told him about the car and the flat and asked him to put four new tires on the car and bill my card on file. He said he could get a guy out there right away. They could pick up the car, change out the tires and put it back in about an hour. Sweet. It'd be a nice surprise for them. I thanked Tim and disconnected.

I got to the hospital and met Joey, Kristin, and sweet little Marissa in their room. We had to wait for the doctor to sign release papers so it took about an hour. I pulled the Jeep up to the the ER doors. They had to put the car seat in and have it inspected by the nurse before we could leave. I was a little taken aback by that. It seemed in the rush, they'd forgotten their car seat, so they were borrowing one from the hospital. When the nurse saw that it was in correctly, we were free to leave.

On the way to the mall. I told Joey and Kristin about the surprise I had for them, and they were ecstatic.

"I don't know how to thank you for everything you've done for us," Kristin said. "The move was expensive and unexpected at this time and then the tire started losing air every day. We knew we needed four new tires but couldn't afford it this month. We don't have great jobs, so it's been tight."

"Yeah we both graduated from college but haven't found jobs yet that make us the big bucks. I've settled on an accounting job for an income tax company but my education qualifies me for so much more than I'm doing. And it doesn't pay much, so I have been picking up hours at the Subway to save for Kristin's maternity leave."

"And I am a dental hygienist, but I haven't been able to find a practice that's hiring. I'm doing reception work at a local dental office, but it's entry level. I keep looking, but nothing yet. I hope to open my own practice someday," Kristen said.

"Well, I'm glad to help out. In return you can allow me to visit and babysit this adorable princess as often as possible," I said.

They thanked me again, and I felt amazing. I dropped Joey off at the mall to get his car, and he was so thankful he was tearing up. He followed us back to their apartment building, and I told Kristin about my new place, just a few blocks away. She was so jealous because she knew the place and wished they could afford it. I smiled and told her to stop over anytime.

I carried the baby, and Joey helped Kristin get in and settled on the couch. I told them again that any time they need anything to just call. I kissed the baby on the forehead and handed her to her mommy and then gave them both a hug.

"Dude," Joey said, "You've been so nice to us. Thank you again so much." I smiled and left. He was funny. Mature and responsible but still said dude like a frat boy.

I sped home. When I got there, Kat had the trailer parked close to the door. I asked her if I could have it until Tuesday, and she said yes. I called my landlord and told him I'd be leaving and worked out the details of how much the early out would cost. Kat tossed me a cold beer.

"Well, sista, let's get to move'n on and move'n up!" Kat said as she raised her beer.

"Cheers to that," I said, not quite sure if I was excited or sad. I hated the gut twisting, emotional, bull crap. We clinked bottles and reached for boxes. We packed everything we could. If I could move in on Monday then I wanted to be ready. At six we called it a day. I promised her dinner and more tonight, so we needed to get ready for the evening. Kat said she'd be back at seven-thirty to pick me up and left.

I called Hom Furniture. They said my furniture would be in Monday morning. I scheduled delivery for Monday at 6:00 P.M. That gave me time to get to the new place and figure out where I wanted it. I made a mental note to go shopping for a couch and kitchen table on Sunday.

Seven-thirty came fast, but I was ready. I dressed in black dress pants and a cute top that showed my assets and went great with the earrings I'd bought at the little shoppe in Nisswa. I slipped on some sweet heels and off we went. Kat took me to a really nice Italian restaurant I loved and then to a martini bar. It was nice. We sat on a little couch in the back and chatted. We had a couple groups of men come and go throughout the evening and buy us drinks and chat for a bit. They were all nice, and Kat did exchange numbers with one of them. I kept a safe distance. I was not in any condition to date right now. We finished out the evening with dessert and then headed home. I thanked Kat for the "hot date" and gave her a hug.

I'd slept well considering it was in the living room on an air mattress again. Sunday came quickly. I couldn't believe I had to work tomorrow. I was a little bummed about that but also looked forward to keeping my mind busy.

I called my mom and asked if she wanted to do church, lunch, and furniture shopping, and she did. I got ready and drove to her house to pick her up.

By the end of the day I had accomplished a lot. I was back on good terms with the Lord. And I had a new living room and dinette set that were both available to be delivered on Monday at six. Unfortunately, I found them all at different places, so I'd have a lot of people in and out Monday night.

I checked my computer before bed to get some documents I needed for my appointments tomorrow. I also had confirmations from the three financial adviser appointments I'd made. I checked the rest of my inbox and there were a bunch from Jake. I stared at the blank subject lines and tried to decide if I wanted to read them. Then made the choice to delete them all unread. Feeling a little weight removed from my shoulders, I headed to the bathroom and washed up for bed. I had a little talk with myself in the mirror, then grabbed some extra blankets for the night alone in the living room. One more night. Only a couple tears later, I fell asleep.

"Sarrrrraaa!" I heard my name. It was her again, I was back in the woods right where I left off last time. "Sarrrraa! Help us, help her." She was again in a long white dress, and she looked like an angel. Was she? I could see her up ahead in the fog. She was waving for me to follow her. "Saaaarrrrraaaa!"

"Who are you?" I asked. I was frightened by my own voice. It was so loud compared to hers. She sounded miles away, but she looked close. I was almost caught up to her. She was by the hole in the mini-mountain again. I thought it was a little cave. I didn't know if it was big enough for me to fit in though. She pointed to the opening.

"Help her. Help us," she said again. Then she vanished. She was gone just like that.

"Who are you? Who do I need to help?" I asked, frantically looking around for her and knowing that I was not going in that little hole. I sat down on the rocks. I was tired and out of breath. I didn't know what to do. I flipped over on my hands and knees and stuck my head really close to the opening. It was pretty dark, but I could maybe see better if I moved to the right a little. I readjusted and looked in again. What was that awful smell? It stank so bad, there must be a dead animal in there or animal poop of some sort. I had never smelled anything like it. I pulled back from the cave and took a breath of fresh air, then went a little further in. I leaned a little more and shimmied in a little ways.

"Hello?" I said, the shaking in my voice not helping. I didn't get an answer. I stuck my body in just a little more and my hand slipped. It was wet. I pulled back and looked at it. It was bright red. It was blood! I closed my eyes, curled into a ball and screamed. I was so scared. It was still dim and foggy, and I was alone. I kept my eyes closed and an image flashed in my eyes. It was there and gone in one second. It was Lily. She was lying on the ground, her head bleeding. There was a huge puddle of blood by her head. She was dead. Lily was dead! I gasped for air and sat straight up.

I was awake, sweating, and panting. I looked at my hand. No blood. "Just a dream, just a dream," I told myself out loud. I got up and grabbed some water, still trying to catch my breath. What the heck was going on with me? I never had bad dreams. I looked at the clock, and it was almost six, so I jumped in the shower and got ready for work.

I was out the door, coffee in hand, by seven-thirty. I only had two meetings with potential clients. After that I had to wrap up the living will and trust for Red Johannson and check the emails from the past week, so I figured I'd be done by about one.

First thing I did was go to an associate's office and get the divorce papers started. Allie said she'd have them ready by Wednesday. That's when I could file them and get a court date for the first hearing.

I made it through the two interviews. Both went well. I finished up the will and caught a quick lunch, my appetite still not good. After a half hour of returning phone messages and replying to emails, I was out the door. I stopped by my supervisor Courtney's office and gave her a quick personal update and my new address. She said sorry. I thanked her, told her I was okay and headed out the door.

When I got to the apartment, Jake was sitting in the hallway on the floor outside my door. My heart started knocking hard on my chest wall.

"What do you want?" I asked, in a not-so-friendly manner. My blood pressure had risen again.

"I just wanted to see your face," he said very sadly. Part of me wanted to give him a hug and tell him I loved him and missed him. I really wanted to feel his touch. Then I pictured him kissing Lily and the good feeling was gone. I felt like I was going to puke.

"Jake, the divorce papers will be served to you on Wednesday. If you don't have a lawyer, get one. I don't want to talk. I'm busy. I'm moving to a new place this evening, so if you want anything else grab it now." I said unlocking the door. He stood and followed me in. I was expecting him to go to a room or closet and grab something he'd forgotten, but instead he grabbed me, pushed me up against the door and started kissing me.

"What the hell are you doing?" I screamed and shoved him away. "Get out!" Geez, my heart was pounding so hard I could hear my heartbeat in my head.

"Sara, we need to fix this. We were meant to be together forever. I'm sorry. I want to make this better. I can't live without you," he said, starting to sob.

I turned around and opened the door. "Leave now!" I said firmly. "You're wasting your time. We'll never be together. You slept with my best friend, Jake!

And you slept with your best friend's girl! You're pathetic and 'I'm sorry' is never going to fix that! Never, Jake. If I ever, for one second doubt that, I'll just replay the image in my head of the two of you on the patio at the cabin and remind myself what a great guy you are." I stared into his eyes. They were so sad. He didn't know I'd seen them. I could see defeat in his heart. I hated him so much right now. I couldn't believe he tried to put his lips on me. And yet I was torn between wanting to hit him and wanting a hug. I wanted him to hold me so much right now. I couldn't let him in though. It was so confusing. He started slowly moving to the hallway.

"Will you at least tell me where you're moving to?" he pleaded.

"It's none of your concern now . . . good-bye, Jake." I said quietly and slowly closed the door. Ugh, I can't believe this! I was having a great day, and then he showed up and knocked me back. I heard my phone in my purse. Mark. He asked if I'd heard from Lily, or if I knew if Jake had talked to her. I told him no and he said her mother couldn't get a hold of her, and she hadn't gone to work today. I told him I knew nothing, and that I just saw Jake but there was no mention of her. I disconnected after I told him to keep me updated. I had assumed that she had gone to her mom's to stay these last few days. I wondered where she went. I didn't think she would've gone too far, at least not without telling her boss and getting her clothes and other belongings. The only thing she had with her was her purse and car. Whatever. I felt the same way about her as I did about Jake. I hated her and loved her and missed her, but we would never be friends again.

It was time to grab the last few items and get on with life. I loaded up the rest of my stuff, and the trailer was full, which was odd because Jake had taken a ton of furniture, I didn't think I had this much stuff. I ran back up to the apartment one last time. The place was completely empty. It was bare and sad looking, so plain, so lonely. And now I was crying again. Shoot, there goes my make-up. I slid my back down the wall and lost it for a while. I spent the next fifteen minutes sobbing, crying, and cursing. Then I got up, grabbed my one live plant and my purse and closed the door. I did it slowly, thinking it was like closing a chapter of my life. It felt like a bad dream. I closed my eyes, shook my head violently and opened them. It wasn't a dream. I marched down to the landlord's office.

The office was empty when I got there, so I left a note on his desk with my new cell number and the keys. I informed him, that if he hadn't already, to talk to Jake, and get his key from him. I left Jake's number.

Okay, off to the new place. The trailer was all hooked up, with help of two young, handsome men in the parking lot. I drove to the apartment and met Jamie in the office and got the keys. She helped me with the first load and then gave me a mini-tour/instruction session on all the appliances. Everything looked and smelled great and it was spotless. I followed her to a storage closet that had a huge cart with shelves and huge wheels. She said I could use it to unload. This way I could haul eight to ten big boxes in one trip, instead of one at a time. Woohoo! Nice because it was already three in the afternoon, and I'd like to get the trailer back to Kat's dad today. He had a remodeling business, and I knew he used it a lot.

Two hours later, the trailer was empty. I had time to drop it off and get back in time to meet the movers. On my way to the Jeep, Kat pulled up in the lot. I told her my plan, and she parked and took my keys and said to go unpack. She'd deliver the trailer and meet me back here to help in a bit. I thanked her and ran back in the room. What a disaster. I ripped the tape off the first box and started in.

Kat arrived about forty minutes later, carrying Subway. What a super hero. I loved her. We sat on the floor in the living room and ate, then got back to unpacking. The first furniture delivery came, and two strong men brought in my bedroom set. They unpacked it and set it up. Just as they left, the table and chairs people and the other guys with the living room set arrived. In less than an hour, I'd had dinner and a house full of furniture set up. It was looking good. I loved it. So did Kat. She threatened to move in with me.

At about nine, Kat left for home, and I went to the bedroom. I had picked up a new comforter and sheet set on Sunday too, so I opened it and threw the sheets in the wash. While I waited, I hooked up the TV, DVD, DVR, and cable. I surprised myself when I turned them all on, and they all worked. I didn't have surround sound, but I could look into that later. I put the sheets in the dryer and went to unpack the bathroom supplies. There was tons of room. The closets all seemed huge, and the drawers looked empty even with my stuff in them. The shoes on the floor looked small, and the hangers were all just a little too far apart.

12

I HEARD MY PHONE RINGING, and it took me a while to find my purse in the mess. It was a number that I didn't have programmed in my phone. "Hello?"

"Hi, Sara, it's Debbie." Lily's mom.

"Hey," I said, my voice dropping.

"Hi," she said in a low, slow, voice. "Sara, let me start be saying, I did speak with Mark, and he told me about the affair. I'm so sorry, love. I had no idea this was going on. Lily never told me anything. I'm as shocked as you two. I can't believe this is happening, I'm so disappointed in her. Are you doing okay?"

"Yeah, best as I can right now, I guess. I have decided to move on with life as quickly as I can and not let them steal another second from me," I said, trying to sound encouraged.

"That sounds like a really good plan, honey. You're a tough girl. You'll get through this. You're beautiful and smart, and I know you'll make it far in life," she said. "I got your new number from Mark, who was hesitant to give it to me. Please don't be mad at him, and I promise not to give it to Lily or Jake. That's actually why I'm calling. I can't get ahold of her. She hasn't called me, and her phone seems to be off. Her supervisor called me today and said that she was a no show at work, and no one I've talked to knows where she is. Have you heard from her?" she asked, sounding very concerned.

"No, I haven't. As far I know, Jake and Mark haven't talked to her either. I assumed she came to stay with you for a while. Honestly, I don't want to talk to her or see her again. I'm really upset about the whole situation." I said, matter-of-factly.

"I know, dear, and I'm so sorry to bother you. I just didn't know who else to try. After I talked to Mark, I started getting worried, because I, too, would assume she would have come here. I don't know what to think. She's a responsible employee, and I'd think if she was going to take some time off, she'd at least let her boss know, and me," Debbie said.

"I'm sorry, I don't know anything, just that she knew I found out about them, got in her car and left. I'm sure she's really upset right now. Mark and I are mad, and Jake, I think, must have told her it was a mistake, because he's been trying to fix things with me and asking me to talk. I told him I'm not interested in working it out. I don't know what to tell you. I'm sure she's embarrassed and hurt and maybe just taking some time to herself," I said.

"Okay, dear. Well, thank-you. If you do hear from her, please call me and let me know she's okay," she begged.

"Sure, I'll call you right away if I see her or hear anything," I promised her.

Well, I wonder where she took off to. I didn't really care but at the same time I wouldn't wish anything bad on her. As soon as I disconnected, I changed my ring tone. FINALLY!

I made my bed and climbed in. Very nice! It smelled great, the sheets were like silk, and the mattress was so soft. I slipped in with a smile. I couldn't seem to sleep though, I kept hearing all the strange, new noises and seeing the new shadows on the walls. It was a wonderful apartment. I loved it so much. It just wasn't home yet. And it was lonely.

I turned on my side and as usual tears started falling. Why? I wasn't even sad right now. It was like my eyes just turned on and off when they felt like it. The problem was that, in my mind, I knew Jake was a jerk and I didn't need him, but my heart wouldn't let him go. And now with Lily missing, it was just too much. I'd like to say I hoped she fell off the face of the earth. In reality I was a little concerned. I just hoped she didn't do anything stupid. I got out of bed and tried her cell phone number. I had no idea what I'd say. Then I remembered mine was a new number. If she answered, I'd just hang up. If she called back, I'd ignore it. I hadn't set up voice mail yet so she wouldn't know it was my number anyway. The call went straight to her voice mail. Oh, well, I tried. I went back to bed. Not my problem. The only thing was, she had been my best friend for so long, I felt a terrible loss, and I really did need to know she was okay. Far away from my life, but okay.

The next few days flew by. I was officially unpacked and could sleep a little easier. Still a few tears now and then, but I told myself it was a process. I let them come and let them go. Jake got his divorce papers served to him. He had sent tons of emails, all of which I deleted before opening.

It was the weekend and I was ready to slow down a little. My vacation had been cut short, my life had been turned up-side-down, I'd lost a friend and a husband, and started a new life with a new home. It had been a lot to take, and I hoped this weekend I could just bake cookies, watch movies, and drink some wine in my new apartment, just breathe for a moment and enjoy what was left of summer. The weather was getting cooler each day, and fall was coming fast.

After a quick store run, I got home and unpacked my bag of cookie ingredients and changed into lounge wear and fluffy socks. I turned the TV on and poured a glass of wine. I was looking forward to a quiet Friday night by myself.

BUZZZ. *Oh, no, who's that?* I answered the buzzer. It was Kat. That's fine, she could help me make cookies. Maybe she brought pizza or subway. It was almost five and my stomach was telling me it was supper time. I swung open the door and told Kat to come on in. She was hesitant and smiling.

"I will, but first we have a surprise for you," she said, all giddy, like a kid at Christmas. "You're going to love it! We've already decided it's perfect for you!"

"We?" I asked, excited and nervous, "What is it? Who is it?"

"Surprise!" she yelled, and pulled my mom from around the corner, who was holding the tiniest, most adorable, cutest, little kitten I had ever seen.

"Surprise!" yelled Mom, a little quieter, as she gently handed me the cute little creature.

"Oh, my gosh!" I said in the highest voice I could muster. "It's for me, really? I get to keep it?"

"Yup, she's all yours! She got her first shots, and we brought a litter box, litter, and kitten chow, but we thought you might want to go 'baby' shopping for the rest," Mom said.

"Oh, you guys . . . I don't even know what to say. Thank you! Thank you so much! I love her!"

"We got her at the Humane Society," Mom said. "She's six weeks old today. Her mother was killed, hit by a car. They said she's the only one from a litter of five that survived. They nicknamed her Ninja Kitty, because she's a fighter. We thought she'd be a perfect fit for you."

"Oh, my gosh, that's the saddest story. I love her so much already and I just met her," I said, holding her up to rub my nose on hers. Then I pulled her to my chest and she started purring. She was gorgeous, gray, white, and black striped. Short haired and her eyes were outlined in black. She looked like a little, black-and-gray tiger. I had wanted a cat for so long, but Jake was allergic so we never had one.

We moved into the living room and played with her for a bit. Then we stuck her in a big purse and took her shopping. I picked her out a new collar, dishes, toys, scratching post, and tons of treats. My mom left for home from the pet store.

"What are you plans for the night?" Kat asked.

"Cookie baking, wine, and girly movies."

"Sounds like a perfect night for you. I have a blind date but wanted to make sure you were okay first," she said. I thanked her for the kitten and told her to have fun, then drove home.

While walking up to the building, I saw two familiar faces and a stroller, at my outside buzzer. "Hey, guys," I said, hauling an oversized purse, a large Petco bag, and a two-foot-tall scratching post, "What are you doing here?"

"Hey, there," Kristin said. "We were just out for a walk and thought we'd check to see if you're moved in yet."

"Here, let me help you, " Joey said, grabbing the bag and post.

"Thanks. Come on in," I said holding the door.

We got inside, and I let them check the place out. Of course they loved it. Kristin asked, "What do you do for a living? How can you afford this palace on you own?"

I told her I was a lawyer and about the recent events, leaving out the inheritance thing. I introduced them to my kitty, which still needed a name, and offered them both a glass of wine.

"I can't. I'm nursing.

"I can't either. We're nursing," Joey said.

"He quit drinking while 'we' were pregnant too," she added, rolling her eyes. Joey lifted the baby out of the stroller and handed her to me.

"We made the baby together, we are both the baby's parents, and I think we should both do everything we can together for the baby," he said more to Kristin then to me. "Dude, it's no big deal. I don't want you to have to miss out on those things alone."

I took Marissa and, oh, my gosh, she was so cute. I was cooing at the baby, and they are cooing at the kitty. It was like heaven on earth. Two of the cutest creatures in the whole world right in my new, super cute apartment! I offered other beverages. They said they couldn't stay. They were just out for a walk and wanted to stop by real quick.

"We brought you a house warming gift," Joey said, while digging in a paper bag in the back of the stroller. "We didn't know what you'd need or what your decorating style was so we got you this!" He pulled out a four pack of toilet paper, and we all started laughing.

"Awe, you guys, you shouldn't have. Thank you."

"We also got you this," he said, handing me a card. I opened it, and there was a twenty dollar gift card to the mall inside. "Sorry it's not much but we wanted to say thank you."

"Thank you," I said. "You really didn't need to, but I love to shop, so this is perfect."

They packed up the baby, and we agreed to get together again soon. Then it was just me and … kitty. I really needed to name her. I set the litter box on the floor, and she used it as soon as I put the litter in. "Good, kitty," I said and gave her a treat. I called the manager, Jamie, and told her the news. She said she loved kittens, and she would be up in two seconds with the paperwork.

Two seconds later, Jamie was at my door. She handed me the paper and stole the kitten.

"Here, fill this out," she said, then added, "the pet deposit fee has already been paid."

"My mom?"

"She called and told me the plan and made sure that it was okay. She took care of the deposit over the phone. If the kitten doesn't destroy the carpet or anything else, the deposit is fully refundable."

I filled out all but breed. I wasn't sure on that. Jamie informed me she was a silver tabby. I finished and handed it to her. She left for the office, only after I promised to call her to cat sit whenever I needed it.

I put the kitty down and turned on the TV. Nothing was on, so I put in *Steel Magnolias*. I loved my new place. I could cook and watch TV at the same time. I got started on chocolate chip cookies. By the end of the night I had enough cookies to eat for the next six months. I put some in the freezer and some in the cookie jar. After about two glasses of wine, five cookies, and a movie, I was ready for bed.

It was foggy again, still dark, darker then before. The cave entrance was cool, and there was a horrible smell. I couldn't take it. I pulled back and coughed. "Hello?" No one answered. I pulled myself up a few inches. My belly hurt from the rocks beneath. I tried to look way down into the cave. I knew I could fit in there, but I didn't want to go in. I just wanted to look. Then I wanted to leave, fast. I didn't like this. I was scared. Why was I here?

"Sara, help us," I heard again, still far away, but it was a whisper. It wasn't coming from the cave though. It was coming from the direction of the lake. I pulled my head back and looked in that direction, but I couldn't see anything but fog. I peeked back into the cave and stretched as far as I could to look. I saw Lily! She was laying there on the floor of the cave. "Lily! I don't know what to do! How do I help you?" I yelled. No answer. She didn't move. "Lily!"

I woke up sweating, out of breath, and pissed off! What was with this re-occurring dream? Was Lily really dead? Was I being haunted? I didn't think I even believed in ghosts. I guessed I'd never really had a reason to believe, or not to, for that matter. Maybe I needed a therapist. Geez.

I heard a scratching noise, and up my brand new comforter climbed a kitty. I reached for her and cuddled with her under the blanket for a few wonderful moments. She laid her head down against my chest and purred. I loved her and needed her so much. I lay there thinking that she was a glimpse of hope for my future. I had faith we would have a great life together. That's it! "Faith." It was a perfect name for her. Faith. I liked it! I told her, and she agreed, so it was official. I looked at the clock and it was only four-thirty in the morning, and it was Saturday, dang it. I was getting really tired of the dream, and the story seemed to be stuck now. I didn't even get anywhere this time, it was almost the same as last time. I couldn't help but think that Lily was hurt somewhere. Was she dead or alive? Maybe it was just a dumb dream that my mind made up, stemmed from my hidden feelings. She'd hurt me and I wanted her to hurt, too. And she was dead to me now. The mind is a crazy thing. But I had to admit it was spooking me. I wondered how much a therapist would have charged for that?

13

AT SEVEN-THIRTY, I DECIDED THAT, since I couldn't sleep anyway, I might as well get up. I hadn't been able to shake the creepy feeling. I had never lived alone, so I had to admit I was a little scared because I'd always had Mom and Dad there, or Jake. But these dreams were very real. And the fact that the first two times I saw that girl I was awake made them even more eerie. My mom once said that when I was little, she thought I could see ghosts. Maybe she was right.

I showered, got dressed and texted Mark that I was on my way over to talk to him. I wanted to talk to him about Lily, her mom, and maybe my dreams. I couldn't decide if sharing the dreams was a good idea. It could make me look crazy or look like I wanted Lily dead.

I got to Mark's about nine, and he looked like he'd just rolled out of bed. "Did you get my text?" I asked, pushing past him with a bag of donuts and two coffees.

"Ah, noooo," he answered. "I was asleep. I'm pretty sure it's Saturday."

"Yeah, Mark, it is, but that doesn't mean that you can sleep all day. Have you even been back to work yet?" I asked, realizing that I sounded like his mother.

"Work's slow," he said as he took a coffee and donut. "Are you going to keep stopping by and chewing me out?"

"Yes, you're my friend. It's my job. This place is a mess again and you look like shit. You have to move on with life. Where are you going to be if you have no job?"

"Okay, Sara, I got it," he said. "After this weekend, I'll go back to work."

"Thank you. There's something else I need to talk to you about, too. It's Lily."

"I don't want to talk about her, Sara," he said, like he was suddenly pissed at me.

"Mark, her mom called me. She hasn't seen or heard from her. Her work said she hasn't called or shown up, and none of her friends have seen her or heard from her either," I said.

"Yeah, well maybe she just needs time alone. Just let it go. Maybe she up and moved out of state," he said, acting like I was annoying him.

"Mark, I know you hate her right now, but don't you at least want to know she's safe?"

"Sara, leave it alone! She obviously doesn't want anything to do with us. She knows where we are. She'll contact us if she wants to."

"I get that, but she hasn't called her mom or boss," I said getting annoyed with his lack of concern. "She still needs to work. Why wouldn't she call her mom back? Where is she staying?"

"I DON'T KNOW!" he yelled at me, "and I don't care, and you shouldn't either, Sara. She totally betrayed both of us!"

"Fine, you don't care. I get it! I'm leaving, but, Mark, I really want you to clean this place up and shower daily." I half smiled and give him a hug.

I marched down the hall to the parking lot, not happy. I couldn't stand all the confusion in my head. I really shouldn't give a crap about her either, but the truth was I did. She had caused a ton of pain and hurt in my life, but at the same time she had been like a sister to me growing up. I knew her better than I knew myself. I just couldn't think of where she would be. It was haunting me, literally.

I called her mom and asked if she wanted to talk more and she did. We agreed to meet at her house for lunch. That left me two hours, so I decided to go get my oil changed. I pulled up to the shop and handed Tim, my favorite mechanic, my keys. While that was getting done, I walked across the street to the mall. I went into my usual salon and talked to Stephon, my hair designer, and asked if he had an opening anytime this weekend. Stephon was the best. He was gay, and that made him better than any woman who had ever cut my hair. I loved him like a brother, and he loved me, too. He had an opening at two in the afternoon tomorrow. I put my name in the book.

"What are we doing, love?" he asked.

"I need a major change," I told him and gave him the quick life update. "I want to go really short, like a tapered bob, maybe." He stood up, and started screaming. He was clapping his hands really fast as he ran over to a shelf and grabbed a book of pictures. He excitedly flipped ahead and pointed to a picture.

"This is it, darling. This one here!" he said in a voice higher than mine. I looked over and I loved the picture. It was exactly what I was thinking.

"Yup, that will work."

"Oh, love, you're going to be fab-u-lous!" he screeched. I laughed, this was why I loved him. He made me laugh, and he was just fun to be around. I had gone shopping a few times with him, and he could dress me better than I could dress myself. I gave him a kiss on each cheek and told him I'd see him tomorrow.

"Have a wonderful day, love. I'll see you tomorrow for your new life trans-formation!" he said as I was walking out the door.

I picked up my Jeep, which they had given a complimentary car wash, and drove over to Lily's mom's. I rolled into the driveway and took a deep breath. I didn't really want to discuss Lily, but I did care about her safety. I think if we put our heads together, maybe we could track her down. While walking up to the house, I saw that Gerald and Debbie were on the porch in the swing.

"Hi, guys," I said, kind of sad. They both looked like they'd had a long night or two.

"Thanks for coming," Gerald said, "We know how hard this must be for you."

"Actually, we can't imagine how hard this must be for you," added Debbie. They were both misty eyed, and so I joined them. We exchanged hugs, and they reminded me that I was like a daughter to them. I thanked them and hugged tighter.

We decided to go in the house and sit at the table. It was set for a light lunch buffet. We all took plates and started in. No one ate much, and no one said a word while we ate. We put the dishes and food away and returned to the table. Gerald started with, "We need to call the cops." My eyebrows immediately shot to the top of my forehead. I hadn't thought it was that concerning. I guess maybe it had entered my mind, but I really kinda thought that we would go through a list of phone numbers and recheck with all her friends and co-work-ers. "We have to. It's been too long," he continued. "She has no reason not to contact us. And no reason not to go to work. The first couple days, I may have understood but not this long. It's too long. She would have called us by now. Maybe not you, maybe not Mark, maybe not Jake, but she would've called us," he said very concerned. "She hasn't answered her phone at all or replied to texts."

"I know, I tried too, from my new number, which she wouldn't have recognized. I spoke to Jake and he said he hadn't heard from her. I don't know that I believe him, but he really has no reason to lie at this point," I responded. "Have you rechecked with all her friends?" I asked.

"We've exhausted all the people she knows," Debbie said, "I've been on the phone non-stop. We're really concerned. She's always called me when she's had a problem. I know she probably feels awful about her behavior and even embarrassed but she'd talk to me about it."

I thought for a moment. "I think you're right. It's been too long. I could understand taking a few days away, but this isn't like her." We all were looking down and shaking our heads. I asked if she had any money stashed in an account, enough to take her anywhere. They said no, and that they'd asked Mark to check phone records and credit card transactions, but he said he wasn't a part of her life anymore and seemed unwilling to help. Mark and Lily had separate checking, savings, credit cards, and phone services. Lily loved her independence, and kept it that way. She had a tough time giving up her apartment and moving in with Mark. I knew she wouldn't have combined any accounts.

"To get that information though we need police help. We've already tried on our own, and they won't give us any information," Gerald said. "I think that something's happened."

He asked me again to go over what happened at the cabin, and I told them what I knew in grave detail. They asked me if I thought that Jake or Mark would have had any reason to hurt Lily. I told them no, I didn't. And I didn't. I thought Mark was very upset about what happened and would be for a long time. But I didn't think he would ever, ever hurt Lily. He truly loved her. I knew Jake too, and he would never hurt her. I had never for a second thought that. Gerald and Debbie had known us all since middle school. I knew that it hurt them to even ask. I could see this was killing them. Had the situation been a little different, it'd be destroying me, too. I was so very concerned, but at the same time, I still hated Lily for what she'd done. I just wished this was all over and done. I needed time to get past my broken marriage and start my new life. This was putting a damper on my moving on. I told them I was willing to help, but I didn't want a relationship with Lily when we found her. There were not enough "I'm sorry's" in the world to fix this.

"Okay, let's do it," I said hesitantly.

Debbie started crying quietly, and Gerald slid his chair closer to her and held her. I picked up the phone on the table and dialed the non-emergency number for the city police.

"Hello," I said. "I would like to report a missing person."

I was put on hold while the call was transferred. "Doesn't Lily have a college friend who works for the St. Paul Police Department?" I asked remembering meeting him at a college party years ago. Lily introduced us, and we spoke for a while at the party. He was really nice. "What's his name?" I asked holding my hand over the phone.

"Um, yes. He's a detective . . . Derek . . . Derek . . . Richards! Derek Richards," Debbie said. "I don't think they've kept in touch lately, but it couldn't hurt to ask for him."

"Can I speak with Detective Richards?" I asked, when someone came back on the line, then waited while I was transferred again.

After a conversation with Richards, I hung up the phone, fighting back tears. It seemed real now. Lily was officially missing. I told Gerald and Debbie that the officer would like all of us to come down to the station immediately to get statements and more information.

"He'll need us to bring at least two pictures that show her face, and pictures of any markings, scars, or tattoos." They nodded, and both were crying. "I'll drive separately and meet you there."

On the way to the station, I called Mark and got his voice mail, big surprise there. I bet he was drunk, sleeping or watching TV. I left a message to call me back, that it was important. I was sure the detective would want to talk to him and Jake, too. I wasn't calling Jake.

I arrived at the station just as the Kowalskis were arriving. We met up in the entry. The secretary told us to have a seat and that a detective would assist us shortly. I sat next to Debbie. She was really upset. Gerald had a couple pictures and another sheet of paper with him. We waited about five minutes, and then a familiar man walked up to us.

"Hello, I'm Detective Richards. I'll be taking your case," he said. He was around my age, give or take a couple years. He had thick, lush, dark hair, dark-brown eyes, and a great smile. His body was well taken care of, and he looked great in his black suit. Derek was taller than I was by about five inches and appeared to be hard, solid muscle. Very easy on the eyes. He was as handsome as I remembered. I hadn't mentioned on the phone that I'd knew him or Lily's name.

He extended his hand, "Thank you for coming in so quickly. It's important to get started as soon as we can. Please come back to my office." He spoke as he shook all of our hands, and then turned to lead us down the hall. He took the picture from Gerald and looked at it, stopped at a desk and handed it to the man sitting there. Then he took a double take at the photo and the look on his face told me that he recognized her. He turned back to me and tilted his head ever so slightly.

"It's Lily Kowalski. Do you remember her?" I asked.

"Yes, I do. We met years ago. We shared the same circle of friends at college," he said.

"She actually introduced us at a party once, too," I said, pointing back and forth between his chest and mine. "Sara Martin. Do you remember me?"

"Yes, now I do. It was at Bill's apartment. That's right! No wonder you looked familiar. It's nice to see you again, not under these circumstances though," he said with a frown. "We had a nice conversation at that party. That was a fun group of people. So, Lily's missing?" he asked, looking concerned. "Come back to my office. Let's get the ball rolling." He handed the paper to the secretary, "Process this right away. Thanks." We followed him down the hall.

We stepped into the office and spent the next forty-five minutes giving him all the information we had. He audio recorded it, with our permission, and he took notes on his computer while we spoke. He asked a lot of questions. Then he collected the full names, and general information on Mark and Jake, and Lily's place of employment. Derek even asked who we thought would want to hurt her. He asked me a lot about my marriage, how long I'd thought the affair had been going on and how I'd found out. He asked so many questions that, by the time I left, I felt like a suspect. He was nice and professional, but I could tell he was serious about doing his job. I felt he trusted me, and I was glad we had someone who cared about Lily working on the case. But he left no stone unturned. It was humiliating to sit there and tell him I'd had no idea my husband and best friend were having an affair.

"Okay, I have what I need to get started. I want all three of you to stay close to to your phones. Call me if you think of anything, big or small that you think I should know. I'll be in touch as much as possible but feel free to call if you want to," Derek said gently. "I'll be bringing Jake and Mark in for questioning immediately. If you notice anything strange amongst them or anyone Lily knows, please let me know right away. Here's my card," he said as he handed them out. Then he shook our hands while he said, "It's very important to continue your day-to-day schedules and take care of yourselves and let us take care of this."

I thought that was very personable of him. He was very kind. We thanked him for his time. He smiled softly and held eye contact with me just a second longer then Debbie and Gerald. "It's nice to see you again, Sara," he said.

"Thanks for your help. It's nice to see you again, too," I gave him a closed lip smile and turned to leave.

When we walked out to the parking lot, the sun was very low in the sky, and I was exhausted. I gave Gerald and Debbie a hug. I loved them dearly, they'd been like my second parents growing up. I hopped up in the Jeep and took a left out of the lot. I drove home slowly. I needed another kitty encounter.

I grabbed my ringing phone out of my purse and checked the caller ID. It was Mark. "Hey," I said, "a detective will be calling you soon. We went to the police station and reported Lily missing."

"What? What the hell did you do dat for?"

"Excuse me? I went with Gerald and Debbie. They're really worried, and so am I."

"Waay can't you just leave it alome. She doesn't want to be with us, so let her be. She's probaby just on a bacation to get away or somfing. She wanted a new life. Lem her have it," he slurred.

"Mark, are you drunk?" I asked. "You better make yourself a pot of coffee. The police are going to call you and have you go in. If you don't go, they'll bring you in for questioning. Sober up, and do it fast. And maybe, for your own sake, you should start acting like you care just a little!" I disconnected and slammed my phone back in my purse. Ugh, what a jerk!

14

FIRST THING IN THE MORNING, I checked my email. Detective Derek Richards had left a note saying he was getting started on the investigation, that it was a pleasure seeing me again. Nice . . . very nice. There were also a few messages from Jake that I deleted, except the one that said, "POLICE" in the subject line. I opened that one.

"Did you call the police? Why? Stay out of it, Sara! You want your divorce, fine! I know I hurt you. Are you trying to repay me?"

I went to hit delete and then decided not to. I turned off the monitor and got in the shower. I dressed in casual but cute clothes. I fed Miss Faith, and she thanked me by rubbing against my leg and purring. I threw my purse over my shoulder and left.

On the way to church, I talked to God for a while and asked Him to help me find Lily. I told Him I hoped I was handling this situation the way He wanted me to. Never in a million years did I think I would be dissolving a marriage I'd vowed to keep in good times and bad. I really hoped God understood that this was a special circumstance. There wasn't much I could do. I thanked Him for friends and family and my kitty, and then spent the next hour at church praising Him.

After the service, I sped to the mall. I was a little excited. I had an hour and a half before my hair cut, so I went to the food court and grabbed some Chinese food. When I finished, I headed to a home decorating store and picked up a few new things for my apartment.

Stephon was in his black smock, waiting for me at the front when I walked up. He started jumping up and down and clapping when he saw me. He screeched, ran up and threw his arms around me.

"Girlfriend, I'm so excited!" he said kissing me on each cheek. "I've been thinking about your makeover all night. Are you ready for a whole new look?"

"Yup, I'm ready," I said. "Make me fresh and new and beautiful."

"Right this way, love. Sit, sit and tell me about all these going-ons in your fabulous, soap-opera life," he said, while draping me and fingering my hair.

We talked first about color and then cut. Then we moved to the shampoo bowl. When I was back in my chair, I told him some of the "going-ons" in my life. I got to the part about filing for divorce, and Stephon stepped back, put one finger on his tightly pursed lips and the other hand on his hip.

"Now wait just a minute, girl," he said. "Are you telling me that Jake Martin is a free man?"

I laughed. "Ah, yeah, he will be soon enough, and you can have him."

"Mmmm, mmmmm, he's a nice slice of man pie! I wouldn't mind none at all taking a nibble on that. Mmmm." He got quiet and still, staring off to the corner of the room. A few seconds later he was back. "Oh, sorry. Go on, love. What else?" he asked shaking his head, trying to refocus.

I giggled and continued. Three hours later, Stephon was up to date, and willing to cat sit anytime. And I was a blond, with golden-honey low-lights. It was a short bob, with a bit of an angle getting longer in the front, tapered up the back and lots of texture throughout. It was amazing. I loved it.

I paid Stephon a very generous tip and gave him a kiss on each cheek. I grabbed my purse and walked out to the mall hallway. I called my mom and Kat and told them about my new do. They were both very excited for me. It felt a little weird when I turned my head, it was so light. I think it added a little bounce in my step. Just what I needed. Goodbye, old me and old life. Hello, new me . . . with a great hair cut! Ahh, spa therapy!

I spent the rest of the day unpacking boxes while listening to music. I got down to the last box and realized that I now had a stack of flattened boxes, that were really nice and I didn't want to throw them away. It felt like a waste, an all-too-familiar story. There was a bulletin board in the entryway of my building with items for sale and services, for the tenants to use. I grabbed a half sheet of paper, and made a quick "Free" poster, with my phone and apartment number on the bottom and ran it down the hall to the board.

When I got back to my apartment, I was hungry and realized that I had no food in the house. I made a quick list of things to pick up tomorrow after work and grabbed a couple cookies. I unpacked the bag of decor I'd bought earlier and put the items out. Then I decided that I was officially unpacked, closets too this time.

At nine-thirty my phone rang. It was Mark. He said he'd just got back from being questioned, and he wanted to talk to me. I headed over there and sure enough the place was a mess. But he was at least showered and dressed and seemed sober this time. I looked to the counter and there was a half a pot of coffee. Guess he took my advice.

"Holy crap, I almost didn't recognize you! Wow, you look great. I like it," he told me.

I thanked him. Just when I was about to sit down on the opposite end of the couch, someone walked out of the bathroom. Jake. "What's he doing here?" I asked. "Mark, you know I don't want to talk to him."

"Sara? Wow, nice hair," Jake said, looking stunned. This was perfect. He thought I looked great, which I did, and he'd lost me forever. Revenge is sweet. I smiled on the inside.

"I wanted to talk to you," Mark said, "I saw Jake coming into the police station just as I was leaving and asked him to come over to talk. We need to go over what happened so all our stories are the same," he said, motioning me to sit.

I uncomfortably sat. "Why would we need to get our story straight? It is straight."

"Look, Sara," Jake said, "we're all being investigated in the disappearance. We need to be consistent with what we tell the police so we are all cleared of suspicion. This is serious."

"Being investigated? Were they the words the detective used?" I asked, wondering if Mark knew Derek. I knew that Jake hadn't been at the party where I met Derek. I was alone, which was why I spent so much time talking to Derek. But I didn't know if he and Mark ever met.

"Not exactly, but that's how we both feel," Mark said. "I think we should go over the details of the day and and make sure we're all on the same page."

"You sound like you have something to hide. Just tell them the truth, and you'll be fine. Anyway I was already questioned. They aren't investigating us.

They're just looking for leads," I said. "Look, Mark, I'm leaving. If you two want to stay and 'get your story straight' then go ahead, I'm going to answer any questions the police have and help in anyway I can. I didn't see anything different than what you saw that day." I grabbed my purse and walked to the door. "I didn't miss anything while I was napping, did I? She did get in her car and leave, right?" I asked.

"Right," Jake said. Mark nodded in agreement.

I closed the door behind me and exhaled. Man, the nerve! Why would he want to be anywhere near Jake? He knew I didn't. So he invited us both over? Geez.

Back home I scooped up my kitty and climbed into bed. We played until she pooped out and then I watched her sleep for a little bit. She was so precious and sweet and getting bigger every day.

In the morning, I got ready for work quickly and threw a few things in a bag for my meetings that afternoon with two of the financial advisers. I had a light day at work and then lunch with Kat. I checked emails, and there was nothing new there. I unplugged my phone from the charger and noticed I'd missed a call while I was in the shower. It was from detective Derek Richards. His message said that he'd like to speak to me again, so to call or stop in sometime today. I returned his call and got his secretary. I asked her to tell Derek that I'd be in about four and if he needed me earlier he could call me on my cell.

I'd put some more cat food in the bowl and then scooped the litter while I had a quick talk with Faith about what work was and how we behave when mommy's at work. I tossed my purse into my shoulder bag, tossed it over my arm, then grabbed the garbage and litter and headed out. I left the TV on for Faith so she wouldn't feel lonely.

People at work loved my new hair and said I looked totally different. It felt good to be back there. And to smile again. My meetings went quickly. I was suppose to be in court next week and had a bunch of paperwork to get ready for that, but I had passed the two big projects on to associates who were more than willing to take them. In my mental condition, I had no business being in charge of serious cases right now. I needed to talk to my boss too and let her know that I was planning to drop back to part time. I figured I'd do that next week.

Morning flew by, and I had a great lunch with Kat. Thank God for her. She loved my new hair too. We enjoyed lunch, and while we ate, I told her about all the cute things Faith was doing. After we paid, we promised to get together soon.

I headed to my first financial adviser meeting and immediately checked that one off the list. She was a rude, old lady who expected a check from me today. I think not. The next meeting was only about a mile away in a really nice, new building. About an hour later, I'd walked out with a lot of literature and a schedule of introductory classes that they held there in the evenings to help teach their clients how the whole investing system worked. The man I met was really nice. Blake Conner, a little older than I was and very friendly. He looked great in a suit and smelled amazing. He was very kind when I told him I was nervous and didn't understand a lot about it. He gave me the class schedule and assured me that it was his job to worry about the money and to handle the paperwork. It was my job to bring concerns to him and learn as we go. He told me, if I did well, he got paid well, and if I lost all my money, he didn't get paid. So it was in his best interest to work with me and for me. I liked him.

My next meeting was tomorrow night at five. So I'd hoped to make a decision after that. I climbed into my Jeep and headed to the police station. Derek's secretary smiled when I walked up. I said that I was there to see Detective Richards. She told me to have a seat and help myself to coffee. After looking over at the coffee bar, which was pretty lame, I decided to pass.

Moments later Derek walked over and took my hand. "Hi. Thanks for coming in," he shook my hand and helped me to stand. "Right this way," he said, motioning me towards his office. His hands were so soft and gentle, just like his smile.

I sat down in the same chair as last time, across the desk from him. I saw all kinds of things pertaining to Lily spread on his desk. "Have you found anything out yet?" I asked.

"No, nothing new. I've spent the day going over the statements from yesterday and verifying their details. We did bring Jake and Mark in last night." He said setting everything aside, and folding his arms. He leaned back in his chair and said, "My concern starts with them. They are the last two to see her alive. I can see a woman running away from that situation and going home or to a friend's or relative's house for a while, but she's been gone too long. It's like her mom said—it's normal to not want to talk to the three of you, but her mom shouldn't be a person to hide from. So that's why I called you back here. You, Mark, and her mom would have known her best. So I want to ask you a few more questions. Is that okay?"

"Yeah, that's fine, I think. Well . . . actually, I'm a little concerned. Let me ask you something first. Mark called me last night after he left here and said that we were being investigated. If that's true, I need a lawyer. Am I being investigated, Mr. Richards?"

"You are a lawyer, aren't you Ms. Martin?"

"Yes, but Criminal Law is not my expertise, and you haven't answered my question."

The corners of his mouth turned up a little. "I don't see you as a suspect in this case. I'm not charging you or holding you, and you came to me, so I think you're okay without a lawyer. You do have the right to one if you would like," he added, to cover his butt.

"Okay, Mr. Richards, what would you like to ask?" I said, smiling and relaxing a bit.

"First of all, you can call me Derek if I can call you Sara," he said, with a wink.

Smiling, I told him okay and we started. He asked again how long my nap was, if I remembered what Lily had been wearing, and if I heard her start the car and leave. I answered all those questions and then he asked about when I woke up, who I saw first and what his behavior was. I told him, again, what I remembered and that I was so angry and everyone was so upset that we all had weird behavior.

We spent the next hour talking, and I had the feeling that he was looking hard at Jake and Mark rather than looking around town for Lily. Feeling concern all over again, I told him I'd help in anyway I could and left feeling like we were on the same team. Derek was a lot nicer today than yesterday. He felt like a friend again. He promised to call me if anything new came up and I did the same.

I got home and Faith came hopping over to me. I dropped everything and scooped her up. "Oh, I love you! You're the highlight of my day," I told her while I rubbed my nose on hers. This must be how parents felt when they picked their kids up from daycare.

I settled in for the night and called Lily's mom and told her about my trip to Derek's office. She was grateful for the update and thanked me for my compassion and help through all this. It was such a weird place to be stuck between hate and worry for the same person. I needed to know Lily was safe though. I didn't tell anyone about my dreams yet. I was really considering it in Derek's office, but I didn't want to look guilty if they found her. And I didn't want him to think I was crazy or losing my mind. After all, I was the wife of the man she'd cheated with. I was just glad I wasn't the last one to see her alive. At least Mark and Jake were there to help clear that up, but Derek said their stories had holes and that I should be careful around them. He said not to act differently but just to watch my back. I told him I trusted Mark completely. I knew he'd never hurt her. And Jake made a huge, selfish mistake but he would never hurt anyone either. Derek didn't seem convinced but that was his job, and it seemed like he was good at it. He then shared some statistics with me that were not very promising. Derek said that tomorrow he would work on phone and credit card transactions but that he needed to pressure Mark for information or get a search warrant.

15

I T WAS A GOOD NIGHT FOR A BUBBLE BATH. I kind of liked the freedom being single brought. I could sleep in, go to bed early, stay up late, eat cookies for supper, and no one was around to shake their head at me. I poured a glass of wine and sauntered to the tub, disrobed and slid in slowly. Faith walked on the edge of the tub and leaned over to bat at the water. Then she hopped over to the toilet and walked around the seat a couple of times and leaned down to bat at the water but fell in head first! She was out as fast as she went in and was drenched! Laughing, I tried to reach for her but she shook water everywhere and took off running out the bathroom door and out of sight. I called for her, but she didn't come back. I reached over and put the lid down, and made a mental note to always put the lid down.

I read in the bath for a while and then got out and put on my jammies and fluffy socks. I threw a load of laundry in and watched TV while waiting for it to dry. When it was done, so was I. I put it away and then climbed into bed. I loved my bed.

"Saaarrra," I heard the voice again. The fog was gone now. It was a bright, clear, cool day. The sun was high in the sky. I was by the cave, sitting just outside of it. I knew she was dead. The puddle was too big. It was too much blood. I was crying and rocking and hugging my knees to my chest.

"Sara, help us," I heard. "Tell them, tell them, so they can know." I looked around, and I saw two girls, one I didn't know, the other was Lily. They were both in white gowns and misty looking. They were about fifty feet away.

"Who do I tell? What do I tell them?" I asked, sobbing.

"Help us, Sara," they said together. "Tell them, so we can go."

"Tell them what?" I screamed, "What do you want from me?"

Sitting straight up in bed, I was panting and sweating, completely out of breath. I was awake now but I wondered if I'd yelled that last part out loud, because Faith had just went running from the room. What was my problem? This was getting really weird. It concerned me, a lot. It was only midnight, so I decided to go to the fridge and get some food. Maybe if I ate I'd sleep better. The dreams were scary. Pretty soon I wasn't going to want to go to sleep. At least not alone in this big apartment.

After I finished a bowl of cereal, I went to my computer. I checked my email and there was a bunch of junk and one from Derek:

"Thank-you for coming in today and helping with the investigation. I want you to know that with all you've been through, no one would blame you if you didn't. I'm doing everything I can to find Lily and I will keep you posted on any new developments. I think that you're doing a really nice thing helping Lily's parents and I can't imagine what you must be going through emotionally. Please let me know if you need anything, anything at all. It was nice to see you again."

Derek.

Well, that was nice of him. I debated responding and decided not to. It was the middle of the night for one thing. I hit the bathroom and headed back to bed. I closed my eyes and had a moment with God, asking Him to guide me through what all this meant and help me understand what I was suppose to do. Then I closed my eyes.

Oddly, I was ready way ahead of schedule. I'd hit the coffee shop and ordered an extra for my boss, Courtney, who I called on the way to work and as always, she was there early and was in need of a cup too. I asked her if we could talk before I had my meeting.

When I got to the office I was the only one there besides Courtney. Courtney had been at the firm since the first day it opened. She was a great supervisor and a great partner too. The firm did very well. We got along well so I wasn't worried at all about the meeting.

"Coffee and company!" I sang, as I entered.

"Sara, my hero, come on in and have a seat," she said smiling. "How are you, dear?" She took the coffee and drank.

"Well," I said, letting out a big exhale, "not great. I know you know about my recent separation and divorce filings."

"And your so-called friend's behavior!" she added.

"Yes. It's been a lot to take. Courtney, the reason I'm here is because well, it's all too much. I'd like to drop way back on my work load, back to part time, maybe less," I said in a questioning voice.

"Why, what are your future plans, dear?" she asked, sitting down in the chair next to me.

"Well, my future has a lot of change in it, and I'm not sure where I'll be led to, but I don't need the money so much anymore. I'd still like to work some, but small, easy cases, here and there . . . on my own schedule. I'd like to drop back to hourly and take what comes in that the others don't want. Maybe I could help assist with large cases. Basically . . . I would like to set my own, part-time schedule. Maybe eventually, just do probono." I gave her the I don't know shoulder shrug and waited for her jaw to close.

"Sara, we don't want to lose you. If you need some time to work past things, we can give you time off. You don't have to worry about your security here."

"No, Courtney, I know. It's not that at all. I have just changed my wants and needs, and I don't want to work as much anymore. I have other income to live on and this is a new chapter in my life. I want to be able to fully enjoy it without the responsibility of a job that requires so much time and effort. "I love this firm and everyone here is amazing. It's not that I want to leave, it's just that financially I don't have to stay," I said.

"Okay, Sara, if that is your wish that's fine. I'll approve you for part time, hourly, and you can come and go as you please. But you let me know, when the time comes, if you want to move ahead in your career because there is room for you here, Sara."

I kinda knew that, but that wasn't where I wanted to go. I saw the partners at this firm, and none of them were married and none particularly happy. They were all rich and lonely, had no kids and no life other than work and an occasional after-work cocktail, if there was a place still open when they got done for the day. Not at all what I wanted in a job or in my life. That was just it, I wanted a job not a career. I wanted kids, a husband and a dog, not a fancy sports car and big paycheck.

I thanked Courtney for her understanding and left for my meeting. It was a sweet young couple that wanted to set up a living will and trust before they went overseas for a month backpacking. I got them all set up and told them I'd have the paperwork ready by the end of the week. As they walked out, I looked at them and felt a huge wave of sadness come over me that had me wishing I had a best friend to go backpacking with.

After a quick lunch, I headed to my last financial adviser meeting. It was good but not like the company from yesterday. They didn't offer any classes or try to reassure me of my decision to invest my money with them. I felt like a total number there. So I thanked her for her time and left. Moments later, I was on the phone with "Mr. Smell Good," Blake Conner, my soon-to-be financial adviser. I let him know that I was very impressed and that I would like to be his newest client. I told him I would let him know when the money came in, and we could go over more details later. He said he was excited for me and glad to be working with me. He took my number, email, and address and told me he'd get some of the paperwork started and send it out for me to look over. I thanked him for his time and disconnected. I swear I could smell him over the phone. I needed to find out what that cologne was.

When I got home I went to my office and got my paperwork done for the backpackers. I set it by my purse so that I'd remember to bring it to the office to be packaged and mailed. I sat down on my deck with Faith and an ice tea and couldn't stop thinking about Lily. I had this incredible urge to go to the cabin. I didn't know why. To feel closer to Lily, to see the last place she was? To look for her body? I didn't know, but I just couldn't wrap my mind around the fact that she might be dead. I knew Jake and Mark were innocent. I knew in my heart that neither of them were capable of hurting her. I had no idea what I would do when I got there but I had to go.

I went to my office and dug out the number to the manager who had rented it to us. Harold said that the place was available tomorrow after 2:00 P.M. for the rest of the week. And I could stay as long as I need to.

I called my mom and told her I was going, and then I filled her in on my dreams. She thought they were just silly dreams and that I shouldn't go to a cabin in the middle of nowhere by myself. I assured her that Faith and I would be fine. I told her I needed to go. It was eating at me, and I really needed to find out what happened. She was not happy and made me promise to call every few hours. I agreed.

I decided that since it would take forever to get there and it was miles from nowhere, I needed some food. At the grocery store, I loaded up with breakfast stuff, some lunch items, chicken breast, salad fix-in's, tons of junk snacks, a variety of beverages, and a few bottles of wine—in case I had trouble sleeping.

Back home, I had just started packing when there was a knock at my door. I opened it to Mark, who was looking very stressed.

"Sara, I don't know what to do. That detective was at the apartment today and wanted a bunch of papers from Lily's desk. I said no, and now he said he'll get a search warrant and be back," he said, panicked. He was breathing heavily and looked really nervous.

"Sit down, Mark," I said, pointing to the couch. "Why would you tell him no?"

"Because, I don't know. I guess I don't want to be investigated. I just want to be left alone," he stuttered.

"Mark, they're just trying to find Lily. You didn't do anything so you have nothing to worry about. Just let them take what they want. If you don't, you're just going to look guilty."

"What did you tell them, Sara? Why are they looking at me so hard?" he asked.

Now I was offended. "I didn't say anything, Mark. I don't know anything. I told them what I know. That's it. You're the only one making yourself look guilty." I paused and looked into his eyes. "Mark, do you know something?" I asked.

He looked away, "No, I don't. She got in her car and left. That's all I know."

"Mark, have you been back to work yet?" I asked, noticing he hadn't shaved.

"No, and that's another thing. That detective was at my work and Jake's work today interviewing our co-workers."

"Wow, really?" I guess they really were looking at Mark and Jake closely. I wasn't sure how I felt about that. I wanted Lily found but to have my two closest friends questioned was discerning.

Mark stood to leave. "Sara, I didn't do anything. This wasn't my fault," he said in tears.

"I know," I hugged him. "This'll all be over soon."

He left and I felt ill. I slowly went back to my room to finished packing. I hadn't told Mark I was going to the cabin. I flipped on the TV and checked the forecast. The temp had been in the sixties lately and looked like it wasn't going to change, so I packed lots of stuff for layering. I got Faith's stuff ready too and then went to bed.

In the morning, I Map Quested my route and then swung by Target and bought a GPS. I wasn't taking any chances. I could got lost in a paper bag.

I got out on the road at nine-thirty. It was about a two-and-a-half- to three-hour drive. Faith was pacing back and forth in the car. She looked like she liked it, but she wouldn't sit still. I gave my mom a call and told her I was on my way and that I'd call her as soon as I got there.

I arrived safely with the help of my GPS, checked in with mom, and then I unloaded the car. Faith was running around the cabin like a kid at a McDonald's Play-Land. It was really nice out and the afternoon sun was warm. After I got settled, I grabbed an iced tea and sat on the patio. And I was instantly sick. I had an image of my husband's hands and lips on another woman almost as soon as I sat down. I closed my eyes and told myself to move past it. It would destroy them, not me. I could move forward. I would be fine. I gave myself a mental slap on the face, closed my eyes and inhaled the fresh country air. I instantly relaxed. I could totally live here. After about twenty minutes, I went inside to make some lunch.

After I ate, I decided to go for a walk in the woods. I took my phone with me and thought that maybe I should have brought some bread crumbs too, so I could find my way back. I just stayed on the trail. I didn't really know what I was doing. Looking for a cave maybe. The woods looked exactly how it did in my dream, except it was bright and sunny. No way I'd be out here in the dark. I wasn't what anyone could refer to as brave. While I walked on the semi-beaten path, I had another talk with God. I asked for protection, courage, and guidance. What was I doing? It's almost as if I was having an out-of-body experience, like a different force was pulling me and my thoughts somewhere. If someone would had asked me a month ago where I'd be today, the answer wouldn't have been anywhere close to this.

I came to a point on the trail where it started to go up hill and my fear suddenly kicked in, and I froze. I suddenly lost my breath, my body went stiff, and I was panting and started to sweat. I couldn't see much, just the dirt and grass in front of me. It was getting rockier, like I was getting close to the top ... close to the cave opening. I didn't know what to do. I tried to catch my breath, but I was at the point where I wanted to wake up from this dream. I took a few more deep breaths and turned around. There was no way I was going to do this. If I got to a cave and saw what I'd seen in my dream, I didn't know what I'd do. My dreams led me there, but I really didn't want to see the rest of the dream in real life. I turned and walked quickly back down the hill towards the cabin. It didn't take me nearly as long on the way back. Nothing like a little fright to keep up the pace. It was only about and hour walk there and back.

Back at the cabin, I grabbed a water from the fridge and relaxed on the couch, it was four o'clock when I lay down. Faith had finally curled up in a sunny window and fallen asleep. I lay there thinking. I knew what I needed to do.

16

I SPENT THE REST OF MY NIGHT LOOKING out the window. Thinking, contemplating, wishing I had Internet access. After I made a fire in the fireplace and lay down by it, I called my mom and told her about my trip in the woods. I had a text from Kat, "Just checking in." I replied back that I was fine and passed on telling her I was at the cabin. I knew her and she would have been in her car and there in a flash. I didn't want her to come. I needed to figure this out on my own.

The next morning, the sun woke me at the crack of dawn. I decided to go out for a morning run. I hadn't done that in a really long time, so it ended up being more of a morning walk. I stuck to the long driveway and county road this time. When I got back, I showered and dressed in jeans and a t-shirt and then threw a sweatshirt over top. I pulled on socks and my tennis shoes and headed to the kitchen for a bowl of cereal. Faith was up with me and was doing a great job at remembering where her litter box was. She had already ate her breakfast of kitty kibble and was giving herself a bath on the sunny window sill.

Making the most of my time in the country, I took my cereal out on the patio to eat. It was the most amazing thing watching the country wake up in the morning. The trees turned on and started to glisten, the ever-so-calm lake sparkled in the sun, and the crisp smell of morning in the country was wonderful. In my experience, waking up consisted of the neighbor's toilet flushing, hallway doors slamming and cars revving up in the parking lot. I absolutely loved this.

After breakfast, I headed out the door and into town. First stop was gas then on to Main Street, back to the little shop to talk to that old man, Reggie. I hoped he was there, I needed to get more information from him about the lake, what people saw, what stories he'd heard. I needed to know more about the history.

I walked into the shop at about nine-thirty. It was the middle of the week and early, so the town was pretty quiet. I headed towards the back of the store and took note that not much had changed. Reggie was in the back talking to a woman about a bear statue. I looked around while they finished the transaction. When he was done he came over and smiled.

"Well, hello, pretty lady," he said with a wink. "I recognize you. You did something different with your hair, nice. I thought you'd be gone by now."

"Hey, Reggie, thanks," I said with a quick smile. "I was gone, and now I'm back. I was hoping you'd remember me. I need to talk to you. Is there a good time when you can talk to me. Maybe I can buy you a cup of coffee?" I asked.

"Talk to me? About what?" he asked. "Did something happen?"

"Yes, something happened, and I was wondering if you could tell me more about what you said about the lake. I would rather not do it here. Is there somewhere we could go?"

"Yes, we can go to the bakery, but not 'til ten. At ten my employee, Ginger, will be here to watch the store. Maureen—that's my wife—is in the back office doing the books. We'll meet you two doors down at the bakery at ten. Is that okay, dear?"

"Yes, thank you so much. I'll meet you there," I said and turned for the door.

"Wait, young lady. I didn't get your name," he yelled.

"Sara, Sara Martin," I smiled and gave him a finger wave.

I went to the bakery and read through the morning paper. Nothing exciting happening here, which was a good thing. I guess Wednesdays were slow everywhere. I ordered a cup of coffee and told the waitress I was waiting on two more. At five after ten Reggie and Maureen walked in. They were just the cutest little couple in the world. They sat, and the waitress brought them coffee. We waited to order. Reggie reintroduced Maureen. She said she remembered me from the shop. I updated her on the conversation I'd had with her husband at the till that day, then told them both about the "vision" I had at the lake, and by my Jeep. They both looked at each other and didn't seem surprised. I asked them if they knew what it was that I had seen.

Reggie told me that the girl ghost had been seen a lot . . . by many. She seemed like she was a friendly ghost, but still a bother to a quiet town.

"People thought it was the ghost of a young girl who had been missing for a long time. She was never found. She'd lived here on the lake with her family for many years. She went out to play one day and never came back. She was thirteen. They presumed she'd drowned, but they never found her body. They drug the lake for two days and even had divers searching the depths," Reggie explained.

"Her family still lives here. She was their only child, and it tore them up. The mother still holds hope for her being found alive. We see her in church most Saturday evenings. She still hasn't moved on," Maureen said sadly.

Continuing, I told them why I was there: Lily missing, my separation, the police report and then the reoccurring dreams. I asked them if they knew of a small cave in the area, and they both said no. But they admitted they had never been able to hike the trails in the area because of Maureen's bad hip.

"If there is a cave up there, it's small, nothing for anyone to get excited about. I've never heard anything about it," Reggie said.

"What was the girl's name?" I asked.

"Carrie Sanders. Her parents are Bill and Nancy," Reggie said. I took out a notepad from my purse and wrote that down.

"Do you remember when that happened?" I asked.

They looked at each other, talked it over a little and decided that it was about sixteen years ago when she'd disappeared, in the late spring-early summer. I wrote that down too. We each ordered a slice of pie and talked a while longer. I told them about my job and thoughts on a life change. I told them about wanting a quiet, slower paced life and how I wanted to get out of my hectic schedule. They asked how I planned to do that, and I filled them in on my grandma and my inheritance. They were excited for me. I didn't know why I decided to tell them all that, but it felt safe. They felt like grandparents. They were full of concern and advice and were very happy and successful, so I listened carefully. After thanking them for their help, I got directions to the local library. It wasn't on Main Street, but it wasn't too far, so I thought I could find it.

I pulled up to the front of an old, faded red-brick building. It was very small, and there was a peeling, hand-painted wood sign out front. The cement steps were getting crumbly, and the glass in the windows was dark and stained. The building was almost creepy looking. I parked on the street and walked, carefully, up the steps. The entry was grand. It had an antique chandelier hanging overhead. The ceilings were really high, and the place was freshly painted and tastefully decorated. The budget must have been used on the inside. There were tall shelves against the back walls and low shelves throughout the room. The librarian's desk was in the middle of the room, and an older woman stared at me from behind it. I noticed three computers on desks over in the corner. I hoped they had Internet access.

"Hello, dear. Is there something I can help you find?" The librarian asked.

"Yes, I'm looking for a newspaper article from about sixteen years ago. It'd be from the local paper here in Nisswa, and if there are any surrounding papers I'd like to look at those too."

"Well, dear. I'm going to need a minute to gather the micro-fiche slides, the projector is over there behind the computers," she said. "Nisswa has the only paper in this area for a fifty-mile radius. Do you know what the dates are that you need? "

"No not really, I know it was sixteen years ago, and it was late spring or early summer. So it looks like I have some work to do," I said with a wink.

"What is it you're looking for exactly?" she asked, looking kind of annoyed, her hands on her hips, eyebrows swished together and lips pursed tightly.

"I'm looking for information on the missing girl, Carrie Sanders. She was thirteen when she went missing, and she's never been found. She grew up around here so it probably was in the local paper," I answered.

"Yeah, sure. I remember that. It was such a sad time around here. Her parents still live in the same house, ya know. Her mom, Nancy, says she'll stay until her daughter comes home." She shook her head sadly. "I'll go in the back and get the slides you need, dear. I'll meet you over by the projector." She turned and headed through a door in the back of the library. I went over and set my stuff down by the projector. The library was quiet. There was only one other person in there with me. A quick watch check showed it was almost noon.

The librarian returned with a pile of slides. "Here's from April through July. It should be in here. I remember it was front page every day for at least a week," she said, turning on the machine. She showed me how to turn off the projector. "My name is Vikki if you need anything else," she said and walked away.

I spent the next hour going over the information. I found it right away. It had been in May. It was front page for six days, but the story got smaller and closer to the bottom as the days went on. It seemed Carrie went out to play with a neighbor boy who was in her class. They'd played together daily since they were young. She simply went out and never came back. The boy was questioned, and released to his parents. His name was not mentioned, however. He was thirteen too and said that he walked her part-way home, like he always did, and that was the last he saw of her. The case was left open, assuming the child was kidnapped. They dragged the lake just in case, because she and the boy often walked around it and played by it. She normally walked the waterline back to her house, so there was the possibility of a slip and fall. The townspeople thought it was a kidnapping because she was a great swimmer and had grown up on the lake.

I took tons of notes and then returned the slides to Vikki and thanked her for her help. When I left it was after one, and I was taking my dreams a lot more seriously. It was all seeming too real, too much of a coincidence. I knew what I needed to do but wasn't sure how it would look.

17

"Hello, can you transfer me to Detective Richards please?" I said, into my cell.

"Richards," Derek answered.

"Hey, Mr. Richards. It's Sara Martin," I said sounding a little uneasy.

"Hey, Sara," he said. I could hear the smile in his voice, which made me smile, too. "What's up? Everything okay?"

"Ummm, well. There's something I need to talk to you about. It's about Lily. Well, about me actually. It's kinda weird, but I don't want you to think I'm weird. I'm just worried, and now I'm scared. I'm, uh . . . I'm at the cabin." I felt like a total dork. I wished I could hang up and start over.

"Whoa, slow down. Sara, I'm not going to think you're weird. Just tell me what's going on. What cabin? The one up north that Lily disappeared from?" he asked suddenly sounding concerned. "Start at the beginning."

I spent the next twenty minutes telling him about the boat and the girl or ghost, and then the dreams. I gave him all the details of each, then I told him how concerned I'd been feeling throughout the days and nights and how I just couldn't shake the feeling that Lily was dead. I told him that I was scared I'd be considered a suspect if I "magically" knew where she was. What if she was there? What if there was a cave and it was just like my dream? Would I be held responsible. Would people think I'm crazy? I continued on and told him about my walk and how I chickened out, but that, more than ever, I was worried that she might be up there.

"I'm also worried that this may just be my brain's way of processing information while I sleep, and I'm being stupid and wasting my time," I said in a whinny voice.

"Sara, you're not stupid. You're a concerned friend or ex-friend. You should have told me this before. Are you alone at the cabin? You went up there by yourself?"

"Yes, just me and my kitty," I said. "I don't know why I called you…I guess I really think that someone should check out the path and see if there really is a cave and then…look in it. I can't do it alone, and I think someone should be here just in case…"

"Sara, Sara, Sara," he said, sounding like my dad. I bet he was sitting there shaking his head too. "Okay…geez, um…all right I'm going to come up there. I can easily clear your name with a quick lie detector test. I'm not too worried about you though. I need some time to get things in order here first, and then I have to get clearance from my captain, which should be fine. He's already aware of the case, and I told him I wanted to check out the cabin anyway. I need to talk to the Nisswa police too. Umm, Sara, I don't like you up there by yourself. I need an hour or so to get things together here, and then it's what, a two-hour drive?" he asked, sounding a little overwhelmed.

"Yeah, it's about two-and-a-half hours, depending on city traffic. Here's the address," I said. "I'm sorry, I didn't come up here to get in the way or make you mad. I just really felt the need to come, but now I'm scared. I didn't know who else to call. I'm sorry."

"It's okay, sweetheart. You did the right thing calling me. I'll be there as soon as I can. In the meantime, stay in or near the cabin and keep the door locked. I'll talk to you soon."

"Okay, thanks. I will." I disconnected and held the phone to my chest. I was kinda nervous and excited at the same time. He called me sweetheart…I wondered if he said that to everyone.

After I picked up the cabin and grabbed some lunch, I headed out on the patio again. The weather was nice, but it cooled down quickly at night, and it got dark too early. I wondered what time Derek would get here. There was no way I was going into the woods in the dark. I wondered what the plan was. Was he coming with the force or just him? Was he starting as soon as he got here, or waiting until morning? If he waited 'till morning, was he staying here? I wondered if he wanted me to take a lie detector test and if that would be something he would be packing too. Were lie detector machines portable?

I went back into the cabin and made a cup of hot tea, grabbed my sweatshirt, then returned to the patio, to enjoy the peace and quiet for the next hour or so.

My phone rang. It was my mom. I told her about my day, and she asked a lot of questions about the detective. She was taking notes, I knew it. She asked all the same questions I'd asked myself. I answered, "I don't know," to all of them and reminded her that I was a grown woman and could take care of myself. She paused for a bit and then in a smirky tone asked if he was cute. I laughed and told her I was hanging up and I would update her later.

I sat there smiling, thinking to myself, he was cute. Really cute. But that was beside the point. I needed a detective, not a new man. It had been hell lately. I didn't need any more complications. I went in and grabbed my shoulder bag, took out my notepad and looked over my notes again. It was so sad. I couldn't imagine what it would feel like, not knowing where your child was. Every day wondering if they would walk through the door any minute or if the police had found anything yet. It must be agony. They probably kept her room the way she'd left it. Wonder what I would do? It must be so hard to go on each day without any answers.

Six-thirty. I would assume that Derek was on the road. I just thought he would've called by now. I was bored, and it was already getting darker, so a walk/run was out of the question.

I decided that my hair and make-up needed a touch up so I went in the bathroom and threw some curls in my hair and added some eyeliner and mascara to my eyes. I loved my new hair. This was the first time I'd tried it curled, and it looked good. I went into the bedroom and pulled on a shirt a little more worthy of my hair and make-up, and walked back out to the living room, which had gotten dark. I turned on a few lamps and lit a fire in the fireplace. The sound of the crackling wood melted my soul. A quick check of my cell showed seven-twenty. I poured a glass of wine and sat by the fire, in the overstuffed chair, all settled in. I looked around. Faith was still exploring. She had tons of energy. She walked by. I scooped her up and played with her for a few minutes. Finally, there was my phone!

"Hello?" I answered, with a smile.

"Hey, you," Derek answered back. He sounded like he was talking to an old friend, so relaxed. "I'm about ten minutes away. Did you eat supper yet?" he asked.

"No, I haven't. You?"

"Nope."

"Don't. I'll make something. Are you coming by yourself?" I asked.

"Yeees," he said. "Is that okay?"

"Yeah, it's just after I hung up, I wasn't sure if you were just coming to check it out or if you were bringing the whole force to tear the area apart."

"No, just me. I think it's too dark to do anything tonight, but I'll check out the cabin and join you for dinner. We'll work out all the details when I get there. Actually . . . I'm here, I think. Do you drive a Jeep?"

"Yup," I said running to the window to see lights coming up the driveway. "You're here. Come on in."

I clicked the lock on the front door, then pulled some chicken breast and salad from the fridge. I went out to the patio and turned on the grill. Just as I came back through the sliding door, I saw Derek letting himself in the front door. He was in dark jeans and a black polo shirt with the St. Paul Police Department logo on it. It went great with his black hair. The shirt hugged his chest and arm muscles perfectly. I felt a rush of heat and had to take a deep breath to steady myself. Geez.

"Hey," I said. "Thanks again for coming. I feel like such a baby, but it gets really dark and scary up here, and with the dreams and everything . . . I just didn't know what to do. And I'm not use to being alone," I said with a half smile.

"Wow! I almost didn't recognize you. I love your hair!" he said smiling.

"Aww, thanks," I said. "I needed a change."

"And don't worry about it. It's fine. You did the right thing. I was glad you called me, and this is the right way to go about it. I should be here when you go to the woods, just in case . . ." He shook his head and looked down and then back up to me. "And if it turns out to be nothing, then you got me out of the office, and I got time on the clock for hanging out with you in this little piece of paradise," he said looking around.

"It is great, isn't it," I said. "I just love it here. The lake is back here," I said, waving him to follow me to the patio door. "The patio and the back yard are really great, too." We walked outside together and stood there looking out to the lake. Derek stood next to me. It felt so good to have someone there with me, and, dang it, he smelled good. I felt an instant connection to him, like I'd known him my whole life. I felt safe next to him.

"So," he said, "what's for dinner?"

"Grilled chicken breast salads, if that's okay?" I said, picking up my wine glass. "I packed some food but not a ton because I didn't anticipate staying for more than a couple days at most."

"Sounds perfect. Yeah, I suppose the nearest store is not so near out here."

"At least twenty minutes in either direction. And they don't deliver pizza out here either. Can I get you a glass of wine?" I asked.

"Yes, thanks. And while we're still in our right minds, I thought that we could discuss the arrangements for tonight," he said in his business voice, folding his arms across his chest. Tipping his chin down slightly.

"Okay," I said. "Well, I don't know what you were thinking, but the nearest town is twenty minutes away. They do have a small motel there, or there are two bedrooms here. If you want to stay here, you are more than welcome to," I said pouring his wine and handing it to him.

"Is it okay with you if I stay here? It doesn't make you uncomfortable, does it?"

"No, no not at all. Actually I'd prefer it. I'm kinda a chicken when the sun goes down," I said. "And you're an officer of the law so you seem safe enough. I imagine you've been background checked. Plus, we have a lot of catching up to do since the last time I saw you was at a college party," I said, with a wink. "You can make yourself at home in the bedroom on the right. The bathroom is just before it. All the towels and linens are clean, and housekeeping is included."

"Okay, thank you," he said. "Glad we got that cleared up. I need to call my supervisor and let him know that I arrived, that I will be staying here and that we'll go on our walk in the morning, so if you'll excuse me for one second," he said, as he pulled his phone off his belt and stepped into the living room. I sat at the island counter and watched him. He talked to his supervisor about the details and answered, "Yes, sir," in a respectful manner. He paced around the room as he spoke. He spun in my direction caught my eyes and winked at me, which caused butterflies. Oh, boy. I decided to get up and grabbed some more wine from the fridge. I heard him say goodbye so I quickly tried to look busy.

"Can I do anything to help?" he asked, sauntering back into the kitchen.

"Sure, you can get plates out, and forks." I said, grabbing stuff from the fridge. I seasoned the chicken breast and put them on the grill. We spent the next fifteen minutes chatting out on the patio, sipping wine and enjoying the evening while the chicken cooked.

When we pieced together our salads, I asked him if he'd learned anything new on the case. He hadn't, but we talked for a bit about other stuff then cleaned up together. Derek started the dishes and looked very comfortable in the the kitchen. So I asked him about it.

"I've been a bachelor for the last five years. Before that I lived with a girl-friend for six months but it didn't work out."

"Why's that?"

"Well, as a surprise, one night on my 10:00 P.M. lunch break, I picked up her favorite ice cream, and walked in on her half dressed on the couch on top of the college guy that lived across the hall. I've been single and working on my career since."

"Oh, wow. I'm sorry. Did you have any idea?"

"None. I was actually looking at rings with her and talking about wedding plans."

"It's so unfair," I said shaking my head.

"Anyway, I tell you that because I know what it's like to be in your situation, thinking everything in life is going great and then suddenly, through no fault of your own, your world is turned up-side-down," he said holding eye contact. "Except your situation is harder because it was your best friend. And you were married," he added, draining the water from the sink.

And there I was in tears, thinking how could people do this? I don't get it. I wasn't planning on crying either, dang it. Derek saw my eyes filling, and tilted his head.

"I'm sorry, I didn't mean to upset you. You must be so lost right now. I hope that tomorrow we can get things figured out a little more." He dried his hands and stood in front of me. "It took me a long time to move past what she did to me. It was hard, but looking back, I wish I would've washed my hands of her and moved on quicker. She stole a whole year of my life . . . my livelihood, my ambition. That's what impresses me about you. You picked yourself up, moved to a new place, got this new friend," he said smiling and grabbing Faith, who had just climbed up his pant leg. He put her gently on the floor. "You even cut your hair and got a new look. You should be proud. You're being very strong."

I half smiled and dried my face. Here he was telling me I was strong and just him talking to me put me in tears.

"And the kicker, you're here looking for a woman who you still care about, and most people think you should hate. You're a brave, good-hearted woman, Sara," he said.

"Thanks," I said. "That's nice of you to say."

"I mean it too. I see a lot of junk in my job, and you're a real stand-up person to be doing this. And I want to help you in any way I can," he added in a soft, gentle voice. "I didn't know Lily well, but I was shocked to hear that she cheated on Mark. They'd been together for so long. I thought for sure they'd be married by now."

Half smiling, I jiggled the wine bottle. He nodded and I topped him off. We walked into the living room, and he threw some more wood on the fire. I grabbed a seat on one couch and he took a seat on the other across from me.

"So how have you been holding up?" he asked with genuine concern.

"I don't know. I'm trying to stay strong. I'm trying hard to push through the hate and anger stages and hopefully skip the self-pity stage. I just take it day by day. I keep telling myself that they stole part of my life, but I'm not going to give them one more day."

"You look great, really. You could be a total mess right now and everyone would understand. You're doing so well."

"Thanks, but sometimes I wonder how long I can keep this up. I wonder if I'm just pushing all that messy stuff off. I feel like I'm very fragile and could break if a feather hit me at the wrong moment," I told him.

"I think that if you were going to be weak and break, you would have already," he said with a closed-lipped smile. "And there's nothing wrong with it if you do. You have every right to be angry, and sad and all the other emotions that pile on without notice."

I took a deep breath and changed the subject. "So tell me about yourself. I mean besides the horrible ex-girlfriend," I said with a wink.

"Well, I grew up in the Cities, Eden Prairie actually, and I've never left. I did my training for the police academy there, too. That's when I met you at that party. I never went to college, just straight from high school into the academy. I got my own place as soon as I got my first job as a cop in St. Paul, and have worked my way up. I've been a detective for the last seven years, and for the most part I like it. I had that one serious girlfriend who moved in for about six months. I've been on a few dates here and there, but, other than that, I'm single. I hope to have a wife and kids and a nice house in the country someday, but we'll see what God has in store for me," he added, with a smile as he shrugged.

So mister handsome cop was a man of faith too, he seemed so genuine and grounded. He took a sip of wine and then looked at me.

"So, how about you? What's your story?"

"Hmm, well, I grew up in the Cities too, in Brooklyn Park. After high school I went to three different colleges in the cities area to complete my law degree. I got a job offer a week before graduation from the same place I did my last internship. After graduation, I married Jake, my high-school sweetheart, and we got the apartment a month before the wedding. I currently work as a lawyer for Robertson-Dubey, but I told my boss this week that I want to move to part time because I'm not sure what I want to do with my life anymore, and she basically told me I'm next in line for partner at the firm. I told her thanks but no thanks ... and the rest you know," I said. "I'm kind of a mess right now."

I looked at my watch and noticed it was already eleven. I was starting to feel the wine. I started to think about tomorrow. It was going to suck, there are only two things that could happen. One, I was right, and we'd find a body, which would be horrible. And, two, we wouldn't find a body, and I'd look stupid. I was being haunted and had no idea why or what to do about it. Both outcomes sounded really bad to me.

"Hey," Derek said gently, as he set his glass down on the coffee table, "where did you go there? What's on you mind, sweetheart?"

Sweetheart? He's so sweet but was that professional? Did I want him to be professional or did I want him to be sweet? I didn't know. I was so confused

I didn't know what I was suppose to feel about anything. My heart and head never agreed anymore. My head told me he was a cop and here on business, but my heart was hurt and lonely and wanted a big, strong, handsome man to hold me and call me sweetheart. Ugh! I was such a case.

"I don't know," I whined. "I guess I'm just worried about tomorrow. It's going to be bad if we find a body, and it's going to be bad if we don't. I'm not sure which I want to happen. I wish I could just back up and start over, or wake up from this awful nightmare," I said starting to tear up. I couldn't even look up at him. It must have been the wine. I couldn't seem to shake it. I felt the rush coming that I felt right before a complete melt down. Dang it. I really didn't want to look weak in front of him or anyone for that matter. I couldn't stop though, I was starting to shake. "I'm sorry," I cried. "It must be the wine and I'm tired, I didn't mean to start . . . it's just . . ." I kept looking down and shook my head not knowing how to finish.

Derek got up from his couch and came over to mine and sat next to me, I had my face in my hands, bent forward, sniffling. "Hey, it's okay, " he said. "If you're trying to be strong for me, you don't have to be." He put his hand on my back and moved it in slow circles. "It's okay to cry," he said softly. He rubbed my back for another minute, then said, "Why don't we call it a night. Between the stress and the wine, it's no wonder. Come on. Let's get you to bed," he said helping me to my feet. He walked with me to my bedroom door.

"I have to run out to the car to get my things. I'll lock the place up when I get back in. I'll be right back," he said gently, his eyes full of concern. He tipped my chin up and wiped my tears with his thumbs. The corners of his mouth curled a tiny bit, and my heart softened even more. Then he turned to the door.

I felt like a baby but at the same time it felt good to be cared for. I closed my bedroom door and changed into my lounge wear. Derek came back in, and I heard the door shut and lock turn. I heard him pull the vertical blinds on the patio, too. I opened the door to head to the bathroom and ran into him in the hall.

"Hey," I said, "I just wanted to say thank-you for coming here to help me. I know you didn't have to, and I know you don't have to be as nice as you're being either. I just wanted you to know I appreciate it." I smiled softly at him.

"Look, I've been there," he said softly. "Just let me know if there's anything you need or if you just want to talk. I'll leave my door open. If you get scared, or have another bad dream or just want to talk … I'll be in there if you need me, okay? I'm right across the hall," he said, with a slow blink.

"Thank you. Goodnight."

"Goodnight."

I went into the bathroom and did my routine, then climbed into bed. It was hard to be there. So much had changed. I lay there remembering what Reggie had said. "People leave there different. It changes people." It did, it had completely changed my life. I came here one person with one life and left a different person with a whole different life. We all had. I let myself cry. Then I heard my phone. Shit, my mom. I grabbed my phone but missed the call, so I texted her back because I didn't want her to hear the sadness in my voice. I let her know I was fine, going to bed and would call her tomorrow. I closed my eyes and talked to God for a while, and finally fell asleep.

18

I SLOWLY OPENED MY EYES. It was light in my room so I knew it was after seven. I glanced at the clock. Seven-forty-five. My eyes felt swollen from crying right before bed. Was that a pan I heard? I secretly hoped Derek was making breakfast. I heard the fridge open and close, I knew I'd stocked the fridge with breakfast stuff. Yes! I grabbed my bag and tried to sneak into the bathroom unnoticed. I didn't want him to see me without makeup and hair. I jumped in the shower and as I was drying off I heard a light tap at the door.

"Sara, breakfast will be ready in ten minutes," Derek said.

"Okay, I'll be right there," I yelled back. I liked him. I smiled and then suddenly I remembered what today might bring, and it wasn't going to be easy.

I quickly dressed in jeans and a fitted, screen-printed t-shirt. I brushed my teeth and combed through my wet hair. I decided to wait on styling my hair until after breakfast. I did put on my makeup though. When I finished with the second coat of waterproof mascara, I headed out of the bathroom and into the kitchen. Derek was in the kitchen, dressed in the same look as yesterday, but freshly showered and shaved. He smelled good, even from across the room, and so did breakfast.

"Good morning, sunshine!" he said, all chipper, holding a spatula.

"Good morning. Thanks for cooking," I said. "I didn't set my alarm. Sorry. You could have woke me up."

"No, it's fine. I love to cook. I'm not used to cooking for anyone other than myself, though, so you'll have to bear with me on the service aspect," he said with a wink.

"Well, it smells great," I said.

We ate and discussed our plans. We decided to head into the woods and see if we could see anything like what had been in my dreams and play it by ear from there. If we did find something, there would be small hang ups with jurisdiction issues, which would require the assistance of the Bureau of Criminal Apprehension. We would need to get clearance before we could do too much. Derek's supervisor was aware of all the details and already had a start on communications and paperwork with the locals and the BCA. The BCA headquarters was in the same building as the Minneapolis police department, so Derek knew some of the guys who worked the scenes that would maybe help us speed things along.

I fed Faith and then headed to the bathroom to dry and style my hair. It turned out really well, which I was thankful for. I gave myself a little pep talk in the mirror and then met Derek in the living room. He was putting a gun into a holster under his police jacket.

"Just in case," he said with a reassuring smile.

I must have looked nervous because he walked up to me and said, "Hey, don't worry. I'll keep you safe, but I have to wear this. I'm here on official police business."

"I know. I'm sorry. I'm not against guns or scared of them. It just suddenly seems much more real than it did a second ago."

We laced up our shoes, and then he threw a backpack on.

"What's in that?"

"A first-aid kit, digital camera, gloves, bottled water, and some other junk we hopefully don't need," he told me.

I ran to my room, grabbed a sweatshirt, and we headed out. We locked the cabin, and Derek threw the keys in his backpack. I led him out to the backyard, and we stopped to look at the lake for a minute.

"This is my dream property," he said.

"I hear ya. It's so beautiful and peaceful. I love it out here too."

"Okay, little lady, lead the way."

We headed through the woods chatting in detail about my dreams. The more we walked the more Derek sounded like a detective. He was in work mode now. We climbed and climbed, slowly getting closer to the top of the hill. When we got to the where I had stopped last time, I told him I didn't know what was beyond there.

"Well, we've come this far. Let's keep going," he said and he took the lead.

We came up to a rocky area, and he turned and asked if it looked anything like in my dream. I told him yes, and I was frozen. From where we were, I could see the lake, and there was a little fog over it.

"Hey, it's okay. I'm right here," Derek said, as he grasped my hand. "Which way now?"

"Over here," I said, turning right, toward the lake. I wasn't really sure where I was going, but it felt right. I looked around. The ground was getting rockier, and we were very high above the lake now. I looked up and noticed the hill didn't seem to go much higher, so we must be close. Then, I saw it. I stopped in my tracks. I suddenly felt like the air had been sucked out of my lungs. I looked at Derek who was looking at me and waiting. I took a deep breath, my eyes wide, my heart beating hard. I could see it! The flat part of the cave that I sat on in my dream, just off to the side of the opening. Oh, crap, it existed!

"There it is!" I gasped, holding my hand over my mouth. It was all coming true. I had kinda doubted it, and now it was true! I climbed slowly closer, while explaining to Derek, "It looks just like in my dream. The opening is small and around to the left side." My voice was getting shakier by the second, and tears were on the way.

"Sit down and stay here." He moved up to the opening and took off his backpack. He pulled out a camera and snapped a couple pics and then grabbed a flashlight. I watched him as he peered in the cave. He scooted up closer and lay on his belly to stick his head in just like I had in the dream. I squinted my eyes shut and started crying because I just knew what he's going to see. I was quietly chanting, "Oh please, oh please, oh please." As much as I hated Lily, I loved her and I didn't want her dead. I wanted her to be okay. I squeezed my eyes tighter and prayed to God that she was okay. I looked again and he was leaning way in, his one arm and all of his upper body inside. I sat there looking at his butt and legs, waiting.

He pulled himself out and sat up. He looked at me and shook his head. "There's no body here. I can't see all of the cave, but there's no body and there's no smell either. But … I do see stains on the floor of the cave that look like blood. It looks like they lead up to the entry, like something was dragged in or out," he said in his official voice. "I'm going to make a call and get a crime scene unit up here to take samples, but for all we know it could be an animal."

"Oh, my God, okay," I said, starting to cry again. "I put my face in my hands and pulled my knees to my chest. My mind was racing, I didn't know what to think. If there was no body, now what? Was it blood? Whose blood? If it was Lily's, where the hell was her body now? Was she alive or dead? Who or what moved her? No, it's probably just an animal that got old and died and another animal came and dragged it out and ate it. Yeah…yeah right. I started sobbing. Now I was more confused and lost than ever. Derek walked a few feet away and made a call.

I felt a hand on my back. Just the gentle touch made me lose it even more. There it was, all the emotion I had been holding back and putting off now flooding me all at once. I felt Derek sit down behind me, he straddled me and slid up close. He wrapped his arms around me, I leaned back against his chest and let the tears come. He rocked me gently back and forth and didn't say anything. About ten minutes passed, and I was settling down. I stretched my legs out and leaned back further into him. It felt so safe, so warm. He whispered in my ear that he'd called his supervisor, and they were sending a team from the department immediately. The locals would be here soon to set up a perimeter and assist, but the investigation was started with the St. Paul Police Department and was, at that point, still a missing persons report they were investigating. The Nisswa Police didn't have the budget, men, or resources to do it alone. The BCA would be assisting the SPPD in collecting samples, photos, and any evidence.

"We can stay and wait for the locals, or we can go back to the cabin. My team, along with the BCA won't be here for about three hours," he said softly.

"I want to go back to the cabin."

We walked back to the cabin, and Derek made some tea. I hit the bathroom and noticed all my makeup, except my waterproof mascara, had washed off. I touched up my hair and skipped the makeup. What was the point? I'd probably cry it off again anyway. I walked into the living room slowly.

"How are you feeling?" he asked.

"Exhausted and confused."

"Drink this," he said handing me a cup. I took a sip but felt like a zombie. It was like I'd just run a marathon. I sat on the couch, and he sat next to me and was drinking a cup too.

"When Crime Scene gets here, I'll take them up to the cave, and they'll do their thing. It shouldn't take too long, maybe a couple hours. When they're done, the area will remain taped off and no one will be allowed in until we know the forensics on the stains and everything else they may find. If it is blood, it'll only take a moment to know if it's human. If it's human, it could take up to a week to get the DNA back. The team will consist of three to five people, and they may send additional men or even a dog. They have already gotten a sweatshirt from Mark and Lily's apartment to give to the dog to get a scent. It's a big stretch because she's been missing for so long, but they may try," Derek explained.

Faith jumped up my on lap and meowed over and over and then ran off. That made me smile.

"I don't think Faith want's a dog here," I said.

"Well, then I'll have to tell them that the dog stays outside," he smirked.

We sat on the couch in silence, and I leaned my head down on his shoulder. I looked at the clock on the wall and saw it was ten. I closed my eyes. When I opened them, I was lying down on the couch with a throw on me, and Derek was gone. I heard a car door and commotion outside, so I got up and walked to the window to see a bunch of men getting out of two black SUVs. They were all busy unloading stuff. Derek was out there talking to them. One of the guys had a dog. There were two Nisswa police cars, but I didn't see any local cops in uniform around. I guessed they were up at the cave. Derek looked like he was explaining things to the crew. They were all gathered around him and listening intently. He looked so professional and tough. They all nodded, and he said a few more words and then put his hands up as if to tell them to wait there. Then he turned toward the cabin, and they all gathered suitcases and light poles and other equipment. A few seconds later, he walked through the cabin door.

"Hey, are you okay?" he asked, walking up to me.

"Yeah, I'm sorry. I guess I was tired. The crew is here I see."

"Yup, they just got here. We're headed up to the cave now. I just wanted to make sure you knew where I was. I'll be on my cell phone if you need anything or get scared," he said.

"Thanks. Will you call my cell if you find anything or if it gets too long?" I asked.

"Yes, I will," he said. "Lock the door."

"Okay, be safe," I said. I closed the door behind him and turned the lock.

I called my mom and told her about my morning. She was very concerned and asked if she should call Lily's parents. I told her no, because we weren't sure of anything yet, and I didn't want them to worry any more than they had to.

I hung up and paced the room for a while. I didn't know what to do with myself. I sat on the couch and prayed some more, and then I put a movie in to try to help pass the time. It helped a little. I heard my phone, and it was Mark. I didn't know if I should answer, so I didn't. I let it ring. Then he sent a text.

Sara, just checking in. What are you up to?

I responded that I was at the mall shopping for a gift. I didn't want to tell him the truth because I wasn't sure if I trusted him. I just didn't know what to think about anyone right now. I really couldn't believe he hurt Lily, but he was with her last, and they had gone on a walk in the woods. I just didn't know.

I sat down and watched some more of the movie, which seemed like a waste of time because I was looking at it, but I wasn't listening. My phone rang again. It was Derek. He said he and the team were on their way back. I looked at my watch, they had been up there for three and a half hours.

It took them a good thirty minutes to walk back with all the equipment. I looked out the window and saw a bunch of men loading stuff into the SUVs. Derek talked to them briefly and then came to the door. I unlocked it and met him.

"Hey, relax," he said gently and reached out and rubbed both my shoulders. I guess I must have looked really tense.

"Just tell me," I demanded.

"Okay, well the stain we found was blood. We took lots of samples, and, like I said, it takes a bit to find out details. They can do a quick test to see if it's human, and they're doing that in the truck right now."

"Okay," I said breathing heavily. Man I do not handle stress well. I couldn't breathe again . . . I needed to throw up.

"There's something else, Sara, " he said, leading me to the couch and pushing me to sit.

"Oh, God, what?" I said, scared to death to hear the answer.

"The cave opening was tiny but my men were able to get in and out and so was the dog. The dog was confusing us a bit. We thought that he may have shown signs that he picked up her scent. But then he went into a corner of the cave and started digging . . ." he said, slowly.

"What? What, Derek? Tell me!" I almost yelled.

"The dog found bones . . . human ones. There was a shallow grave in the cave."

I grabbed my mouth and gasped, "What?" Tears instantly filled my eyes.

"They were old, Sara. We know that they're not Lily's. The bones appear to be that of a young female, but the decay is many years old. We don't know for sure. We have to do tests in the lab to determine all that. The blood seems new, and the bones old, so we aren't sure what's going on right now. We need to get back to do more testing and investigating. The local cops who were up there mentioned Carrie. They think these might be her remains. Again, we don't know for sure, but they don't have any other missing persons that would match. We have a homicide now, but it's tricky because it seems there are two stories and two jurisdictions involved in this. So we'll have to see how the BCA wants to handle it."

I was still crying, but trying my hardest not to. "I don't believe this is happening. Do you have to leave now?" I asked.

"I do. I need to go to the Nisswa station with the team and get some paperwork, then head back to the department and tear into this," he said. "Do you want to stay longer or are you coming back too?"

"I don't know," I said, trying to process everything I'd just heard. "I guess I'll go home, too. There's really no reason to stay."

"Okay, let me go talk to the men quick, and you start packing. You can follow me back later."

I went straight to the bathroom and threw up. Then I headed to the bedroom and tossed my stuff in my suitcase. I gathered all the things from the kitchen and set the cooler by the door and then grabbed my bathroom stuff. Derek came back in and took two seconds to get his bag. He packed my stuff in my Jeep, then headed to Nisswa with the boys in tow. I paced the cabin and patio while he was gone.

Three hours later, Derek was back. He came in and got the garbage and the litter box. I grabbed Faith and locked up.

At my Jeep, Derek leaned in the window, "Drive careful and stay focused on the road."

"I will."

He smiled, tapped the window sill, walked to his car and slid in.

I followed him out of the driveway, and as we started down the road, all I could think about was poor Carrie. It had to be her. What could have happened? I called my mom and told her that I was coming home. An hour into the drive, Derek called and said that we were stopping to eat, to help us stay focused. He left me no room to argue. I thought about the fact that I had no makeup on, and I really didn't want to go out in public. He said to follow him, so I did. We pulled up to a pizza and beer joint in a tiny little town that desperately needed to have a sale on paint.

The two SUVs from his team were in the lot when we pulled up. Derek parked on the street, so I pulled in right behind him. He got out and waited for me.

"I'm really not hungry," I said.

"You have to eat. No one is hungry after a day like this, but you have to stay strong. And the boys and I are going to be pulling an all-nighter, so we need to eat," he said, holding the door open for me.

The place was old and in need of updating. It smelled like old smoke and stale beer. The lighting was horrible, which was good for me in my current condition. We joined the C.S. unit sitting at a big table in the middle of the room. They were the only ones there. We walked up to the table, and Derek introduced me to everyone. They were all drinking pop and said they'd ordered a few pizzas. We took off our coats and joined them. Everyone started talking about the case, and Derek told them about the research I had done the day before. He asked if he could have a copy of my notes. When the waitress brought the pizzas. I asked if they had a copy machine. She said yes and that I could use it. We ate, and it tasted surprisingly good, but I didn't have much of an appetite. When we were done, I asked Derek if I could talk to him for a second. We stepped away from the table.

"Hey, I'd go out to my Jeep and grab my notebook, but I'm afraid of the dark. Will you walk with me?" I said, smiling. He looked at me like he was confused. "Really, I know it sounds dumb, but it's true."

"Okay, sweetheart," he said. He looked amused.

I took my notebook and met up with the waitress, she led me to the back office, and I made copies of the five pages I'd written on and brought them to Derek. After he thanked me, we all got our jackets on, and Derek walked me to my car.

"Follow me back to the Cities, and then I'll touch base with you in the morning and let you know what we find out. If you need anything or want to talk, you have my number. Don't worry about bothering me. I'll be up for a while yet tonight. And I'll be in the office a lot this week. Just call if you need to," he said. "Oh, and none of this information is public yet. I need you to keep it that way."

I stood there leaning on my Jeep. I nodded and thanked him. He put his hand on my shoulder.

"Are you going to be okay?"

"Yeah, I'm just tired. Thank you again for all your help and for your company," I said. "I'll talk to you soon."

I angled in my Jeep and pulled out behind him. An hour and some later, I was pulling into my lot, exhausted. Faith looked tired, too. It took two trips to get everything in. I threw the food in the fridge and fell onto my bed, fully clothed and not caring. I was just about to fall asleep, when my phone rang.

"Hey, are you busy Saturday night?" Kat asked.

"I'm free."

"Keep it open," she said and disconnected.

I called my mom and told her I was home safe. After I turned all the lights off and climbed into bed again, I though about Kat. I should have told her, then again I wasn't sure I should. Derek said to keep quiet. Ugh, I just wanted to sleep.

19

I WAS ON THE HILL AGAIN. It was foggy and dim. I was sitting by the cave entrance crying. I looked up and saw the two ghosts. It was Lily and Carrie, both in long, white dresses. They were just standing there looking at me. They didn't say anything, just looked like they were softly smiling. Slowly they grabbed hands, turned and walked away, fading into mist as they went.

I woke up calm. It was still dark out. I looked over at the clock. Two. My face was wet from tears, but I wasn't out of breath or scared. Faith was asleep next to me. She picked her head up and looked at me, then went back to sleep. I lay there wondering what that meant. Now I really felt that Lily was dead. With every passing day, I thought that more and more. I also wondered if I could be wrong about Jake and Mark. I didn't know what to think anymore. It didn't seem fair to even think that, I had known them so long. The facts were just so few and far between and there was no body. Where was her body if she was dead? There's no way it was Jake and Mark because they wouldn't have had time to move a body. I was only asleep for three hours, and she got in her car and left . . . ugh, I didn't know what to believe. And I didn't know what the dreams meant. So far they had panned out, so I wanted to trust them, but I didn't want to believe that Lily was dead. It was like a bad movie. I closed my eyes and tried to fall back to sleep.

The next time I opened my eyes, it was eight-thirty. Friday already. Did I just hear my phone? I got out of bed and checked it. Two missed calls, one from Mom just checking in, the other from Kat, wondering about a lunch date. She didn't even know that I'd dropped to part time. I should probably catch her up on my week. I felt like a bad friend. There was major drama going on and I wasn't keeping her informed. Plus, I'd gotten a divorce lawyer from work, and it wasn't her. I had told her right away I didn't think she was a good idea because she was friends with Jake, too. And if the divorce got messy it would be really hard for all of us. She'd probably called because she wanted to do lunch to prep me on the events planned for Saturday night. On the rare occasion that she did get me to go out, she had it all planned, and it was usually tons of fun. I was actually looking forward to getting out and getting this mess off my mind for a bit.

First things first, I called Kat back and told her that I'd meet her for lunch and that my mom was coming, too. We agreed on Buffalo Wild Wings at one. I jumped in the shower and did the jeans and sweatshirt look with tennis shoes and hair as usual. That's the one nice thing about my new look. I didn't have to figure out what I was going to do with my hair. I could really only wear it one way now. Limited makeup too. I wasn't feeling up to much primping today. The whole situation had been so exhausting. I'd just gotten up and already I felt tired, and my headache was back. I tossed back some Tylenol and spent some time on the couch with Faith until it kicked in. After I ran the vacuum through the apartment, I did a once over with the glass cleaner and surface cleaner. I was quickly reminded of how big the apartment was. It didn't get nearly as dirty when it was just me.

Next, I grabbed the number to my investor's office and sat at my nice, new table with a pen and notebook.

"Hi, can you transfer me to Blake Connor, please?"

"Sure, can I tell him who's calling?" the receptionist asked.

"Yes, it's Sara Martin."

"Hey, Sara. How are you?" Blake said, in a friendly voice when he came on the line.

"Hello, Mr. Connor," I replied. "I'm good. How are you?"

"Please, Sara, call me Blake. If you're calling, you must have more questions or the money came in."

"Both actually."

"Well, let's see, I'm free for lunch at twelve-thirty. We could meet somewhere and go over details," he said. Wow, this was not what I was expecting, but it sounded nice.

"Actually, I have lunch plans with my mom and a friend," I said.

"How about dinner? Are you free for dinner? My treat," he offered.

"Ummm, yeah. I'm free. Sure. Where should I meet you and when?" I asked, smiling.

We agreed on seven at Applebee's, which was good because I didn't want anything too formal. It almost seemed like a date. Maybe I was way out in left field. Professionals took clients out for meals all the time. I was sure he was just being nice.

I yanked my purse onto my shoulder and headed out the door for lunch. Kat and my mom beat me there. They both were set up with tall beers, so I ordered one, too. Mom jumped right in.

"Spill it. I want all the details about the trip, and that includes the details on the detective."

Kat put her glass down and almost choked on her beer. "What trip? What detective? What did I miss?"

"Okay, " I said, then I took a long pull on my beer. "Here's the story."

I spent the rest of a two-hour lunch filling them in on everything from my dreams, to Reggie, to the library, to the actual cave, to the sleepover, and the emotions that fit with everything that happened. They told me I shouldn't trust Jake and Mark and agreed that I should keep my distance from both until things were figured out. Then they informed me that I was falling for Derek, to which I responded that they were wrong, but they both said they could see it in my eyes. Whatever.

"I think you should talk to Lily's parents and tell them what you know before the police do," Mom said.

I thought about it. "I'll check to see if there are any new details first."

"You should go there personally to check and then you could say hi to Mr. Detective," Kat added.

"Stop." We all laughed, which felt good. I swore them to secrecy until further notice. Then after taking care of the bill and collecting my hugs, I drove home.

When I got settled in, I called Derek to see about any new details.

"Hey, Sara, how are you feeling?" he asked.

"I'm okay, thanks. Have you got any labs back or found anything out yet?"

"We are still waiting on the labs. They're backed up. They told me within the hour, so I'll let you know. We did a phone interview with Bill and Nancy Sanders this morning, and they said Carrie and her childhood friend played and walked around that area a lot, but they never knew of a cave and doubted that Carrie did either," he said.

"Did they seem upset?"

"Yeah. It's never easy to ask more questions when you have no more answers for them. I told them to hang in there, that I'd call them later," he said.

"What about Lily's parents? Do you think I should talk to them?"

"That might be a good idea. It'd be better coming from you than a cop they don't know," he said.

Derek instructed me on what I could tell them because the case was still under investigation. He also asked me to see if they knew her blood type and to call him with it right away. Otherwise he would get an order for release of her medical records.

I jumped in my Jeep and drove to the Kowalski home. I sat down with them and told them that I had just spoken with Detective Richards, and he was wondering about blood type. Debbie went to the office to see if she had it in a file. I decided not to tell them anything about my trip to the cabin. I wasn't sure where to start or stop and I didn't want to worry them if I didn't have to. I talked to them a little on what they had been doing, and they said Lily's credit cards had not been used and her cell records had no outgoing calls since the day she left the cabin. They seriously thought that something was terribly wrong. They both looked horrible. I told them that Derek put an APB out on her car, but they hadn't had any sightings yet. Debbie gave me a copy of her medical bill from years ago that included her name and blood type. I left and told them if I learned anything new, I'd let them know. They thanked me and gave me hugs.

I drove to the police station and walked right into Derek's office. "Here ya go." I said, setting the paper in front of him. He hadn't seen me coming because he was busy staring at his desk and the mess of papers on it. The bulletin board to his left was even more filled up with details of Lily. He looked up at me and smiled.

"Hey, you! You're a breath of fresh air," he said leaning back in his chair. He looked awful.

"Have you been here all night?" I asked.

"Yes, but I'm heading home for a recharge in about an hour, I'm just waiting on labs," he said, just as his phone rang. He gave me a "wait a minute" finger and pointed to the chair. I sat as he took the call. He was listening intently, then reached for the paper I'd given him, scanned it and said, "It's a match on blood type."

He hung up and looked at me with concerned eyes. "The blood in the cave was the same type. It'll take a bit for DNA to confirm that it's Lily's for sure. We have her hair sample from Mark's apartment so the lab can get started right away, but we won't know for about a couple days."

I nodded, and he continued, "We got a search warrant for Mark's apartment. We took information on cell and credit card records, and it showed a lot of calls back and forth between Lily and Jake starting back five months ago." I nodded again. It felt like someone had a fist around my heart and was squeezing it.

He moved to the chair next to me. "I'm sorry," he said and patted my leg. "If there is anything I can do, let me know."

I stood up and reached for my purse. "Okay," I said with a deep breath and a forced, tight-lipped smile. "Thanks, for telling me. Will you call as soon as you hear?"

"I will," he said with a small smile.

When I walked out, the receptionist said goodbye and called me by name. I got home and watched TV for a while, not sure what to do with myself. I knew if I sat still, I'd cry, so I had to keep my mind busy. I checked my watch. Six. I went to my room and switched the sweatshirt out for a blouse with ruffles on the front. I added cute heels and jewelry, and tossed on some extra eye make-up. Voila!

I arrived at Applebees at ten after seven and checked with the greeter. She said she hadn't seen a single guy come in for a while. I grabbed a spot at the bar, by the door and ordered a drink. While sitting there, I was trying to think of questions to ask about money stuff, in case we didn't have anything to talk about. I was kind of nervous and excited. Geez, it's not like it was a date.

I felt a hand on my back. I turned, and it was Blake. Gosh, I could smell him already. Yum. How do men smell so good all the time?

"Sara? Hey, you look amazing," Blake said from over my shoulder.

"Thank you," I said. "So do you," noticing he was in a black dress shirt and jeans. He'd lost the suit.

"I changed. I hope you don't mind the business dinner being more casual. I actually hate wearing a suit," he said with a wink.

I smiled and giggled. "Nope, I don't mind at all. You look fine." Mighty fine. "I didn't know where you wanted to sit, so I just grabbed a drink here."

"That's great. Sorry I'm late, I got stuck on the phone. How about we move to a table in the back," he said, grabbing my drink for me and offering me his arm. I smiled and took it. Chivalry was not dead. We got a table in the back of the restaurant near a window.

"How about we go over paperwork and enjoy a drink, then order dinner," Blake suggested.

"Sounds perfect."

We spent the next forty minutes or so talking money and strategy. I felt really comfortable with him, like I was in charge, too. We agreed that, with a portfolio of this size, it'd be good to meet at least once a month and take a look at what was going on with the investments and make any changes we needed to make in a timely fashion.

"Do you want to set it up month by month or set a specific day of the month?" he asked me.

"How about the last Friday of the month," I said with a wink.

He smiled and suggested that we make it a dinner meeting just like tonight. We both wrote it down in our planners and then reached for our menus.

Blake ordered a chicken pasta bowl, and I ordered the same. We were talking about his office and how long he'd been there, when I noticed Jake at the bar. I hoped he hadn't seen my Jeep in the lot. He looked really tired and appeared to be alone. I kept peeking at him and noticed that he ordered three shots of something. When they arrived, he paid the bartender. I expected him to take them to a table. Instead he shot all three in a row and walked out. What the heck? I had never seen this side of him. He must not be handling things well. Dressed in old raggedy sweats and tennis shoes and a dirty t-shirt, I hoped he was going straight home.

When I turned my attention back to Blake. I realized he must have noticed that I was watching Jake.

"Do you see someone you know?" he asked.

"Yeah, but he's gone. Sorry," I answered. The waitress brought our food and refreshed our drinks.

"It's okay. You just looked so sad all of a sudden," he added. "So tell me more about yourself," he said, taking bite.

"Well, I was born and raised in the area," I started. I gave him the shortened life story all the way up to college. Then I pondered continuing. I did. What the heck? I liked him and I trusted him with my life savings. Why not my life story? He listened intently, nodding here and there, tipping his head and adding puppy-dog eyes once in a while. So cute. I liked how he made me feel so comfortable, so confident, so important. I skipped all the day-to-day stuff lately and ended with a simple separation/divorce story. "And that's about it," I said. "That's me in a nutshell," I added with a wink.

"I like it!" he said as I felt my cheeks turn pink. Must be the second drink. We finished our dinners, ordered another drink and sat there talking like old friends for a while. I found out that he married right out of high school, was divorced a year later, went on to college, got his degree and started working for Edward Jones right after graduation. He'd been there for nine years. He was thirty-five and couldn't wait for retirement. I looked at my watch.

"Wow, it's almost ten," I said. "Do you have to get up early?"

"No, I have nothing going on tomorrow. Well, I have paintball with the boys at eleven but other than that I finally have a weekend free. How about you? Do you need to get going?"

"I don't have too, but I probably should. I'm really tired, and these drinks are going to kick in pretty soon. I had so much fun. It was really nice getting to know you," I said.

"The pleasure was all mine, Sara," he said with a grin. "I'll walk you out to your car."

We slipped into our jackets as he put cash in the money folder. I thanked him for the drinks and dinner, and we walked out together. We got to my car, and I unlocked it. He leaned up against the back door, briefcase in one hand. He looked so different out of the office and out from behind his desk. He was in very good shape.

"You gonna be all right to drive?" he asked.

"I'll be fine if I leave now," I said. "Thanks again for the dinner. I'll drop off the funds next week."

"Great. Thanks for allowing me to be your adviser. I'm looking forward to working with you and growing your money," he said, trying to sound professional. He smiled and I laughed out loud.

"I'm looking forward to it too," I said, putting my hand out to shake. He took my hand and shook it, then turned it over and kissed it. Then he opened my door for me, and I got in.

"Goodnight, Sara."

"Goodnight," I said feeling all giddy.

I headed for home and hoped I'd make it. I had a big smile on my face while I drove, and butterflies in my tummy. When I got two blocks away from my apartment, my phone rang.

"Hello?"

"Hey, it's Derek. I have some bad news," he said. "Where are you?"

"I'm almost to my apartment," I said, suddenly losing my smile.

"Okay, call me back when you're in your apartment." He disconnected.

I parked and walked inside, dreading calling him back. I wanted answers but only good ones, and he'd said bad news. I said a short prayer while I dialed.

"Hey, what is it?"

"We got a call from the Nisswa police station this afternoon. A man on lake Hawsawneekee, reported a strange object on his fish finder and noticed a large shadow in the water. He's a regular on that lake and had never seen it before. He called it in, and the police went out. Long story, short, they found a car in the lake. It's Lily's."

"Oh, my God," I said, sinking into the sofa.

We had it brought here. The C.S. unit is testing it now. What we know already is that there are blood stains in the trunk. Not sure on type yet, and I don't have DNA for what was in the cave yet either. I'm so sorry ... are you going to be okay, Sara?" he asked.

"No," I said crying. "I don't know how I'm suppose to feel."

"I'm going home for the night. Do you need me to stop by and check on you?" he asked.

"Okay," I cried. "Apartment four," and I hung up. What the heck was that? Did I just invite the hot cop over to my house, late at night, drunk, crying, and make-up washed off? What was I thinking? Geez. This guy had only ever seen me at my worst. Poor guy. I must seem kinda scary.

Fifteen minutes later, I heard the buzzer. I hit the button and after a quick mirror check, I opened the door to hot cop, leaning on the door frame, arms crossed.

"Hey," I said.

"Hey? Hey? Do you always just buzz people in before you check who it is?" he asked, sounding like a cop.

"Get in here," I said as I fist-grabbed his shirt and yanked him through the door. I pulled a little too hard because now he was right in front of me. Oops, awkward. I stepped back.

"What are you, my dad?" I asked to break the silence. I smiled and then turned and walked to the kitchen. "Can I get you something to drink?"

"Yeah, a beer if you got one."

I handed him a beer, and invited him to sit in the living room. I flipped on the gas fireplace and joined him.

"Nice! Beats the wood one at the cabin, doesn't it?" he said, looking at the fire and sipping his beer.

"It does for ease, and it's clean, but it doesn't have that nice crackling sound."

"So this is the new place … it's nice. Is it better than your old apartment?"

"Yes, it's tons bigger, and our old apartment was on the third floor too, which was awful. So tell me more about what we know," I said, as I settled back on the couch across from him.

Derek told me again what he'd already told me. He thought that the blood was Lily's, and now he was investigating who put the car in the lake.

"They're checking the car for fingerprints which may or may not help. We already know we'll find Mark's and Jake's prints in there, so that doesn't tell us anything. We have a man watching Mark, and he's not coming or going much from his apartment. If he does, it's for groceries or alcohol. Jake is over a lot, and that's a red flag because they should hate each other, not be buddies, considering the situation. Have you talked to them lately?"

"No."

"Something isn't adding up. I've been doing this a long time, so trust me and my gut when I say I think you should keep a distance from them. Don't trust just the fact that you know them. People can change in a heartbeat," he said. "I think the reason they still talk is because they both have something to talk about. Normally in this situation they'd never speak to each other again, but with these two, they only speak to each other. And Jake has missed a lot of work. We've been keeping tabs on him, too."

I shook my head. It was so surreal. My mind was spinning, trying to figure out what was going on. If Mark and Jake were involved, what did I feel about Lily? What about the two new men in my life? How did I sort what they felt about me? Should I be feeling anything at all? The fact that I was in the beginning of a divorce might be a clue. Where was Lily? On and on. Ugh.

"So," Derek smiled, "were you out drinking when I called?"

"No, sir," I lied. "Just a business dinner with my financial adviser, a three-drink dinner is all," I added, trying my best to look innocent and not buzzed.

"Financial adviser? What's this financial adviser's name?" he asked, in his investigator voice, with his squinty eyes, arms folded across his chest.

"Ummmm, Blake Connor," I said, biting my lip. "He's helping me plan my future. We have to meet a minimum of once a month so we do it over dinner, since we both have to eat."

"Really…should I be worried?" he asked, as he took a long pull on his beer.

I had no idea what to say to that, so I just sat there wondering if he liked me or if I was looking into this too much. Was he jealous? I just shook my head and gave him a smile. I suddenly wished I had reapplied my makeup. We sat there in silence for a few seconds, occasionally locking eyes. He finished his beer and placed it on a coaster on the coffee table. On the coaster. I loved him.

He turned to me and said, "Well, sweetness, thanks for the beer. I have a big day tomorrow, so I better get some sleep." He stood to leave, and I stood with him. He grabbed his empty and put it in the garbage. Nice. While he headed over to the door and put his shoes on, I stood there leaning on the wall. When he looked up, the thought flashed in my head that I really wanted him to kiss me. It was so wrong, but I really hoped he would. He looked at me and the corner of his mouth curled. From the look on his face, I wondered if he was reading my mind, or if I'd said that thought out loud.

20

I WOKE UP IN THE MORNING, having had no bad dreams, just tons of good, un-interrupted sleep. Good thing too because I'd promised Kat I'd go out with her tonight. A phone check showed eight-thirty, and I had a text from Mark:

"Hey, how are you? Fine here. Have you heard anything about Lily? Maybe we should get together."

I decided to ignore it. I didn't know if it was a good idea to respond. There were just too many reasons not to, and I promised Derek.

I called Kat and got a wardrobe, venue, and time from her. She said she'd pick me up at eight, and told me to dress hot. *What the heck does hot mean? I don't think I own any hot.*

A couple seconds later my phone rang again, "Yeah, you need hot clothes don't cha? Make it six, and we'll go to the mall first. I'll find ya sum'n," Kat said.

I laughed and agreed.

I spent the day cleaning and organizing my new apartment with the iPod cranked. Then I took a quick trip to the liquor store and grocery store to stock up. My phone rang. Derek. "Hey, sweetness, how's the hangover?"

"Hey," I said, with an instant smile. "Fine, no hangover. I wasn't drunk." Lie.

"Riiiight. Anyway, I'm calling with an update, but as always this stays be-tween you and me," his voice in serious mode now.

"Of course," I said, loading the groceries in my Jeep. "What do ya got?"

"Well the DNA is back, and it was a match for Lily. I'm sorry. The blood in the trunk of her car was hers as well."

"Oh, my God," I said covering my mouth, "So she *is* dead." I sat down in my driver's seat and rested my head on the steering wheel.

"Yes, at this point we believe she is, but we don't have a body yet. We have a dive team in the lake, but they haven't found anything yet. We'll keep them out there through today but if they don't find anything by tonight, we'll call it off. We doubt at this point that she drove the car into the lake, being her blood was in the trunk, and the trunk was closed when we took the car out. We think the car was put there after she was moved."

"So what now? Are you going to tell her parents yet?" I asked, in between sniffles.

"That's another reason I was calling. I do need to update them, and I was wondering if you wanted to go with me," he said.

"Umm, sure. I guess I could. When?" I asked, not sure that it sounded like something I really wanted to do, but they were like second parents to me. I felt like I should help. I told Derek I'd be at the station in fifteen minutes.

The drive over there was horrible. When I got there, I asked if we should call ahead, and he said no. It was protocol to just show up and get straight to the point. Talk about a bad part of a job. This was the worst job in the whole world. What, we just knock on someone's door and tell them their child is presumed dead? On second thought, I didn't know if I wanted to do this.

I settled into the black sedan with Derek, and we drove to her parents house. When we pulled up, I noticed Gerald was on the riding lawn mower and Debbie was on her knees in the garden near the front door, taking out the half dead flowers from summer. Fall yard prep, I couldn't wait until I had a house with a yard.

Gerald saw us pull up and drove the lawn mower over and got off. Debbie, at a garden, stood up and took her gloves off. They both had horrified looks on their faces. They looked at each other and then at me. My eyes instantly filled with tears. I was trying not to cry, but I knew what was coming, and I didn't want to see them hurt.

Gerald stepped up and puts his hand out, "Detective Richards."

Derek shook both their hands and asked, "Is there somewhere we can sit down?"

You could see they were both already preparing for the news. I could see both of them breathing, the rise and fall of there chests very exaggerated, and their eyes fearful. Debbie motioned us to come inside. We all sat at the table, and Derek started at the beginning with my dreams and my returning to the cabin, and went through the whole story. All of our eyes, except Derek's were filled with tears. When he said that the blood and DNA were a match to Lily, they both broke down, they hugged each other and cried, hard. It was the single, worst moment of my life, right up there next to finding out my husband was sleeping with my best friend. The girl I went from loving to instantly hating, the girl I secretly wished dead the moment I found out, and now I wished with everything I had that she was alive and well. I started sobbing too. I got up and grabbed tissues from the kitchen counter and four glasses of water and set them on the table.

After a few minutes, Derek continued and told them, "We are now investigating a homicide. If you hear anything unusual about her or those involved, please call me right away. Also we need you to keep this as quiet as possible. That means not calling all your extended family yet. I know that's asking a lot, but it should only be another day or two before we have more figured out. None of us want to have to deal with media attention or have it mess up the investigation. And don't make or take any calls from Mark or Jake. We just don't have all the answers yet, and the investigation is in a critical time. I promise to let you know anything we learn right away. And when the investigation is done, you can let your families know."

I went over to Gerald and Debbie and gave them big hugs. Derek told them that he would be in touch. Derek walked to my side of the car and opened my door for me, I got in and he closed it. When he sat down in the driver's seat, I was face to tissue.

He patted my thigh and said quietly, "You were great. Thanks for coming, it made it easier to have you there. They had someone who cared about her too, to share in the pain."

I nodded and cried quietly all the way back to the station. When we got there, he opened my door for me, walked me to my Jeep and helped me in.

"I'll give you a call later," he said.

"I'm suppose to go out with Kat tonight, but I'm not sure I'll be up to it now," I responded.

Derek smiled gently, "I think you should go. It'll do you more good to go out and have fun than it will to sit around and cry. There's nothing you can do about the situation now anyway."

I nodded. "I'll talk to you later," I said sadly and got in. I drove home slowly, thinking about Lily and wishing I'd had a chance to say goodbye. I bet her parents did, too. Now I hoped we'd find a body so her parents could lay her to rest and have some closure.

Faith, my bundle of joy. I was so grateful for her. She came pouncing over to me when I walked in. I picked her up and instantly felt loved. Carrying her against my broken heart, I walked to my room, climbed into bed and closed my eyes for a bit.

Two hours later I woke up. I still felt exhausted. I knew that it was the stress and emotions, but I hated it. I just wanted to feel happy and content again and have a normal feeling in my body. My stomach felt hollow all the time. From the moment I saw Jake kiss Lily, I'd felt like I had the flu.

It was only four o'clock, so I decided to pass the time and keep my mind busy by baking cookies and then delivering them to the people in the apartments on either side of mine. It was a good idea. The ones on the left were a younger couple with two young kids and were very excited about the cookies. The one on the right was a single male, young, maybe twenty-three or four, cute. He said he loved me. He said he'd smelled them an hour ago and was drooling. He seemed nice. He was very funny, and he looked great. Thick blond hair, light-brown features, he had a day-old beard that gave him a perfect rustic look. Let's just say he was easy on the eyes. I should have gotten his name. I ziplocked the rest of the cookies in sets of a dozen and stuck them in the pantry.

I showered, threw on jeans and a sweatshirt, not too worried about my fashion right now because I knew that Kat would find me something nice at the mall. I packed a variety of shoes in a bag. That way I'd have a pair to match whatever I bought. Then I spent some extra time on my hair and make-up. When Kat called and said she was in the lot, I grabbed a dozen cookies, my purse, the bag of shoes and ran out the door.

21

K AT LOOKED AMAZING AS ALWAYS. I gave her the cookies, and she thanked me. We spent about an hour at the mall in three different stores, trying on tons of clothes. We even tried on some prom dresses, then got really depressed because we were too old for prom, and we had no boys in our lives to take us to prom or even out on a fancy date. So we took the gowns off and put them back on the rack. It was super fun, and for a moment I almost forgot about my problems. Finally I decided on a shirt that was very cute. It was black-and-bright-blue rayon and was off one shoulder. The print was small squares, and it was fitted across the stomach. That's one good thing about stress, it burns a lot of calories. My stomach was almost flat right now. I bought the the second- and third-place shirts and some jewelry too.

After we were in the car, I threw on my shirt and some black, strappy heels, and the silver jewelry I'd bought to match. We settled on dinner at Olive Garden and spent the next hour or so drinking and eating and catching up on the weeks events. After I told Kat everything, including the blood match, I asked her not to tell anyone and mentally prayed she wouldn't. She was trustworthy, so I wasn't too worried. She then told me my divorce lawyer, Allie, her co-worker, said that the court date was set. I asked her if she remembered when, and she said no, but she knew that Allie would be calling on Monday to go over things.

"It sounds like Jake has a lawyer and isn't planning to fight for anything. He told his lawyer that he loves you deeply and wants you to have everything," Kat said and then sipped her martini.

"That's good. I wonder if I could ever forgive him. Not that I would ever work things out with him, but to move on for my own sake. I still have so much hate, I don't know when I'll feel better. I'm just glad there are no children involved, I don't know how people with kids get through this," I responded.

"You're not drinking very fast? Are we not getting spritzed tonight?" She winked, trying to change the subject.

"I'm still recovering from last night."

"Last night? What, hot date? Spill, girlfriend," she demanded.

I filled her in on my night, including Derek swinging by.

"How do you do it? With everything you've got going on, how do you hook two men in the process?" she asked, shaking her head.

"Uh, no. I'm not trying to hook men. I'm still legally married, and it's way too early to even think about that. I'm total rebound material right now … do they still say that? That I'm on the rebound? That usually scares guys away doesn't it?" I asked.

"I'd think so, but, girlfriend, it seems to be working for you." She shook her head again and motioned the waitress for another round. We decided to move to the bar area so someone else could have our table to eat while we hung out. At ten, we hit the club downtown, I hadn't been in a club for about two years, maybe longer. Lights, music, dancing and everyone was smiling and having fun—it was the perfect place. I felt my phone vibrate as we walked in. I grabbed it while I followed Kat to the bar, she ordered shots. Great.

"Hellooo!" I sang, suddenly realizing how drunk I sounded.

"Hey, there," Derek answered. "Are you and Kat having fun?"

"Sure are. We went shopping and ate and now we are apparently doing shots and dancing at the club."

"Wow, sounds like fun! What club are you at?"

"Flash." I answered. "It's packed."

"Well nothing new here. We do have a lead that we'll follow up on in the morning. Other than that, nothing. I'm off for the night. I just wanted to check in and make sure you're doing okay," he said.

"Hey, do you need a night cap?" I asked, as I looked at Kat who was handing me my shot. We clinked our glasses then threw them back. I raised my eyebrows in an effort to question if that was okay, she nodded, took my shot glass and gave me two thumbs up with a big smile. "Why don't you come join us? You can meet my friend Kat and hang with us," I yelled in to the receiver.

"I don't think so. Isn't it ladies' night?" he asked. I could barely hear him above the noise.

"Nope, it's just go-out night. Anyone can come. Even you!" I said trying my best to convince him.

"Well, I will think about it. If I see ya, I'll see ya. If I don't, you enjoy your night," he said.

"Okay," I yelled. "See ya in a few!" Then I hung up before he could answer.

Kat and I both laughed. She gave me a high five and then handed me another shot. We clinked and shot yet another. An hour later, I was buzzed but steady. Kat and I were on the dance floor twirling and shaking our goods. She was really close to a young guy, and they were yelling in each others ears, smiling and laughing. I suddenly felt someone dancing really close behind me. I didn't turn around but kept dancing, thinking how nice it felt to be this close to someone. Whoever it was could dance, they were moving with me and right on the beat of the music. I felt him move his head up against my hair by my neck, and I fought the urge to tip my head and let him kiss me. Oh, please be Derek! That's when I smelled him. I inhaled deeply and knew it was Derek. Slowly, I turned my head slightly and it was. I smiled and turned my head away again. His right hand slid slowly across my belly and around to my left hip. Our hips swaying to the beat of the music. I swung my arm back, up around his neck and he pulled me in close. I happened to catch Kat's eyes, and she was smiling and looked shocked. She mouthed, "Is that him?" I nodded. She smiled and fanned her face with her hand. I mouthed, "I know." Then, sadly, the song ended, dang it, and they started the electric slide song. Yuk! Sliding my arm off his neck, I turned to meet his eyes. I blinked slowly and smiled softly.

"You're quite the dancer, sweetness," he said, as he grabbed my hand and led me off the dance floor to the bar. "Can I buy you a drink?"

"Thank you. Yeah sure. I'll have Windsor, diet," I said. By the expression on his face, that impressed him. As the bartender started our order, we both turned our backs and leaned on the bar, watching Kat and her new friend dancing. I pointed her out to Derek.

"Is this someone she knows," he asked.

"Nope."

"So is this how you meet people?" he asked, with a snide smile.

I played along. "Usually I just get really drunk, go out there and wait for someone to push up on me from behind, and that's the guy that gets to come home with me for the night." I smiled matter-of-factly, then grabbed my drink and took a big gulp. He turned and paid the bartender.

"Well, lucky me," he winked. "Come on, sissy, let's go dance!" He grabbed me by the hand and twirled me out on the dance floor. We spent the next few songs out there making friends and talking to Kat. While I introduced Kat to Derek, her boy toy headed to the bar for refills. After about an hour, Derek grabbed my hand and pulled me off to a quieter corner.

"I'm going to head home. It's been a long week," he yelled into my ear, his face close to mine. He smelled so good. I tried to keep my lips from touching his cheek. They were really fighting me. I nodded and said, "Okay, thanks for the drink and dance."

He smiled back. "Do you need a ride?" he yelled in my ear with a quick glance at Kat.

"No, but thanks. We'll grab a cab in a bit," I leaned forward and hollered back. I felt his hand on the other side on my head. He pulled me close, and now our cheeks were touching. He whispered that I looked amazing, kissed my cheek, then walked out. I watched him walk away and tried to mentally will the blood in my body to go back to where it belonged. That's when I heard Kat's voice.

"Close your mouth, dear."

I closed my mouth, caught my breath and clinked glasses with her. We both took a long drink.

"Are the two of us really leaving together?" she asked, kinda sad.

"Aw, yeah," I said. "Did you think I was going to split with Derek and leave you here with frat boy? Not a chance, sis-ta."

She checked her watch and said, "We should probably head out."

"Are you going to get frat boy's number?" We both scanned the dance floor for him.

"Oh, there he is, lip-locked with the blonde over there," Kat said. "I'll just check back later," she winked.

"Awe, young love."

We headed for home in a cab. Kat crashed at my place, on the couch. In the morning, I came out to the kitchen for water and noticed she was gone and there was a note on the counter that said, "Thanks, call ya later."

22

SUNDAY ... UGH. I SUPPOSE I SHOULD HIT CHURCH. If I got ready fast, I'd be able to make the late service. I jumped in the shower and dressed quickly. I did a simple yet effective make-up and grabbed my purse and shoes on the run. I got to church just in time, and I noticed that Blake was there too. He was sitting far to my left and next to a beautiful brunette. She made me feel very simple. As soon as church was over, I rushed to my car before he spotted me. Who was he with? He said he wasn't married. I guess I hadn't asked about a girlfriend but I just assumed since he was in no hurry on Friday night, he had no one to hurry home to.

I called my mom. She warned me that I was living my life in fast forward, and it could bite me in the end. I mentally agreed with her, but I also felt like everything was happening without my control so what was I suppose to do about it? I was making choices that felt right. After I reminded her that I was a big girl, I told her I loved her and disconnected. I was actually looking forward to some quiet time at home, but I wanted to make one stop first. I pulled into the lot and rang the buzzer. The door unlocked and I headed in.

"Hey, Joey!" I said, "How's my baby?"

"Dude, thanks for stopping over. We were just talking about you," he said, stepping aside to usher me in. "Kristin, it's Sara Martin," he yelled.

We walked through the kitchen and into the living room. Kristin and Marissa were on the couch. Quietly, I walked over and sat down and she passed me the baby. Oh, my gosh, she was the cutest thing ever!

"She's so beautiful! I think she gets prettier every time I see her," I said in a squeaky baby voice. "Isn't she just a sweetheart?" Pulling her in close to me, I squeezed her gently and kissed her forehead.

"Dude, we were just about to call you, when you rang the door bell," Joey said.

"Really, why?"

"We need a baby-sitter for tomorrow night, and we thought of you. We don't know very many people, and the few friends we do have, we'd never leave a baby with, so we thought we'd ask you," Joey said.

"Oh, I'd love to. What time?"

"We have a baby CPR and First Aid class for new parents at the hospital from five to ten, but if you came earlier, we'd like to go out on a mini date for a nice dinner, too. We haven't been out in so long, and we don't want to bring a baby to a nice restaurant," Kristin said.

"Sure, no problem. That's great for you guys. How about three in the afternoon. That'll give you lots of time together before the class," I said, smiling at the baby.

"Thanks so much. Do you want to do it at our house or yours?" Kristin asked.

"How about my place? That way if she sleeps, I can clean or bake or something."

We sat there and chatted for another half hour and then I left. I just had to get my baby fix. As I said goodbye, I thought about how instantly excited I was for tomorrow. I couldn't wait to have a tiny baby for the whole afternoon.

I went home and changed into lounge wear. I checked my email, and there were two new messages. The first was from Jake. I was just about ready to delete it, but then I was curious as to what he knew, so I opened it. It just said that he missed me terribly and couldn't go on living without me, that it'd been too long, and we needed to talk and get this worked out. He added that he was so depressed he couldn't work, was about to lose his job, and drank to mask the pain. While I hit delete, I got sick to my stomach. I couldn't believe he thought we still had a chance. I opened the one from Derek. It just said last night was fun and had a smiley face. And now I was smiling too. I thought it was funny that I was catching my breath at an email. Geez, I really must like him if his emails gave me butterflies. I sent a winking smile back, then did a mental head slap—what, was I fifteen again? I turned off the monitor and went into the living room. After starting a movie, I climbed on to the couch with hot chocolate and a blanket.

I watched movies for three hours, then I had to get up. I was getting so tired I needed to move or I'd be asleep by six. Maybe I should check out the fitness room. It was one of many amenities here at the complex, and I got free use. I should maybe use it. After I changed into shorts and a t-shirt, I put two barrettes in my hair to hold it out of my face and headed out the door. I thought on the way there, how nice it was that I didn't have to go outside, just down two long halls. The room was empty when I got there. Good, if I was the only one, then I wouldn't feel so awkward since I had no idea how to use most of the equipment.

There were mirrors on two walls so the place looked huge, but really wasn't. There was a big flat screen TV on the wall, I found the remote and turned it to HGTV and muted it, then went to the stereo and cranked up some music. It was a satellite radio, so I put some old school rap on. I was happy. Good music, good show, and I had the whole place to myself. I made a mental note to come here more often on Sunday afternoons.

I lay down on the weight bench and lifted very little, then did some thighs and some other machines. I didn't even know what muscles they were working I just knew I hurt … everywhere. Gosh, I was out of shape. I was in definite need of toning. I decided I'd had enough of the sore muscles, so I got on the treadmill and found a comfortable speed. I was walking for about three minutes when the door opened. Lord give me strength. It was my neighbor, the hot, single guy, from the right!

"Well, hey, neighbor," he said. I never noticed how muscular he was. Holy crap, this guy was huge! He was wearing shorts and a tight tank that hugged every ab ripple and there were a lot of ripples. His arms were large! "Thanks again for the cookies. They were great. You're an excellent cook. Anytime you have extra, you can just walk your narrow behind over and knock on my door," he said with a wink.

Narrow behind? I liked it. "Okay, that's a deal." I said, wishing I could start over. I sounded like a dork. "So did you eat them all yet?" I asked.

"Yup, pretty much in one sitting. I called it supper," he smiled and wrinkled his nose. "Nice tunes. Did you pick this out?" he asked.

Oh, gosh, what's the right answer? "Yup, it's got a good beat," I said, again wishing I could choose a different answer.

"I like it," he said, as he sat back on the weight bench getting ready to lift the circle of weights he'd just put on there. I looked over at the reflection in the mirror and watched him lift. I totally just saw him check out my butt! He didn't know I saw him, and I guess there I was checking him out, too. I just hoped my butt looked good in these shorts. I turned my machine off and spent a few minutes on the floor stretching. Then I stood and grabbed my water bottle.

"Well, see ya later," I said, with a smile and a quick finger wave.

"See ya, cutie," he winked. I walked out and jogged back to my room. I had a ton of energy now and no idea what to do with it, so I settled on a much needed cold shower.

23

MONDAY, OHHHH, OUCH! Slowly moving from the sore muscles, I dressed in black, dress pants that fit just right and one of the cute tops I'd bought Saturday. It was a fitted, rayon and silk, sleeveless blouse, with a v-neck and it tied at the waist. I threw on some matching jewelry and I looked good. My hair had worked out well. Good thing, too. I had to make an appearance at Blake's office today.

I checked my email, and there was one from Derek. It said: "Stop in and see me today. I have information." Shit. I looked at when it came in and he'd sent it at nine-thirty. A quick glance at my watch showed ten-fifteen. I grabbed my coat and headed to the station. I wondered why he hadn't called. While I was driving, I was stuck between excited to see him, especially after Saturday night, and nervous that they'd found Lily. The drive seemed to take forever. When I did finally pull into the police station, I parked and started walking across the lot quickly. About half way I had to slow my pace down and try to catch my breath, my heart was beating so fast that I was short of breath. The receptionist said to go right back.

I knocked softly on the open door. "Hello," I said to Derek, who was facing away from the door towards the computer. He swung his chair around and smiled, leaning back in his chair.

"Hey, you, have a seat," he said as he made a gesture to the chair. I sat down, trying to take a few deep breaths. "Wow, you look really nervous."

Great that helps. "I am," I smiled uncomfortably. "I'm not sure why." I laughed softly. "So, Saturday night was . . . fun."

He walked over to the door and closed it. "Yes, it was. I saw you in a whole new light. I got to thinking, the whole time I've known you, you've been sad and upset. It was good to see you having fun and smiling. You looked good," he said, looking hard into my eyes.

"Thank you. It was a good night, just what I needed," I said. "So what's your news? I saw your email, and all the way over I was thinking it must be really bad if he want's to tell me in person. So what was it?"

"Or, maybe I just wanted to see you again," he said, still looking into my eyes. Wow, that hit me like a rock. Was he joking? I couldn't tell if he was joking or not. I smiled but squinted my eyes at him, thinking hard. He smiled back with his eyebrows up, but after a moment his face changed.

"I do actually have news, too," he said. "We're on the move in about an hour to Jake's work site. I'm just waiting on the search warrant. We questioned his co-workers, and one of them made mention to a project getting done ahead of schedule. He told me that a small portion of a foundation on a commercial project, that Jake was in charge of, was done ahead of schedule. At the end of the day when he left, it wasn't done and when he got back the next day it was poured and half dry. He asked Jake, who's his supervisor, about it, and Jake told him that he'd done it himself overnight to speed things along. The employee thought it was strange because with the mixing, hauling and the finishing, it'd be impossible for one man to do it and get it done that fast and that well. Over the next week he noticed that Jake was very snappy and stressed out. And then after the police had questioned everyone, and he started noticing that Jake was missing a lot of work and seemed drunk a lot. He started getting suspicious when he heard that the girl Jake was seeing was missing.

"Sara, he also mentioned that Jake had been picked up by this girl for lunch dates more than a few times. He knew that the woman in the car was not you, so he called me and said he felt someone should look into it.

"Nice. So tons of people knew my husband was having an affair. Just not me."

"So anyway we put two and two together and we both thought the same thing. I checked the time cards and no one else was punched in that night."

"Oh, my God," I said, covering my mouth. "You think they put her body in the cement?"

Derek slowly nodded, with a sick look on his face. "When we get the search warrant, we'll be going to the site with that employee and using a scanner that can give us an x-ray-like image of the cement. If there is anything unusual in the cement, it'll show up. They use them frequently for finding cracks and weak spots in foundations for large structures, like bridges and parking ramps."

In total shock, I caught my breath. "I can't believe this. No way. It'd take a really sick person to do something like that, and I know Jake and Mark. They would never," I said, shaking my head, trying to convince myself.

"Sara, this was the same Jake, your loving husband, that you would never ever think would cheat on you, and it turns out he did. We don't know for sure, so until we do, don't ... feel anything yet. This is just a lead we're checking on. I just wanted you to know. I really don't want you anywhere near those two. And this has to stay between you and me, too. This is not pubic information."

"Holy crap," I said, my knees were shaking, and hands waving. I stood and started pacing.

Derek stood and grabbed me by the shoulders. "Look, I didn't bring you in here to scare you or upset you. I promised to keep you in the loop, and that's what I've been doing. Now, you need to go home and get on with your day. I'll call you if we find anything. Okay? Can you promise me that?" he said, tipping my chin up. "Do not tell anyone. I'm stepping over some serious lines here for you."

Now I had a whole new set of emotions whipping through me. He was so close to me. I could feel his breath. I nodded and pulled away, before we both got ourselves in trouble. I grabbed my purse and gave him a half grin.

"I'll check in on you later," Derek said softly.

"Okay, I'll be baby-sitting this afternoon and evening at my place."

I slid into my Jeep and cleaned my face up in the mirror. My face was so blotchy. I had to go to the bank and get some of the funds to bring to Blake. He warned me that, when I got there, I'd have to go through all the security stuff. I was making a large withdrawal, so I'd get to see the big wigs for that. I didn't want to look like I had just been crying when I got there.

It took about thirty minutes, but I passed the inspection and left with a check in hand. Upon arrival at Blake's office, I noticed his secretary was on the phone.

She disconnected and she said, "Have a seat, Ms. Martin," as she gestured to a waiting area. She walked down the hall, came back a moment later and said, "Follow me, Ms. Martin. Mr. Connor will see you now."

24

NERVES CAME OVER ME WHEN I started walking down the hall. What the heck was my problem? I hadn't had this many butterflies since high school. I was not interested in a relationship right now, and yet everywhere I went, I felt rushes for all the hot men I kept running into. Geez. This was an investment firm not a matchmaker's lair.

I walked in to Blake's office, and his secretary closed the door behind me.

"Hello, Sara," he said with a smile. "So how was the rest of your weekend?"

"Good I guess. It sure went fast. I went out Saturday night to a club with one of my single friends, and we had a really good time. It was a little much for this girl, I can't remember the last time I went out on a Friday and Saturday night," I laughed. "I had fun though. It was nice getting to know you on Friday."

"Yes, Friday was a lot of fun. I thought about it a lot over the weekend. I had a really good time," he said with a smile.

I had no idea how to respond, so then we had the whole awkward silence going for a moment or two. I broke the silence by saying, "Well, I have some money for you."

"Great, let's have it," he said half giggling. We sat down, and he pulled out a bunch of papers for me to sign, and then gave me copies of them.

"You probably want to start a file at home to keep all the mail you get in. It's kind of a lot," he warned.

"If you have any questions on anything, just call me or bring it to our dinner date every month, and we'll go over it. Did you sign up for any classes yet?" he asked.

"No, I haven't yet. I've had a lot going on the last few weeks, but I intend to."

"Well, if you can hold out, next month I'll be teaching the class. We all kinda rotate the job, and my turn is coming up."

"Really? Well, I'll have to sign up for that one then and make sure you know what you're talking about," I teased. "I have you down in my calendar for our next dinner meeting, so I'll get the details on it then." After thanking him for his help, I stood to leave. Blake opened the door for me and then walked me to the entryway.

"Take care, Sara. Call me with any questions. You have my number," he said with a really nice smile.

Again with the butterflies. What the heck? I must be getting my period or something. My hormones were all over the place. I stopped to think for a moment . . . when was I going to get my period? I hadn't had it in a while. Shit, I better take a peek at the calendar when I get home. It seemed like it'd been a while . . . too long, gosh. *No way. I am not going to think about that. That would be horrible.*

The grocery store summoned me on the way home, so I stopped to pick up a few things. When I got home, I ran across the apartment to look at my calendar. Shit, I was due for it three days ago. I was always very regular. Fuck! Now what? I paced around wondering what I would do if I were pregnant. That would be the worst thing that could happen to me right now. I started crying and sat on the couch. The door bell rang, and I looked at the clock, it was only one-thirty. I didn't have to babysit tell three. I went to the buzzer, and it was Kat. I buzzed her in.

"What's wrong?" she said, as soon as I opened the door.

"I'm three days late," I sobbed, throwing my arms around her.

"Oh, shit! Did you take a test yet?" she asked, as she set my bag of shoes that I forgot in her car in the entry closet.

"No, I just noticed a second ago that I was late. I'm never late. It's three daaayyys!" I cried.

"Oh, honey. You wait here and don't drink anything. I'll be right back, and we'll put your mind at ease . . . I hope." She ran out the door, and fifteen minutes later she came in with ten pregnancy tests. "I got some extras just in case," she winked.

I grabbed one and walked to the bathroom. I peed on the stick, replaced the cap and set it on the counter. I opened the door, and Kat and I hung over it for a full three minutes staring in silence. Only one line. We checked the box, not pregnant. I looked at her.

"Okay, well that's good for now, but these things don't always show up right away. I think you should do another first thing in the morning," she said.

I nodded. "I don't feel any better than I did before. This sucks," I said.

"Do you want a baby, Sara?" she asked.

"I do, but not Jake's and not now," I said, as I sat down on the toilet. "I hope I'm not, not with Jake." Even as I said it, I couldn't believe that a month ago I would have been thrilled to be pregnant with his baby, and now it seemed like the worst thing in the world.

We sat in the living room and talked for a while. She was such a good friend. Thank God for her. She reminded me that stress can throw off a woman's cycle, and I had been under a lot of stress. Feeling a little better, I hugged her goodbye, and, just as she left, Joey and Kristin arrived with Marissa. They brought her stroller in case we wanted to go for a walk, and a huge bag with everything a person could possibly need to take care of a baby for one evening.

I invited them in, and Kristin walked me through the bottles and other stuff in the bag, while Joey took Marissa out. He took her coat and tiny shoes off and handed her to me. I could literally feel love come out of my heart and wrap around her tiny body. I loved her so much. I cooed at her for a few minutes and kissed her forehead. I inhaled deeply and smelled her head. For a second I thought it might not be so bad, but the next second I pictured passing a baby off to Jake every other weekend. Or telling a kid their dad was in prison. Yuck, no way. Joey and Kristin made sure I had their numbers and they both checked to make sure their phones were on.

"Just call if you have any questions at all," Kristin said. "This is so nice of you. It's nice to know someone is willing to help and mature enough to be trusted with a baby. Most of our friends are not, and our families are so far away . . . so thanks. It'll be nice to have a break."

"Yeah," Joey said. "But if we need to come back we can, just call if she cries or gets sick." His voice was strange. Kristin and I both looked at him and then at each other. I smiled. He was crying. Kristin walked over to him and put an arm around him.

"Joey, are you crying?" Kristin asked, "Geez. We're only going across town for a few hours. She'll be fine, she won't even know we're gone. We will call and check on her in a little bit okay?"

"Okay, yeah, we'll call in a little bit." He gave Marissa a kiss on the cheek. "We'll be back very soon. Daddy loves you so much." Mom gave her a quick kiss and told her to be good. They turned to the door, and Joey looked back one more time and then shut the door. Two seconds later the door opened.

"Dude, you should lock this," Joey told me.

"I will." I said and when he left, I turned the lock. I looked at Marissa and told her she had a very good daddy. She just looked back at me.

I spent the next half hour looking at her and talking to her. I changed a poopy diaper and then looked at the weather channel. It was fifty-eight degrees and sunny for another couple hours, so I decided a walk sounded like a good idea. I got her bundled up and then myself ready. After loading her into the stroller, I covered her with her blanket. As I opened the door, I pushed it out to the hall and almost crashed right into hot, neighbor guy.

"Oops, sorry," I said. "Didn't see you coming."

"That's okay. Aww, who do we have here?" he asked, bending over to look in the stroller. "I didn't know you had a baby."

"Oh, no, I don't. I'm babysitting for friends," I said, defensively.

"Oh, okay. Well she's a cutie. If you need any help let me know. I helped raise my three little sisters, and babies love me," he said with a wink.

"I'll keep that in mind, Mr ..."

"Jared, Jared LeBlanc, and what's your name?" he asked, extending his hand.

"Sara Martin," I said with a smile.

"It's nice to formally meet you," he said, as he kissed the back of my hand. "You two enjoy your walk."

"Thanks. We will," I said with a dorky grin and a finger wave.

We rolled down the hall and out the front door. My encounter gave me something to think about on the way. Wow. He was hot and so smooth, and I seemed to lose all my skills around him. Why was it everyone I met was incredibly sexy? Being married must have blinded me. We walked six blocks to the nearest park and stopped at a bench when I heard my phone beep. A text from Derek:

"Hey, I'm off in an hour or so. Got news. Are you home, have plans for dinner?"

I replied, "Babysitting, no plans ... something at my place?"

Moments later he responded with a smiley face and, "I'll bring some take-out".

I returned a smiley face and put my phone in my pocket. I told Marissa about my feelings for Derek and how I really liked him but it was too soon to get involved with anyone. She looked deep in my eyes and listened intently. I sat back on the bench, and Derek was all I could think about. Well, Derek and Blake and Jared that is.

I needed to talk to my lawyer. Kat said she'd call today, and she hadn't yet, so I dialed her number.

"Jake's lawyer asked for an extension and was denied," she informed me, "The court date is set, and our first hearing will be on Wednesday morning. I apologize for not calling earlier. I've been on the phone all day trying to get that set up. I'm pushing hard for a quick divorce."

"I know the work that goes into it, and I really appreciate it."

"Jake isn't fighting for anything and will cooperate, so we should be in and out on Wednesday. Then it's just paperwork to finish it all up. We're hoping for less than a month," she said.

"Thank you so much. I'll see you on Wednesday."

I disconnected and sat another thirty minutes and enjoyed the park. There were not very many people out. The sun was getting low in the sky now, and the temp was getting cooler. I looked over at Marissa, who was now sleeping, then turned the stroller around and headed for home. It was a perfect evening. I loved just walking through the park pushing a stroller. Before I opened the apartment building door, I took one last deep breath of the cool, crisp, fall air.

Once inside, I laid Marissa on a blanket on the couch and turned the radio on to soft rock and set some nice, soft lighting throughout the apartment. I lit a pumpkin spice candle in the kitchen and then went to the bathroom to freshen up. As I walked out I heard the buzzer growl.

"Who is it?" I was sure to ask.

"Delivery boy."

I buzzed him in.

Moments later my phone rang. It was Kristin, wondering how Marissa was. After updating her on the poopy and the walk, I told her as soon as she woke up I'd give her a bottle. "How's our little boy doing?" I asked.

"He cried all the way to the car, but he's okay now."

I reminded her to call as often as she wanted, then hung up as Derek walked in.

25

EREK, WHO WAS STILL IN HIS SUIT, was carrying Chinese take-out and a six pack.

"Well, hello, prince charming," I said, grabbing the take-out bags. "Come on in, but shh. The baby's sleeping." I pointed to the couch.

He looked over and his eyebrows went up. "Oh, my gosh, she's a new one," he said, in a tiny voice I'd never heard before. "Wow, she's gorgeous! What's her name?"

"Marissa. I have her until about ten tonight. Her parents are taking a baby CPR and First Aid class."

"So these are friends of yours?" he asked, coming back into the kitchen to help get food ready.

"Funny story," I said. We spooned the food onto plates and sat at the table. I handed him a beer and opened one for myself while I told him my "moving box-baby story." That got him laughing pretty hard. I'd never seen him laugh. I smiled and shrugged, "What do ya do?"

We finished eating and then picked up the kitchen. Derek grabbed two more beers from the fridge and went into the living room and sat on the couch at the baby's feet. After I turned off the radio, I grabbed the remote and turned on the Twins game. They were playing the New York Yankees, and it had just started. He looked at me like he was impressed again.

I smiled and said, "What, a girl can't like baseball?" He just smiled and took a pull on his beer. I sat down by him. "So what's the news?" I asked.

"Well," he said taking a deep breath, "we spent the day at Jake's construction site. After we'd brought him in for questioning, it was pretty obvious he was lying. We held him until we got the warrant and then brought him and the co-worker, Scott, with us to the site. Scott showed us where we should scan. Jake just stood there and didn't say a word. As soon as the scan started, he asked for a lawyer.

"Oh, no," I said, staring into his eyes. "And?"

"And, we told the company that does these x-rays to continue. They shine a laser type, light beam across the cement and then there's a monitor that shows different colors on the screen that measure strength, depth, density, and will show any cracks or breaks in the cement.

"Did you find anything Derek?" I demanded.

He looked at me and put his hand on my thigh. "We did, Sara. I'm sorry. The monitor showed an unusual image, and it was enough for us to dig it up. We found a young woman's body matching Lily's description. It went to the county morgue about three hours ago."

I started crying. I went the kitchen counter and grabbed Kleenex and sat back on the couch. Derek put his arm around me and pulled me to him. I leaned my head on his chest and cried for a while. I couldn't believe that my best friend was dead. I would never ever see her again.

"Sara," he said after a few minutes, "we need someone to identify the body. I was hoping you'd do it. It can be a really hard thing for parents to do. Mark isn't credible, because he's listed as a suspect and the rest of her family is too far away. You don't have to, but I thought I'd ask you before her parents."

"Oh, my God. I don't know if I can. Is it bad?" I cried.

"It's not great, but we'd just need a quick peek at the face and you to say yes or no. If you can't, we'll have to ask her parents, but we don't like to do that, especially in a case like this. Our other option is dental records, but that will delay our case a minimum of another day. So you'd be helping everyone out. But no pressure."

"When?" I asked still crying, trying to get under control.

"We can go tonight after the baby's picked up. I have access to the morgue. Tonight is the best, if you can. Then the guys can get started on making official arrests, and we can keep Jake in custody."

"Was Mark there too?"

"No. We had a man outside his place watching him, but we need an identity and lack of alibi to charge him. Even then, it's only a temporary hold. Once they get lawyers, it's harder to hold them, and Jake has already been assigned one. We really need a confession or some solid evidence."

"Okay, I'll do it, but you'll be there with me the whole time right?"

"Right," he said. I put my head back on his chest, and he kissed the top of my head.

Marissa made a squeaky sound, and Derek shoved me off him and picked her up. So cute. He was smiling at her and talking to her. He put her up on his chest, and she tucked her legs under her belly and curled right into him. I was so jealous. Not sure who I was jealous of, but I definitely wanted a part of that. I whispered that I'd go get a bottle. Derek nodded, settled back and put his feet up on the table. I grabbed the beer he'd brought in for me and put it back in the fridge. One was probably enough. I made a bottle and handed it to him. He turned her over, and she started eating right away.

"Wow, you're a pro. Have you had a lot of experience?" I asked.

"I roomed with my brother and his wife for a couple weeks in between my parents and my first apartment. They had a newborn, and I helped out. I love kids," he said with a smile.

"I can tell. She looks good on you," I said leaning over and petting her head. "She's so sweet." I saw him smell her head, and I thought, *he's perfect*.

I heard my phone. It was Joey. "Hey, the class is really small, so we'll be out early. I'm thinking we'll be there about nine. How is she?"

"She is doing amazing. She just woke up and a friend of mine stole her and is giving her a bottle right now," I said, trying to sound like I wasn't crying earlier.

"Oh, good. Thanks again for watching her. We'll see you about nine," he said and disconnected.

I went back over to the couch and sat by Derek, who was now gently burping her. I told him that we could go early, then sauntered into the kitchen and made some Iced-Tea. When it was ready, I brought Derek a glass.

"Thank you. Would you like to hold the baby now?"

"Yes, I'd like that very much." I smiled and took her. Derek got up and went to the bathroom. When he got back, he took her away again. "Hey," I said. "I'm the one who's supposed to be babysitting here."

"I know. I'm just helping out," he said, with a wink and set her on his chest again. I looked at him and instantly thought that I wanted to marry him and make lots of babies with him. Then, I was reminded that I may already be pregnant. Gosh. I couldn't wait until the funeral was over and my marriage was over and the murder trial was over and I wasn't pregnant, and I could just be happy . . . and not cry everyday. I watched the game quietly next to Derek for a half hour, then I stole the baby back. She, of course, didn't want to cuddle anymore. She wanted to stretch. Derek grabbed her blanket and laid it out on the floor. Faith came from out of nowhere and instantly lay on it.

"Geez, where did she come from? I didn't know there was a kitten in the room with us."

"She's the other baby of the house. I think she wants some attention, too." I said with a wink. We all ended up on the floor, Faith and Derek playing off to the side, and me and Marissa on the pink blanket. He looked over at me and smiled softly. I smiled back.

Derek's phone rang, and he took the call in the hallway.

He came back in and said, "The uniforms will meet us at the morgue at nine-forty-five." I nodded and got up to fix my make-up, and touch up my hair. Then went to the bedroom to switch out my blouse for a cozy Twins sweatshirt.

At five after nine, the buzzer hummed. I buzzed Joey and Kristin up. They both shoved past me and raced across the floor to the baby.

"Miss her any?" I asked. I introduced them to Derek. They all shook hands and Derek told them how pretty their little girl was. They agreed and started to pack her up.

Joey tried to hand me money. "No way. Put it in a college fund for her and call me anytime." They loaded the stroller with all her stuff and left.

Derek grabbed his jacket and asked, "Are you ready for this?"

"No."

He walked up to me in the kitchen and put his arms around my waist. That sent heat through my body. He stood there looking at me. I got lost in his eyes. Then he took my face in his hands and kissed my forehead. "You can do this. You're a strong woman," he said.

I nodded, on the verge of tears, not convinced. He held my hand and said he'd drive and pulled me through the door.

When we got to the morgue, about fifteen minutes later, there were three uniforms waiting, two of them looked familiar. We walked into the building, which was dark and quiet. Derek went first, flipping on lights. We all followed him down the hall to the back. We entered a cool, cement-block room painted bright, glossy white and had a wall of stainless steel vault drawers. I was a little taken aback, it was just like in the movies. The drawers were big and had large, steel handles on them. I took a deep breath and suddenly felt faint. I must have looked faint too because one of the uniforms I recognized from the cabin reached out for me and called Derek's name. I looked over at Derek and the room went from dim to dark.

26

"HEY, SWEETNESS," DEREK SAID IN A SOFT, slow voice. "You fainted. Are you okay?"

"Um, yeah," I said trying to sit up on the floor. My heart beat was pounding so loud in my ears that I could barely hear him. "Geez, I'm sorry. It suddenly occurred to me that I was going to see a dead body, and I guess I lost it."

"It's okay. You don't have to do this," Derek said, looking really concerned. "I didn't know you would be affected this much."

"No, it's okay. I can do it. Let's get it over with quickly." I stood up, with his help and took a deep breath.

One of the cops handed me what looked like an air sickness bag and said, "Just in case," with a wink.

I took it, just in case, and thanked him. Derek nodded and pulled open a drawer. There was a skinny body on the table, covered with a white sheet. He pulled back the sheet, and I saw her face. I gasped. It was scratched up and her hair was really dirty and tangled and still had chunks of cement in it. The tone of her skin was a ghoulish, blue-gray. Her lips were dark blue. She looked horrible. I knew that it was her, but I had never seen her look so bad. It took me by surprise. I nodded and covered my mouth, instantly crying.

"That's her," I managed. "That's Lily."

Derek quickly pulled the sheet back over her and closed the drawer. Then he came over to me and asked if I was okay. I shook my head, crying. He walked me out the the car, helped me in the passenger's seat and told me he'd be right back. He closed my door and went back into the building. I watched him through the window. He was talking to the three uniforms, and they were nodding occasionally. Then one of them smiled and said something to him, and he gave a half grin. Derek said a few sentences back and the other two smiled. One of them socked him in the arm as he turned away, flicking off the lights as they shuffled out of the room. I had a feeling that conversation had something to do with me. Derek was the last one out, he locked up the building and sat down in the car with me. The three uniforms got in the patrol car parked next to us and drove away.

Derek patted my leg, "You did great. Thank you."

I just nodded.

"What you did was hard," he spoke softly, "and I can't imagine the emotions you must be juggling. But I want you to know, I'm proud of you. You're a real compassionate woman, Sara. And you saved her parents from having to see her like that. We'll finish the autopsy, and then they'll release her body to the caretaker at the funeral home. When she's cleaned up and has make-up on, then we'll let her parents view her."

"When will you tell her parents?" I asked.

"I need to do it right now. I can drop you off or you can come with, if you want."

He looked at me, and I just kept staring out the window. I wasn't sure what I wanted to do at this point. I was still crying hard, and I didn't know if I wanted to be around for her parents reactions. I did want to be there for them, though. It was so hard.

"Okay, I'll go with you. Dang it, this sucks so bad. I don't know how you do it," I said, through tears.

"It's not easy. But you just have to. I don't usually know the victims, so it makes it a little easier, but in this case it's getting harder and harder every day."

I looked at him, and he continued talking while looking out the window, driving slowly. "I care about you, Sara. I don't know how or when this happened, but it has. And it's gotten hard for me to see you hurting."

Wow, I had no idea how to respond to that. I looked at him, and he gave me a quick glance, then back to the road. I sat there quietly thinking about how much my life had changed in such a short amount of time.

"I care about you too," I finally said. He looked at me, smiled, and put his hand on my leg.

We drove in silence the rest of the way. When we pulled up to the house, it was pretty dark. There was a light on downstairs in the family room, so we knew at least one of them was up. When we parked, I saw Gerald come to the window and peek out from behind the curtain. Moments later the outside lights came on, and Gerald was standing with the front door open in his lounge wear. We walked up to the house, and Derek shook his hand.

"Good evening, sir. Sorry for coming so late."

Gerald looked at me and saw that I'd been crying. By the worried look on his face, I thought he already knew why we were there. He invited us in and motioned us to the lower level. He told us to have a seat and said that Debbie was in her pajamas and ran up to change quick. Derek and I sat on the couch, and Gerald sat on the adjacent love seat. We quietly waited for Debbie. Gerald looked so upset and lost in thought, staring across the room. I was trying hard to hold back my tears, but I knew what was coming, and I couldn't stand to see people in pain. This was going to be the worst day of both their lives.

Debbie walked into the room and looked at everyone's faces. She looked horrified, like she, too, knew what was coming. She sat down slowly and cautiously on the edge of the chair next to the love seat. Gerald extended his hand to her, and she took it.

"Okay, Detective Richards, we're ready," Gerald said, slowly. He was staring at the floor, and I could see them both inhale deeply.

Derek sat up and leaned forward with his arms bent on his knees. "There's no easy way to do this, so I'm going to get straight to the point . . . we found Lily's body. I'm so sorry." He left it at that for a moment.

Debbie screamed a bone chilling "No!" and slid off her chair to her knees. She was bent over with her face in her hands and head to the floor. I instantly started crying harder. Gerald's shoulders shook as he sobbed. This was the worst experience of my life. Debbie crawled closer to Gerald and put her head in his lap, balling. He leaned over her, and they both cried hard. Derek sat there quietly looking at the floor. I looked up and saw a box of Kleenex on the end table across the room. I got up and grabbed about ten for me and then set the box on the floor next to Debbie's knees and sat down right there next to her. I put my hands on both their backs and told them how sorry I was. After a few minutes they calmed a little, sat up and grabbed for Kleenex.

"Where did you find her? Who did this?" Gerald asked, looking like he'd gone from sad to pissed off. It made me a little nervous, but at the same time I understood completely. Debbie crawled back up in her chair, and I went back over to the couch.

"We found her body at a construction site. She . . ." he hesitated, "she was buried in a cement foundation." Derek continued, "I had a lead, and did an x-ray-scan of the specified area. The scan showed us enough that we had suspicion that it may be her body. We got a warrant to break up the cement, and we found her. I had Sara identify her this evening just before coming here." Both of their mouths were hanging open in shock, their eyes filled with disgust.

"Who did it? Why? What the hell happened to her?" Gerald demanded in an angry, deep voice.

"Sir, we have Mark and Jake in custody, and they are our only suspects right now, but we haven't figured out all the details yet. We will be questioning them tonight, and, hopefully, we'll get a nice, easy confession. We have some work to do yet, but we're close. There are holes all over this case that we need to fill in. I will be going to the station after I leave here to . . . hopefully close this up. We want to wait until a little later into the night to start questioning, as suspects are more willing to cooperate and confess if they are overly tired. I hope by morning we have all the information we need. As soon as we know what happened, I'll call you."

"Where is my baby now?" Debbie asked. Hearing her call Lily her baby made me start up all over again. It was so incredibly sad. "I want to see my baby!" she said with authority.

"Debbie," I said gently, "I can't begin to understand how you must feel. I know you want to see her and you can, but the police need to finish their autopsy to get any evidence they can to convict whoever did this. Then, after the caretaker makes her nice and pretty again you can see her. You don't want to see her right now," I said shaking my head. "You know how Lily was. She wouldn't want anyone to see her without her make-up on." I added, with a strained smile. Debbie wiped her nose and nodded.

"Mr. and Mrs. Kowalski, I know this is a very difficult time for you, but I do need to make you aware that the press may get wind of this soon. We had a big operation out at the construction site today. My officers have been told to keep it quiet, but there were onlookers that we can't do anything about. If anyone tries to contact you, do not tell them anything. Doing so could have negative effects on the investigation. If you have any trouble with them, let us know, and we can put an officer here. Screen all of your calls and only talk to me about the case. You can tell your families now but, again, do not talk to the press. I will let you know when Lily will be released. It usually takes a few days."

Derek stood, so I did too. "We'll leave you two alone, but I promise to be in touch as soon as I know more. In the meantime, let me know if you need anything. Again, I'm so sorry for your loss."

"I'm sorry, too," I said. I gave them both a hug. "We'll let ourselves out."

At the car Derek opened the door for me, and I angled in. He sat down in his seat and took a deep breath, staring out the front windshield. "You never get used to this."

I put my hand on his leg and leaned over to put my head on his shoulder. I had been so focused on me and my issues that I never thought he might be upset having to tell her parents, too. Derek didn't really know them, but I guess it's not "just a job" when you have to tell parents that their child is dead.

He turned the key and I picked my head up. "Well, sweetness, I'll bring you home, and then I have to go back to the office and probably pull an all-nighter."

"Okay," I said sadly. I wished he could come in for a while, but I wanted him to get this case closed too. We drove in silence until we got to my lot.

"Do you want me to walk you in?"

I shook my head, said, "No, I'll be fine," and exited the car. "Will you call me if you find anything out? Even if it's the middle of the night." I asked, leaning into the open car door.

"You got it, but promise me that you'll get some sleep," he said, tipping his head to the the side and giving me a closed, tight-lipped smile. I nodded and forced a small smile and shut the door.

I opened my apartment door, and Faith came bounding down the hall. I picked her up and mentally thanked Kat and my mom for her. I didn't know what I'd do without her some days. She started purring and climbed up to my neck. I gave her a kiss, set her on the floor and then prepped myself for bed. Bringing a cold washcloth with me, I climbed into bed and placed it on my swollen eyes and fell asleep.

In the morning, I was surprised that I had been able to sleep. I hadn't gotten a call in the middle of the night, so what did that mean? I checked my phone. Seven o'clock, and no missed calls. I ran into the bathroom and peed on a stick. I waited three minutes, took a deep breath and looked at it.

27

ONE LINE. NOT PREGNANT! Thank you, Lord! Geez, that was scary. I felt like a huge weight lifted off my shoulders, until I remembered what Kat said about it taking a while to show up. That I could still be pregnant but the test can't pick it up yet.

I prayed to my King that he would send me a period now and the baby later in life. He didn't answer me back, but I promised myself I wouldn't panic and take it morning by morning until my period or two lines came. What else could I do?

Now what? I had nothing planned today, and no idea what to do with myself. It was Monday, but I didn't have the focus to take on a work assignment right now, so I wasn't going into work. I turned on the TV, but I couldn't watch anything because my brain kept going back and forth between Derek, Lily, her parents, Jake, Mark, Blake . . . Jared. My life was exhausting, yet I had nothing to do. Ugh. I decided to call Derek, maybe that would put my mind at ease a little.

"Good morning," I said when he picked up. He sounded really tired or mad maybe.

"Hi, sorry I haven't called yet, but I haven't had a second to myself all night."

"You've been there all night?"

"Yes, I'm on my way out right now, I get an eight-hour break. What are you doing?"

"Nothing, I'm totally bored and my mind is totally busy. It sucks. Have you learned anything?"

"I have. I can stop over in a few and update you if you want. I should be leaving here in fifteen minutes," he said.

"Sure. Are you hungry?" I asked.

"Yeah, starving."

"I'll have something ready for you . . . wait, do you want breakfast or supper?"

"Breakfast, thanks, sweetness. I'll see ya in a few," he said and disconnected.

Yay, I had something to do, and it just happened to be make breakfast for a hot cop. I did a little, happy dance into the kitchen. The little dance was kinda fun, so I went back into the living room and turned on the radio. I danced back into the kitchen to start breakfast. Quiche it was. I put it in the oven, then went to change into clothes and did a quick hair and make-up routine. The shower would have to wait. I spritzed on some body spray to cover for now. Twenty minutes later, I checked the quiche, it smelled really good. I got the toaster out and put in four slices of honey wheat bread as I heard the buzzer and pushed down the toaster to start.

"Wow, it smells great in here," Derek said as he entered. He put a hand on my hip and gave me a kiss on the cheek. "Thanks for cooking, sweetness."

"No problem. Like I said, I was so bored." I took the quiche out of the oven just as the toaster popped. I told Derek to sit at the table, and I put the butter, apple jelly, and orange juice out for him. We dished up and ate. I felt sick to my stomach and wondered if it was because of stress or a baby. Now that I thought of it, I'd felt sick a lot lately. After we finished eating and Derek helped me pick up the kitchen, we sat on the couch. I was so nervous, it was as if he were my dad and I'd crashed the family car. I couldn't stand it.

"Okay, tell me already!" I anxiously demanded.

"Okay, okay!" Derek took a deep breath and let it out. "Well, after we found Lily's body at Jake's construction site, it gave us all reason to believe that he was either responsible or involved. That, along with all the other stuff, like the affair, he being one of the last to see her alive, the blood where he'd just vacationed with her, the fingerprints and fibers in the car, and on and on. That was enough to bring him in. Same was true for Mark. We held them both in separate cells, all afternoon and evening. After you identified the body, we started questioning them separately. Mark asked for a lawyer, which slowed down the process a lot. However, the exhaustion kicked in, and Mark was the first to confess."

"What? Confess? He killed her?" I asked with a gasp, covering my mouth and shaking my head. I didn't believe it. No way he'd kill her. He couldn't have!

"Not exactly. I'll get to that. Jake then confessed to his part after I told him that Mark had told us the whole story. The stories matched to a tee, and we had no reason to think that they would be lying, so they both remain under arrest."

"Oh, my gosh! So what's the story? Who killed her? Who did this?"

28

SHE DID. LILY KILLED HERSELF."

"What? Suicide? Why? Why wouldn't they just tell me then, or go to the police?" I stammered, all panicky, not believing any of it.

"No, it wasn't suicide," Derek corrected. "It was an accident. When you were sleeping, Mark and Lily had gone on that walk. They walked up to the cave. When they got up there, Lily told Mark that she wanted to be done, that she was breaking up with him. Mark was shocked and upset, said no and suggested a counselor or therapist. Lily told him she wasn't interested in ever being with him and that she didn't love him. He was naturally angry but said that they should try to work on it. That's when she told him she was cheating on him. He walked up to her and slapped her across the face and told her to stop lying. She got pissed and stepped back. She was close to the edge of the cliff and told him she was worthless and stupid and should just jump. He grabbed her by the arm and yanked her back from the edge. Hard. All this left a big hand print on her face and bruise on her arm. He felt horrible and said he was sorry. He admitted that in anger, he grabbed her really hard. Lily then stood up and again walked up to the top of the cave. He continued to apologize and asked her for forgiveness. He asked her to give it time, told her that he really loved her and he could forgive her."

I nodded, crying. He really did love her.

"That's when he stepped up there, to the highest point, with her and said that they'd get through this together. She turned to him and said it was Jake. She told Mark she was cheating on him with his best friend, with her best friend's husband. She asked him if he could forgive that? Then she turned to walk away, and she slipped and fell. She fell down the opposite side of the cave entrance. There's a ten-foot-drop on the lake side of that hill, to a flat spot down below. It's almost impossible to see from above because of the overhang and the foliage. We sent a uniform out there, and he confirmed it. He brought back pictures and and blood samples early this morning, and it was a match. When she fell, she split her head and bled out in moments. Mark tried to grab her, but it was too late. He ran back to get Jake, and he and Jake pulled her up together. After seeing the blood and realizing she was dead, Mark panicked. He thought because his hand print was on her face and arm that everyone would think he pushed her and killed her. He got scared and convinced Jake that hiding the body would be the best for everyone. Jake was not thinking clearly either because Mark had told Jake that it could easily look like Jake did it since he was having the affair. So, after much stupid deliberation, Jake agreed, saying he felt like he was being threatened, that if he didn't help, he'd be blamed for it all. Mark noticed the cave opening, and they put her body in there until they could figure out what to do. Then they came back to the cabin, came up with the story about her taking off in the car because she was mad. They drove her car about a half mile down the road and parked it there, out of your sight. They got back and were talking by the Jeep, when you woke up. They told you their version of the story, and then you guys left."

I was still hand to mouth in disbelief, tears running down my face and my head involuntarily shaking.

"That night, after you dropped Jake and Mark off, they went back to the cabin, got her body out of the cave. They put her in the car's trunk and then drove it back to the construction site. There, they mixed up fifteen bags of cement and put her under it. The next day, Jake told his employee he did it to help the guys stay on schedule. The employee, Scott, who we interviewed at the site, was the one who came forward later and said something seemed off. He also thought it was strange that Jake was back from vacation so early. When Jake was not acting like himself and Scott learned more about the investigation, he got a bad feeling and came to see me."

Derek took a deep breath, then continued. "After they buried her body, Mark followed Jake back to the cabin. Jake remembered the depth finder on the pontoon reading a really deep spot, on the edge of the lake, when they were out there fishing. He said that usually the deep spots in lakes were in the middle. He thought it was weird and thought about it again when Mark asked what they should do with the car. When they got to the lake they found a back road fairly close to the spot. The woods were not as thick there, and they figured they could make it through. They did get stuck a few times but eventually made it. They pushed it over the edge and crossed their fingers. When they saw it go under they thought that was the end of it. But the two old guys in the boat could see its shadow and picked it up on their depth finder too. Turns out they missed the drop off by about ten yards. Mark and Jake drove back home together that same night and agreed never to tell anyone."

I still had my hand over my mouth, and my eyes bulged out of my head. I couldn't believe this. "So it was an accident that they stupidly turned into a crime?" I asked, shocked. "It must have been so scary for them. But still, they're so dumb!" I almost felt sorry for the poor bastards. "Geez, what were they think-ing? They should have just told me. They should have called for help."

"They weren't thinking. Some people panic in the midst of tragedy, and some can't differentiate right from wrong. They get crippled from the anxiety and adrenaline and turn a simple situation into a totally complicated one. They get so deep into mistakes that they can't see a way out. A lot of murder-suicides start out as accidents."

"I can't believe this is happening," I said, crying. "My three closest friends went from greatest, most important people in my life, to dead and criminal overnight. I feel so alone." I sobbed for a few more minutes. Derek stayed quiet and let me cry. He reached out and put his hand on my back.

"I think that God has a plan for everyone," he said, softly. "I don't know why He would put you through this, but I think that everything happens for a reason. It's really hard to think about what those reasons are right now, but I just know that you're a child of God and that He will get you through this. And your life will be better because you went through this. For some reason, God needed you in this. I think Lily's in a better place, and Jake and Mark will come out okay in the end," Derek said.

I looked down at the floor. He was probably right, but it was hard to think like that when you're mad about the situation. I had faith in God. It was just I wished He was here so I could talk to Him face to face and clear a few things up. I slowly raised my eyes to Derek and forced a half smile.

"Sorry, I don't mean to go all churchy on you. That's just how I feel, and I wanted you to know that," he said sweetly. He was so confident. I loved it. He didn't care what I thought, nor did he even know if I was a believer. He just said what he thought. It seemed so easy for him to open up.

"Thank you. I needed to hear that. It's just hard to stay focused on what He would want in your life when you get so busy living it your way." I looked up and saw the corners of his mouth turn up a little.

"There's more," he said as his face changed back to serious.

"There's more?" I responded a bit surprised. "Is it bad? I don't know if I can take anymore."

"It's not bad . . . per say," he said, as the corner of his mouth twisted. He waited, looking into my eyes. I was scared of what he was going to say. He turned toward me, and looked serious. "Sara, it's about your dreams."

"What?" I whispered weakly. I had kinda forgotten about my dreams.

"When Mark finally broke and told us what happened to Lily, he was really upset. He was crying really hard and completely came apart. It was actually really hard to watch. He really loved her, and it showed. When he was done giving us the details on Lily, he made another confession."

"What? Confession to what?"

29

THE GHOST YOU'VE BEEN SEEING in your dreams is an old friend of his."

"What? Who?"

"As it turns out, the little girl, Carrie Sanders, was Mark's childhood friend."

"The boy that saw her alive last? The one questioned and released," I asked, starting to panic. "That was Mark?"

"Yup," Derek said. "He told us about what happened to her," he continued shaking his head. "It's so crazy. It was like deja-vu for poor Mark."

"Derek tell me!" I said turning toward him and pulling one foot under my leg.

"Mark said that he and Carrie had been friends for about four years. They were the only kids from their school who lived on the lake so they spent a lot of time together after school and in the summer. Mark told us that on the afternoon Carrie disappeared, they had hung around the lake and were up by the cave. They often walked there and hung out and talked. The two of them used to sneak cigarettes and beer from their parents and sit up there all afternoon. On that particular afternoon, they ended up having sex. It was the first time for both of them. They were only thirteen, and both were really scared about anyone finding out. They promised each other not to tell anyone. Especially their parents. Mark said that when they got up to get dressed, Carrie was jumping into her jeans, hopping with one leg in and lost her balance. He had just reached down to grab his t-shirt, heard a short scream and looked up to see her fall. Carrie simply slipped, fell, hit her head and died instantly, a foot away from him. His was in complete shock. He bent over to see if she was okay but she didn't move. He couldn't believe it. She was fine one second and dead the next. He tried to do CPR, but it didn't work. Mark said that he was scared of her dad. He feared what would happen if her dad found out about the two of them having sex. He knew that if he went for help, the doctors would see that they'd been together, and her parents and his would hate him . . . maybe worse. He'd be the town's hated boy. Everyone would think it was his fault, and he was scared he'd go to prison for the rest of his life. Not to mention what his parents would do. He was a terrified little boy, so he panicked and hid her body in the cave. And the next day, he came back and buried her in a shallow grave he'd dug in there. The one the search dog found."

"Holy shit! Oh, my gosh, Derek! And he never told anyone before you?" I asked.

"No, he said that he has never told anyone! It's been eating at him his whole life. He was actually relieved to get it off his chest. He cried and said it's haunted him every single day of his life."

"I don't know how to process all this. It's too much. I can't even imagine going through that . . . twice. I feel bad for him, kinda," I said, still crying. "Actually, I'm not sure how to feel about Mark right now."

"I know. I feel sorry for him, too," Derek said, rubbing my arm. "He seems like a really nice guy who's had really bad luck and no self-control in a crisis situation. Mark said his dad got a job transfer shortly after it happened, and that's when they moved to the Cities. That's when he met all of you guys. He never told you because he was a scared little kid. He really needed a friend, and he got three great ones. He feels really bad that he brought all of you guys into this. Mark said that he was really uncomfortable when you told him and Lily about the cabin you had rented. He knew it would be near there. He didn't realize it was the same lake until you gave him the directions. Mark said he felt sick to his stomach the whole time."

"He must have been so scared. I can't imagine what it must have been like for him to go back there." I had to stop talking and catch my breath. "I didn't tell him exactly where we were going. I just said that I made reservations for a small cabin in the woods on a lake up north. I feel awful."

"Don't, Sara. You had no way of knowing. You did nothing wrong," Derek said compassionately.

"For him to find out that Lily didn't love him, and then to lose her . . . in the same tragic way . . . in the same exact spot." I cried hard again for a few minutes. Then I looked up at Derek and took a breath. "Do you believe him?" I asked.

"Yes," Derek said softly. "I do, and the investigation proves it. All the facts and evidence are there. Mark's very remorseful. And he already said he'd plead guilty and do his time."

"What are they being charged with?" I asked.

"Mark will be charged with involuntary manslaughter, and Jake will be charged as an accessory. If they plead guilty, the time should go way down. And they can get out early for good behavior, too. But ultimately it will be up to the judge and jury."

"What about Carrie Sanders?"

"Mark would normally be tried separately for that, his sentencing would be separate and so would the judge and jury. But he was a child when it happened, so I don't think they'll do much about it now. It'll be up to the district attorney to decide to try the case or not. Carrie's parents have options too, though I doubt at this point they'll press charges."

"Have you told Carrie's parents yet?"

"No. I have to go up there later today," he said. He didn't look excited about it either. "I'm going home to sleep, and then I'll head up there this evening . . . if you want, you can ride along. You wouldn't have to come with to tell her parents. I could drop you at a restaurant and meet back up with you," he said, with those puppy dog eyes.

"Can I think about it?" I asked, not really liking the sound of it.

"Sure. I'll call you an hour before I leave, and you can let me know," he said.

"You've just been through a lot. It might be best for you to stay here and rest anyway. I just thought it'd make the long, boring, drive nicer if you were with me." He moved closer and slung an arm over my shoulder. I put my head on his shoulder and closed my eyes. They hurt. I needed eye drops. I didn't want to even think about what I looked like.

Derek sat back and put his feet up on the table. I snuggled in and enjoy his warmth and delicious smell. It was so nice to have him, such a nice guy and so strong inside and out. I closed my eyes slowly, and inhaled deeply.

I opened my eyes because my neck hurt and noticed on the clock across the room, it'd been an hour. I slowly picked my head up and saw Derek was sound asleep. I carefully got up and grabbed a blanket from the closet and covered him up with it. He sank a little lower into the couch. He looked comfortable so I didn't wake him. I turned the radio and the lights off and pulled the blinds on the patio door.

I went to my computer and checked emails. None from Jake. Guess he'd been busy. It made me sick to replay in my mind my conversations and interaction with him. I was glad I kicked him out right away. There were so many nights when I just wanted him to come home and hold me. I couldn't believe that he'd helped Mark. What was he thinking? Then again, what was he thinking when he cheated on me? I thought I knew him. I thought my heart was safe with him.

Mark too, I had been there for him! I even cleaned his apartment! I couldn't believe he'd never told me. All that time I spent talking to him, and checking in on him, not knowing all the while he was hiding my ex-best friend's body in the cement of my soon to be ex-husband's construction site. I guess you never really know a person. I grew up with him, all of them! I spent time almost every, single day of my life with them. I told them all my secrets. I trusted them . . . I trusted them! How do I ever trust anyone again after this. Leaning back from my desk, the tears rolled down my cheeks full speed, I didn't even feel them coming. I was numb. There were so many emotions to feel that I didn't know what to feel.

I stood and looked over at Derek on the couch. He was still sound asleep. So handsome, even when he was sleeping. The sight looked very inviting. If the couch were bigger, I'd have crawled right up there with him. I went to my bedroom and grabbed two pillows off the bed and another blanket from the closet. I put one pillow next to Derek's head. He moved a little and slowly opened his eyes.

"Pillow?" I whispered. He lifted his head, and I tucked it under. "You fell asleep, but it's okay. I'm going to lay down by the fire and take a nap, too." He nodded and smiled. I made myself a little bed on the floor in front of the fireplace. I saw Derek pull his feet up on the couch and settled in. I set my cell phone alarm for two hours and closed my eyes.

It was misty, and cool. I was at the cave entrance. It was rocky but clean looking. It's as if someone swept it and bleached it. It glistened in the early morning sun. I look up into the sun, and there are two shadows, two ghosts. Lily and Carrie in white dresses and glowing.

"You helped us. You did it!" Carrie said.

"Thank-you," Lily said.

It was strange to hear her voice. It sounded just like her. I missed her, but I still hated her, too. "I'm sorry," she said. "So sorry."

I looked at her and didn't know what to say. I was angry and sad and hurt. She smiled gently. They both started to fade, the glow was disappearing. The mist they seemed to be made of getting thinner and thinner. I watched until they were completely out of sight.

I felt a thousand pounds lighter. I could breathe! I took a deep breath and opened my eyes. I was awake! My cell phone alarm was going off. While turning it off, I glanced at Derek. He was lying there with his eyes open and a small grin on his face.

"Hey," I whispered. "Sorry. I didn't know how long you wanted to sleep so I set it for two hours."

"It's okay. Thanks. I should go home and sleep in my own bed for a few more, and then I have to go to Nisswa," he said as he stood and folded the blanket. I stood up and walked him to the door. "Well, goodnight," he winked. "I'll give you a call later to see if you want to go with. Thanks again for breakfast, sweetness."

I nodded, "You're welcome," I said and shut the door behind him.

I missed him already, and he wasn't even to the end of the hall. I smiled and headed to the shower. I spend some extra time exfoliating and shaving. When I got out, I put on my best-smelling lotion and then threw on a thick, plush, bath robe. I put in a chick flick and gave myself a mani/pedi while I watched it, and did a face mask too! I felt great when I was done. After I spent some extra time on my hair and make-up, it occurred to me that I must be mentally planning on going with Derek. I guess that was fine. Really I had nothing else planned and, like he said, I didn't have to go to the house with him. I could just wait at the restaurant. It'd be bonus time together. How bad could it be driving through the country in the fall? The leaves were at their peak, so it would be a beautiful drive.

Cleaning up the apartment took all of an hour. One of the bonuses to being single was it was never messy, unless it was your fault. After that, I paid some bills, which was really fun to do when you have money in the bank, and more coming in every month. I was able to pay all of my debts off in one month, what an amazing feeling! I couldn't wait until next month when the bills came and the balances said zero.

I called my lawyer and asked what she was planning to change, if anything, for the hearing tomorrow now that Jake was incarcerated. She was as shocked as I was and said she'd get back to me.

I decided to walk a couple of blocks to the gas station and get a paper. Sure enough Mark, Jake, and Lily were front page. I was reading it while I walked back when my cell phone rang.

"Have you seen today's paper?" My dad, straight to the point.

"Yes. I heard some of the details last night, and the rest a little bit ago," I responded.

"What are the details?" he asked, "The paper doesn't tell you anything."

"I don't know how much I'm able to tell you yet. I haven't finished reading the article," I said.

"Well, where are you getting your information from?"

"Um, the lead detective on the case. We've been helping each other figure things out."

"Oh, yes. I think your mother said something about you having a thing for the cop. Well, don't be a stranger and stay out of trouble ... and off the front page!" he said and disconnected.

My dad, gotta love him. When I got home, my phone rang again. It was my lawyer. She said that she spoke with Jake's lawyer and everything was still on. Jake wouldn't be fighting for anything, so he didn't really need to be there. The judge said it was fine to continue since he plead guilty and wasn't fighting for anything.

I disconnected and called Kat and my mom to set up a lunch date for tomorrow after my court appointment.

My phone rang again, and it wasn't a number I recognized so I send it to voice mail. It was a reporter asking for a comment. Great. I deleted it and made a mental note not to answer unknown numbers.

Derek called a few minutes later, "So are you in or out."

"I'm in."

He said, "You have an hour."

Good, because I'd been ready forever. I grabbed my camera and threw it in my purse, in case the trees were really pretty.

30

AN HOUR LATER, I WAS DOWNSTAIRS chatting with Jamie at the front office when I saw Derek pull up. As usual he was in the black sedan that belonged to the station. I slid in.

"How was your nap?" I asked.

"Not long enough. Sorry for falling asleep on your couch," he said.

"It's okay. I understand completely."

Derek trailed through town then jumped on the interstate. To pass some time, I grabbed a magazine from my bag and paged through it. We talked for a while. I learned where he lived and even got the apartment number. Derek told me about his parents and the rest of his family. It turned out he had an older brother and two younger sisters. His brother was married and his sisters were both in college. The way it sounded, they all got along.

I informed Derek I was an only child and warned him that I didn't share, didn't socialize, and if I didn't get my way, I threw huge fits. He laughed, but this was sometimes true.

We got to Nisswa at five-thirty and drove down Main Street to the little mom-and-pop restaurant. Derek dropped me off and said he shouldn't be more than an hour or so. I grabbed my bag and cell phone, told him good luck. The hostess was waiting, menu in hand when I walked in. I informed her that I was meeting someone, but I was very early. She sat me in a booth and brought me a coffee. I'd paged through my magazine twice and was already bored. I got up to go to the bathroom, and on the way I checked my watch. I'd only been there twenty minutes.

I went into the stall, and YES! I got my period! I thanked God, and rooted through my purse for supplies. Nada. Nothing! Seriously? I had been hoping and praying for this for days, and I didn't even prepare. I peeked out of the stall door and there was a machine on the wall in the corner. I dug through my purse again, but no quarters. Shit, now what? I thought for a second that I could get change from the waitress, but all I had was a credit card. I really didn't want the embarrassment of running my card for quarters. I slowly walked out of the bathroom and scanned the place. There was only one other couple in the whole place. I happened to glance at the table to my right. It had dirty dishes on it and a tip which included a few quarters. I couldn't believe that I was going to this. I casually walked by, while looking around to make sure no one was watching and swiped a quarter off the table, then returned to the bathroom. A few minutes later, I was back to my table.

The waitress came over and topped off my coffee, then went to the table and grabbed her tip and the dishes. I made a mental note to leave her a bigger than normal tip. I was so relieved. The not knowing had been awful, especially since my baby's daddy would be in prison for a while. How embarrassing would that be. "Who's the father?" "Oh, he's in prison." It was strange how I was proud of where I was at, but embarrassed about my recent past, which I just had been proud of in the recent past. It made me angry to think of how out of my control my life actually was. I had no choice in the way my life changed, the selfish people I was involved with took it from me. I shook my head to rid the thought. *Move on*, I scolded myself.

As I was shaking my head, I heard a voice. "Don't rattle your brain too hard, dear. You'll get a headache." I turned around to see Reggie and Maureen.

"Hey, guys," I said with a smile. "How are you? It's good to see you again."

"What brings you back to town? It doesn't have anything to do with all the drama up on the hill by the lake does it?" Reggie asked, with a suspicious smile.

"Please, join me," I said, motioning toward the booth across from me. They sat down.

"Are you here for dinner?" I asked.

"Just pie. Maureen made a wonderful pot roast for dinner, so as a thank you, I'm taking her out for pie," Reggie said, as he smiled at her. She leaned over and side-bumped him and looked blushed.

The waitress came over, and the three of us ordered pie. I excused myself and grabbed my ringing phone.

"Hey, Derek."

"I'll be about forty-five minutes, Carrie's parents were at the Saturday night church service, so I had to wait for them."

"No problem. I met some friends, and they're having pie with me." I disconnected and turned my attention back to Maureen and Reggie.

We spent the next forty minutes having a very enlightening conversation. I updated them on the lake and the cave and told them about both the girls. I filled them in on everything, including my dreams and my new-found feelings for the detective . . . everything. It was so easy to talk to them. They were like grandparents to me. They were happy for me and glad there was finally some closure for the Sanders family.

I asked them about themselves and their business. They started at the beginning when they met and walked me through their life. They filled me in on their thoughts for retirement, which they were way past, but were now thinking that it was time to really slow down. We spent a lot of time on the subject while finishing our pie. The conversation put a huge smile on my face. When they got ready to leave, I told them the pie was on me and exchanged contact numbers with them. And just as they stood to leave, Derek walked in. I made introductions, then gave them each a hug and said goodbye. They thanked me for the pie and walked away hand in hand. Derek slid in the booth across from me.

"Bill and Nancy took it very well. They of course were upset, but they seemed at peace with at least having an answer. They were stuck between feeling sorry for Mark and being angry at him," Derek said. "I gave them some materials on mental health and how people handle crises differently. I also reminded them that Mark was just a scared kid when it happened, and that he was very remorseful and carried the burden of his choices his whole life."

"When will the Sanders get their daughter back?" I asked.

"I spoke to them about that, and they decided that at this point cremation was the best choice. So as soon as the coroner is done, the remains will be cremated and the urn will be delivered to the family by a uniform. They said that they'd plan a funeral for late next week."

"Wow, that must be so hard. Not just to lose your daughter but to have to wait so long for answers and then to find out that it was an accident that could have been dealt with years ago. They lost years of a happy life, waiting and wondering. I just feel so bad for them."

"I know. The death of a child is the hardest of all deaths," he added. "I called the Nisswa police on the way over here. I need to stop by the station on the way home and drop off some paperwork."

"Okay. In the meantime, are you hungry? I already had pie with my friends."

We ordered and talked while we waited. Derek asked me, "how do you know Reggie and Maureen?"

I filled him in and told him that we had a very interesting conversation but left out the details. I loved them like grandparents. Derek smiled. I think I amused him. When our food came, we ate quietly and soon after we were back in the car. Following a quick stop at the Nisswa police station, we were on our way home.

"Considering the mess of the jurisdiction issues and the two separate cases overlapping, this investigation went pretty smoothly. The chief here is a real stand-up guy," Derek said as we pulled out of the Nisswa Police station lot.

The ride seemed shorter on the way home. When Derek pulled into the lot, I started to gather all my stuff and checked the time. Eleven-fifteen. I briefly thought about inviting Derek up but then decided it was late and he looked beat. And so was I. I opened the door, thanked him for dinner and jumped out.

"Thanks for riding along, sweetness," he said with a wink that instantly gave me chills.

"You're welcome . . . handsome," I said, returning the wink and shutting the door. One day soon, I was going to kiss that guy.

I went straight to bed. I felt a sense of relief, so much had happened that day and I felt like the future was looking really bright. I just had to get through the next couple weeks.

31

WEDNESDAY … "D" DAY. While I got ready for court, I felt sick to my stomach. I was glad that Jake would not be in the court room, I didn't want to see him. While driving to court, I got an incoming call. Lily's mom.

"Hello?"

"Hi, Sara. It's Debbie. I hope I'm not bothering you," she said.

"Debbie, you could never bother me. How are you, dear?" I asked gently.

"Awful. I'm awful, but I have to keep going. I know my Lily made some really bad choices, and again I'm so sorry, but I wanted to invite you to her services. I understand if you don't want to come, but I wanted you to know you're welcome there," she said through a cracking voice.

"Okay, thanks, Debbie. I'll stop by. When are the services?" I asked.

I got the info and disconnected. I wondered if Lily would've wanted me to come. I wondered how much of our friendship was real. I wondered when she started just using me to get to Jake. I wondered if she was alive today, if she would have apologized to me or tried to continue the relationship with Jake. I guess I'd never know.

Court was a breeze. Everything was mine that I wanted because Jake knew that he'd be in prison for a big chunk of time and we didn't have a house or kids to fight over. The judge ruled and all was settled. The paperwork would take a couple days and then I'd be officially divorced. It paid to know people!

I called Kat and my mom and told them the good news. We met for a quick lunch. They didn't know weather to be happy or sad for me. I told them to be happy. I couldn't go back so this was a huge step going forward.

I spent the next few days getting phone calls made, papers faxed and plans in line. I talked to Derek a few times, but he had been hard at work with reports on all that had gone down. Before I knew it, it was Monday, the day of Lily's wake. I dressed nice and stopped by. The casket was open and I could see her from across the room. She looked a ton better then the last time I'd seen her but still pretty rough. I found Debbie and Gerald and gave them both a big hug. They were having a really tough time. The place was full to capacity, and there wasn't a dry eye anywhere. I saw a few people from the office and said hi, but it was awkward. No one knew what to say. Tragic death was hard enough to accept, then throw in the affair of a best friend and an accident turned crime and . . . really, what do you say?

I left soon after arriving. I really had no desire to sit around and talk about how great Lily was. I didn't really know what to feel walking in and I guess I kinda let her go a while ago so I didn't need the wake and funeral for closure like the rest of her friends and family did. I decided that I'd go to the funeral tomorrow but like today, I would be in and out. I didn't hold a grudge, mostly because she was dead but also because I knew that I was a good person and a good person would forgive. I had to, not for her but for me. And I needed to know what I did was right. She would have to deal with her wrongs from the Big Guy above.

Derek met me for dinner, and I asked if he wanted to join me for the funeral. He said he'd come with me, if I went with him Wednesday to Carrie's funeral. I agreed. After dinner, he invited me back to his place for a night cap, and I said yes, of course. I wanted to see his apartment. One can tell a lot about a person by seeing where and how they live. Right?

He parked the work car in the lot, took my hand and walked me in. He opened the door and turned on the light. It was very nice and the whole place smelled like him. The kitchen was spotless; even the floors looked washed. Derek went to the fridge and pulled out a bottle of wine. While he worked the corkscrew, I looked around the living room and dinning room. The furniture was nice. A large couch, and recliner were both dark-brown leather. There was a coffee table that looked like the one that I almost bought when I was shopping. There were end tables on both sides of the couch, and the lamps were new and tasteful. The walls were a warm, brownish, and the lighting was soft. He had wildlife pictures hanging here and there, and I noticed that two of them had lakes in them. There was a forty-seven inch, LCD flat screen on the wall, and all the other equipment just below in a black, modern, sleek enclosed cabinet. I loved it. Very manly, yet very inviting and tasteful. I turned around and Mr.

Handsome was holding out a glass of wine for me. I took it, and he clinked my glass, holding my eyes as we sipped.

"So what do you think?" he asked, stepping next to me, his shoulder tight against mine.

"It's okay," I said, being a smart-ass. I smiled, then turned to face him. "It's great. I love it. Did you do all this yourself?"

"Most of it. My younger sisters came with to the furniture store and put in their two cents but for the most part, it's me," he said proudly and took another sip. "There's pictures of my family over here," he said and lead me to a distant wall. There were about twenty photos, all in matching frames of different shapes and sizes, they included everyone, even Grandma. It was touching. Most bachelors would have basketball posters up or half-dressed woman posters and a beer bottle collection. He pointed to a few faces and told me who they were.

"I like it…a lot," I said, turning to him. I blinked slowly and looked closely at his face. He was so perfect—handsome, clean, liked outdoors, a family man, career man, stable, strong, sweet, spiritual. I could go on and on. My mind was spinning, and my heart was melting. "I like you…a lot," I said sheepishly.

He smiled gently and then leaned in and kissed me. It was so nice. Instantly a heat wave moved through me, and my heart beat faster. I hadn't had a first kiss in a long time. I opened my eyes, and he smiled again. I smiled back. Then he leaned in for more, and I let him. Yay, he was a good kisser, too! I was awe struck. I opened my eyes and wondered what he was thinking. Was he feeling all the things I was? He smiled gently, took my hand and led me into the living room.

"Twins are on," he said, as he reached for the remote on the side table.

I got up to leave shortly after the Twins won. Derek walked me out to the lot. After I unlocked the Jeep door, I turned to him. He smiled gently and closed the space between us, leaned the weight of his body against me and pushed me back against the Jeep. He took my face in his hands and kissed me again slowly, and gently and then gave me a full contact hug. Perfect! I slowly opened my eyes and caught my breath. He smiled and opened my door, and I plopped down, bummed I had to leave.

"Goodnight. I'll pick you up in the morning for the funeral. I'll be driving my personal vehicle so you might have to look for me in the lot," he said with a wink.

The thought occured that he'd always been in the black sedan from the station so I didn't even know what he drove, and it never came up in conversation. "What do you drive?" I asked.

"You'll have to wait and see," he said smiling. I squinted at him as he closed the door. Oh, no, it's probably a two-seater, hot shot, bachelor car.

"Goodnight," I said with a finger wave, and pulled away.

The next morning, I was up, dressed in black and ready to go. I was excited to see Derek again and to get this chapter of my life closed. While I was on my way down to the lot, Derek called and said he was down there waiting. I walked past the office and gave Jamie a wave. She was fanning her face like she was hot and then looked out the window to the lot and pointed. I laughed as I walked out the door and right in front of me stood a handsome man, dressed in a perfectly tailored, black suit, arms folded, leaning against a Jeep Grand Cherokee, just like mine. I started laughing and shook my head.

"Nice ride sport!" I said.

"Thanks, cutie. I thought you'd like it," he said, opening my door for me.

His was black and mine was red, but other than that, they were the same!

When we got to Lily's funeral, we chose a seat in the back of the church. The service was full. I spotted a couple of mutual friends and co-workers in the crowd. They gave me small, close lipped smiles. I smiled back but it was really hard to be there. I didn't think it was going to be that bad but it was the most uncomfortable feeling I'd ever had. I had spent so much of my life loving this person and then for a brief moment in life I hated her and the next second she was gone.

Sadness was creeping in, and once the music started and they wheeled the casket into the church, I lost it. Derek passed me a box of Kleenex from the seat next to him and looked at me with concern. I spent the rest of the funeral, trying really hard to focus on the good times we'd had, which proved to be very challenging. I wondered as I looked around the room, how many people knew what she did to me, that she was my best friend and slept with my husband. I wondered if they knew that. I wondered if they knew who she really was. I tried to shake the mean thoughts away, but the anger was more powerful than my will. I wondered how Jake and Mark felt knowing she was being buried today and they couldn't even be there. I dried my eyes and looked at my watch. I just wanted this to be done and over and I never wanted to think about her again. When the service finally ended, I led Derek to the Jeep as fast as I could walk in heels.

"So, sweetness, how are you feeling?" he asked, in a sympathetic voice.

"I don't know. I went from sad, to angry, to wanting revenge, then back to sad," I said checking the mirror. "But you know what? I did it, and it's over. I can move on with my life now and forget about her," I said, with a half smile.

"Do you want to go out to the cemetery or to the luncheon?" he asked, as he started the engine.

"No cemetery. Yes to lunch but not here. Take me far away from here." I said with a deep breath. I put my head back against the head rest and closed my eyes.

"You got it," he said and put the car in gear. "I took the next two days off work . . . how far am I allowed to take you?" he asked.

I laughed and told him, "Not too far right now. I have a kitten at home."

Derek settled on taking me to lunch and then to a movie so we could relax and just enjoy each other's company. We decided to stop by both of our apartments first and change into more comfortable clothes. We went to his place first. He went into the bedroom in a suit and came out in jeans and a long-sleeved shirt that hugged his chest and arms just right. It was tan and made his blue eyes stand out. He grabbed a jacket from the closet, and we headed to my place.

When we got to my door, Faith came bounding over, as always. This made Derek laugh really hard.

"That was the cutest thing I've ever seen," he said laughing. He bent down and picked her up and made all sorts of cute faces and noises at her. I went into the bedroom and put on my best-fitting jeans and a red, fitted sweater, and jewelry to match. Then in the bathroom I touched up my make up and hair. I threw on socks, casual shoes and a dash of perfume. When I came out, I noticed Derek was out on the deck cuddling with Faith. He smiled at me through the glass door and came into the living room.

"Ready?" he asked, setting Faith gently on the floor.

"Yup, ready and hungry," I answered. I tossed some kitten kibble in Faith's bowl and grabbed my purse.

Derek took me to a sports bar that had pool tables, dart boards, ping pong, Foosball, and a ton of other things to do. We ordered burger baskets and a pitcher and spent an hour game hopping, which was really fun because we're both very competitive. After we finished the pitcher, we drove to the movie theater and caught the latest Samuel Jackson flick. It was so nice to just sit quietly and know that Lily was laid to rest, my divorce would be final in a day or two, and I was there with a great man, who genuinely cared about me. I felt at peace, like I could breathe again, like I was in control again. I liked where I was at. I smiled and took a handful of popcorn from the bucket in Derek's lap and mentally thanked God for this moment and this feeling.

After the movie, we stopped by the grocery store and got a few things to make dinner together. Then we went to my place and sat on the deck and talked while we had a few beers and some snacks. The conversation was smooth. I decided not to tell him yet about my money. I'm sure he wondered how I could live like this and work very little, but I'd let him wonder a while longer. A few hours later, we'd both learned a lot more about each other and I felt like I had known him my whole life. I told him that, and he leaned over and kissed me.

We finished dinner quickly since we had to get up early to go to Nisswa for Carrie's funeral. Derek told me that Carrie's parents wanted to meet me. I had no idea what I'd say to them or what they thought of me. Derek informed me they were very spiritual and believed the dreams that I had. Nancy had told Derek that she had a similar dream a year or so ago.

I walked Derek to the door at eight-thirty. He took my face in his hands and kissed me gently and softly.

"I'll pick you up at five-thirty in the morning.

"Yay, looking forward to it," I said with a fake smile.

"We'll stop for coffee as soon as we get out of the lot," he assured me.

As soon as he left, I called my mom. They had declined the invitation to Lily's funeral but wanted me to call when I got home. I gave her the four-one-one and then went to bed.

I fell asleep easily and woke to my alarm clock at four-thirty. Geez, this was not a good idea. I hated mornings. I sauntered into the bathroom and turned on the water. After a long, hot shower, I dressed in black dress pants and a fall-colored dress shirt, threw on some jewelry, shoes, and a cute scarf. I did a quick make-up and hair routine, went to the kitchen and did the Faith routine, then I walked the garbage and litter out to the dumpster and met Derek in the lot at precisely five-thirty.

32

IT WAS A LONG, BORING DRIVE, but Derek made it go by quickly. I told him that while I was in town I had a date to meet my friends Reggie and Maureen for pie again. He said that he had to get somethings taken care of at the Nisswa police station too, so we agreed to a plan. He would drop me off at the restaurant and go do his thing and then meet up with me when he was done.

I loved talking with Derek on the drive. He was so open and honest and didn't seem to care if I agreed or disagree. He just stated what he felt and moved on. Unlike most men I knew, he spoke from the heart. He always told me exactly what he was thinking and how he felt at that moment, and I didn't even have to ask. It was so nice because there were no guessing games with him. He was just cool and confident and strong, both physically and mentally.

"I'm falling for you, Sara, and I don't know what to do with all the emotions I'm feeling. I wonder all the time, what you think about us . . . and if there is an us," he said, hesitantly.

"I think there is. I feel the same way. I wonder all the time what you're thinking too."

It scared me that maybe I was just clinging to him for security. I hadn't dated since before Jake and that was seventh grade, so in reality I hadn't dated at all.

"Do you think we're moving too fast?" I asked.

Derek turned his head and looked me in the eyes and said, "No, I like the pace. And when I'm not with you, I'm thinking about you and wondering when I'll get to see you again. When my phone rings, I get goosebumps and wonder if it's you. I'm actually disappointed if it's not. And when it is you, I have to catch my breath before I answer."

That was so nice to hear. Jake had always been nice but short. More like, "You look nice," not "Wow you take my breath away when I see you." That was a huge difference, and I liked it. I could totally get used to it.

"I'm just nervous that I'm on the rebound and that I'm moving too fast. And that people will think bad of me," I confessed.

He reassured me by looking at me and saying, "if it feels right. It's not wrong. And don't worry about what other people think."

I nodded in agreement and smiled at him and blinked slowly. Gosh, he was so beautiful. I looked out the window and admired the colors of the trees. They were just past peak, and the sun was starting to come up. Derek put his hand on my thigh, and I tipped my head back against the seat and closed my eyes. I felt the car stop, and I opened my eyes. We were at a gas station in Nisswa.

"Morning, sunshine," Derek said with a slap on my leg. "We're a little early, so I'm going to fill up and hit the bathroom."

I nodded and stretched, then exited the Jeep. The air was cool and crisp. I tossed my purse over my shoulder and walked around to the other side where Derek was leaning back on the Jeep waiting for it to fill. He smiled and gave me a "come here" finger wave. I walked over to him, and he pulled me in and hugged me, wrapping his coat around my sides with his hands still in his pockets. He buried his nose in my neck, inhaled deeply and kissed my neck. Okay, I was awake! He smelled so welcoming.

The nozzle clicked, and we parted. I told him I'd meet him inside and shuffled to the building. I gave the cashier my card and told her I was paying for the gas. Then I went to the bathroom. When I got out, Derek was just coming out of the men's room.

"Thanks for the gas, sweetness," he said.

"You're welcome," I said with a wink.

After we both grabbed another coffee, we jumped back in the Jeep. We arrived at the funeral home ten minutes early. After we sat down in the back, Derek pointed out Bill and Nancy and a few local police he'd worked with. I recognized Reggie, Maureen, and the librarian, Vikki. I bet she had some questions for me. All of a sudden I got nervous. My heart was racing, I was hot, and I could feel my face turning red. I knew I didn't cause all this but in some ways I felt I did. Now that I thought that, I felt really sick. I whispered all this in Derek's ear. He turned and looked at me then took my arm and led me to a back hall of the church. He gently pushed me back against the wall and put his finger under my chin and lifted my face to meet his eyes.

"Hey, I don't want to hear that. This was in no way your fault!" he said, in a very stern voice. "This situation happened a long time ago and had nothing at all to do with you. God simply used you as his angel, on earth, to provide Bill and Nancy with closure and give them a way to get their daughter back. You did that! They love you for it. You need to believe that and nothing else. You're an angel for Carrie and Lily, and a lot of people are grateful for what you've done. God knew that you were strong enough to handle it, and I think He was right. Now, take a deep breath and be proud. Keep your chin up," he said firmly, then kissed my forehead.

After a deep breath, I nodded and dried my tears. That was everything I needed to hear. I loved him. I really did. I wouldn't tell him that yet though. He took my hand and walked me out to the main lobby. The lobby was full. People were getting their last chance to pray over the urn. The urn was beautiful, and there were a bunch of pictures all around it. I walked up to them and looked closely. It was so strange to see Carrie in kid's clothes, playing on the swing set in the backyard. There was one of her first Communion and her first day of school . . . I had only ever seen her as a ghost in a white dress and it was always so foggy and misty. She was a beautiful little girl. It made me so sad to think of what a loss her parents experienced. The pain of never seeing her again, and wondering for all those years where she was and what she might have gone through. My heart ached for them. I felt Derek tap me. I looked up at him and he tipped his head toward who I assumed were her parents. The crowd from around them was thinning so he walked over and I followed.

"Bill and Nancy Sanders, " he said gently, "I'd like you to meet Sara Martin."

I smiled a sad, closed lipped smile and extended my hand. Nancy wrapped her arms around me and whispered, "Thank you," in my ear. I returned the hug and said, "You're welcome," back. That put me into full-on tears. Then Bill hugged me and said his thanks too.

"I'm so sorry for your loss," I added, looking at them both.

"Thank you, dear. It sounds like you've had a rough few weeks, too," Bill said.

I nodded in agreement.

Nancy asked if I'd had any more dreams. I told her and Bill about my last one. They were both sad and relieved at my story. It felt weird to tell them. I didn't consider myself psychic in anyway, and I wasn't sure I believed in them either.

The funeral director walked in and said we were going to get started. Derek and I took the same seats in the back. Bill and Nancy walked in carrying the urn to the front alter. I felt weak just watching.

The service lasted about an hour and was really nice. I only cried a little, which I considered an accomplishment. Afterward, we had time so we did the cemetery part. Then when people started getting in their cars we went over to Bill and Nancy and said goodbye. I exchanged numbers with Nancy in case she wanted to talk about things in the future.

After we got in the Jeep, we drove to the diner. I told Derek I would see him soon and hopped out curbside. I was a little early, which gave me time to get my paperwork organized. When Reggie and Maureen arrived, I was really excited to see them! We exchanged hugs. They sat down in the booth with me and pulled out a bunch of papers, too. Then after a few minutes, their agent arrived, and we finished our business.

An hour later, Derek called and told me he was on the way. I met him outside. When I got in the car, I asked how his meeting went, and he said the cases were both officially closed. He looked relieved.

"The chief of police was there and said that he'd heard good things about how well I handled the case and about my professionalism," Derek said. "It seems he's looking at retirement next year and said that he'd love to talk to me about a position."

"As chief of police? Would you consider it?" I asked.

He shrugged. "I don't know. I love it up here. Up until recently, there wasn't anything keeping me in the city. Now... I don't know. I guess time will tell." He looked at me and smiled. I smiled back.

"How was your pie date?" Derek asked.

I sighed. "Perfect. It feels great to have all this done and behind me."

When we got back into town Derek pulled into my lot and dropped me off at my apartment building's front door. I leaned over and gave him a quick kiss.

"I'll call you tomorrow," I said.

33

THE NEXT FEW DAYS WENT BY REALLY FAST. My divorce was final. I ran to my office and got copies of the papers and used the fax there to send them off. I was so excited that I could hardly catch my breath. I went in to a stall in the ladies room and did a silent happy dance and jumped up and down a few times. Then, after I was composed, I stopped by all my friends' offices, said hi and picked up a client file for a living will and trust for a young couple. I checked in with my supervisor and told her I'd have it back in a day or two.

I walked out of the building with an extra spring in my step. When I got to my Jeep, I called Kat and told her I was having a Bar-B-Que on Sunday, and she said she'd be there.

I dialed Derek. "What's up, beautiful?" he answered.

"What's your schedule for the day?" I asked, getting an instant smile.

"I'm at work until ten . . ." he said slowly.

"Do you want to meet for a drink after you're done, at Buffalo Wild Wings?"

"Okay. I see ya there . . . about ten fifteen," he said.

I made a quick phone call to make sure that my fax was received. It was. After I showered and spent lots of time on my make-up and hair, which turned out fabulous. I dressed in my other new shirt that I still hadn't worn and some jeans that fit just right. I threw on some heels and big hoop earrings then downed a beer from the fridge. I gave my mom a quick call to catch her up, telling her that I was going to have a little get together on Sunday to celebrate. She said that she and Dad would be there.

At about ten-twenty, Derek showed up, looking as hot as ever. He walked right up to me, put both hands on my face and gave me a strong, passionate kiss. I thought it was almost like he was making it known that I was his, marking his territory. Which was fine by me.

He leaned forward and whispered, "I missed you the last few days. I'm really glad you called." Then he looked me up and down and made a quiet, grunting noise in his throat.

"What's your schedule like this weekend," I asked.

"I work Saturday from five to nine in the morning to make up a few hours, then I have Sunday, Monday, and Tuesday off."

"Do you have anything planned?" I asked.

"No."

"Keep it open. I have a plan," I informed him and he seemed perfectly fine with that.

Saturday morning I got up early, got groceries, and called Derek.

"I'll be to your place by ten. Be ready and dressed casually. The plan is full of surprises, so you'll be on a need-to-know basis." I smiled as I disconnected. I liked the power.

After packing my Jeep to the brim, I went back for Faith and her things. When I got to Derek's, he started in right away.

"So, what's the plan, sweetness?" he said, arms folded, leaning on the counter.

"You, my dear, need to go pack a bag for an over-nighter or two or three. Pack extra. Who knows how long we'll want to stay."

"Seriously? Where are we going?" he asked.

"Somewhere you'll love. I'll tell you on the way," I said with a wink.

Derek motioned me toward his room. "Come with me. I need help."

Fifteen minutes later we were heading out to the Jeep, bags packed. I opened the trunk of my Jeep, and he saw the cat stuff and the cooler and looked at me funny. I helped him throw his stuff on top. When we got in, he sat sideways in the passenger's seat and folded his arms. "Okay, Chicky, spill!" he demanded.

"All right. There are a few things about me you don't know," I started, as I turned out of the lot. I looked over and he had his eyebrows raised.

"Should I be concerned?" he asked.

"Maybe," I said, toying with him. "I'll start back a generation or two." I winked, and pulled out on the highway. "My grandpa and grandma we're very lucky in the real estate market . . ."

I brought him up to the part where grandma passed and left me a letter. I continued on and told him that, in the letter, she told me to continue working or volunteering and to "find my place in this world." We spent the next half hour driving and talking. Derek remained quiet and smiley. He told me he liked my grandparents and could tell where I'd gotten my drive from. I thought Gran would have approved of him as well.

"So as you've probably guessed, I recently received an inheritance. And I just made my first big purchase with some of the money!" I turned to look at him.

"So you bought us a weekend vacation?" he asked smiling.

I laughed out loud. "You see, when I got to the cabin the first time, I absolutely loved it there. And when I went back with you, I loved it even more. The morning I was there alone, the day I went to the library and researched Carrie, I learned something. Before I went to the library, I met up with Reggie and Maureen from the little shop on Main Street. They helped me learn more about the Carrie story and the lake. When I questioned them about the neighbors of the lake area, I asked why it was so under developed. They told me most of the land was owned by one family, and they had owned it for a long time and didn't want the lake to become busy or to turn too commercial, so they never sold it. Hawsawneekee was one of those quiet lakes that's a hidden gem, and they wanted it to stay that way."

"When you and I went back to Nisswa the night you had to tell Bill and Nancy the news, I saw Reggie and Maureen again in the diner, and they joined me for pie. I learned a lot more about them. It turns out that they are the owners of all that land! They'd had dreams of moving closer to their children and grandchildren in the Cities."

"The problem is, they didn't want to split the land into lots and no one could afford the asking price except builders and contractors. They didn't want to sell to them because the lake would soon get developed, so they felt kinda stuck. They also had the gift shop "Lost and Found" in town, on Main Street. They sell gifts, clothes, handmade jewelry, home decor, candles, and more. They put their hearts into that store, and it does very well, but now it seems harder and harder for them to keep up."

"I think I see where this is going," Derek said with a huge grin.

"I made them an offer! Not just on the lake land, but on the store, too. I can hire a couple part-time employees to help out so I'm not working all the time. I have enough money that I never have to work again, but I want to make sure that I take Gran's advice. So this will give me something to do and be proud of but not control my life and time. It's perfect!"

"Oh, my gosh, Sara! I'm so happy for you! You must be so excited," Derek said.

"I am! And this is the best part . . . the cabin is part of the lake land and the purchase! The cabin is mine! The pontoon too. I get the keys today! All the paperwork was finished on Wednesday at the diner, while I waited for you. I'd been making a lot of phone calls this last week and had everything ready to go when I got there. I had to wait on a couple documents until my divorce was final, but it all worked out. I'm meeting Reggie and Maureen at two this afternoon to get the keys. They're going to walk me through the store operations on Monday and Tuesday next week. I asked them to kinda shadow me for a few days until I learn the ropes. They have a small house in town too, that they're going to list on Monday with a local realtor. They said that the two employees they have there now are interested in continuing to work with me if I'll have them. Which I am, so it's a total 'turn-key' business! I wired them the money yesterday. I now own two-thirds of the land on Lake Hawsawneekee and a cabin and pontoon, and I own Lost and Found!"

"Wow, Sara, that is so amazing! I'm so happy that things are turning around for you. I've never seen you smile this big. It's beautiful," he said and kissed my cheek.

"Thank you. So, we're going to the cabin to celebrate! For Sunday I invited Kat and my parents up for a Bar-B-Que, so you can meet them, and they can see my land, cabin, and store. And then I thought we could all go out on the pontoon and tour the lake," I said grinning. "And you can stay as long as you'd like. I planned enough food to stay until Tuesday."

"Really? I get to meet your parents?" he asked, not looking concerned. "Are you sure? That's a big step," he said.

"I'm sure. I know it's big, but I want you to meet them," I said. "And, more importantly, my parents want to meet you."

"I'm looking forward to it," Derek said with a grin.

We rode in silence for a little while and then I added, "I also think that you should keep your options open for any job prospects that might come up. This is a really nice area."

Derek smiled. "Yes, it is. I do love it up here."

It was noon when I pulled up to the cabin. It was a beautiful, sunny day, sixty-three degrees and a little breezy. I put the car in park, rolled the windows down and inhaled the cool, fresh, clean air.

Derek quickly escaped the Jeep, ran around to my side and opened my door. He offered me his hand, "Welcome home, sweetness."

I took his hand and he pulled me out and into him for a big hug, then he kissed me . . . for a long time. When our eyes finally opened, I took his hand and led him to the dock. We sat on the edge and let our feet dangle just above the water. I looked up at the beautiful, blue sky and mentally thanked God.

They say everything happens for a reason. I wouldn't want to do it all again, but I knew I was stronger and in a better place now. It wasn't very long ago, I felt completely lost. And now . . . well now, everything was falling into place. I guess He knows what He's doing after all.

I looked over at Derek. He smiled. "I think you found your place," he said.

"I think you're right," I said with a smile, then leaned over and kissed him again.

About the Author

Danelle Helget grew up in small town Milaca, Minnesota. In the summer months she loves to spend her weekends outdoors on the lake, camping, boating and hiking. She now resides in Sauk Rapids, Minnesota, with her husband and two daughters. Find more info at www.danellehelget.com or on Facebook: Author Danelle Helget or on Twitter DanelleHelget.

Don't miss the sequel:
Found and Destroyed
and
Destroyed and Detained
coming June 2013